PRAISE FOR *THE ORIGIN OF AVA*

"A well-plotted drama linking three unlikely characters as they make the transition into their lives' next phases."

—*KIRKUS REVIEWS*

"A tough and gritty and richly observed story. All the more powerful when notes of compassion, camaraderie, grace and beauty break through. A remarkable piece of writing."

—PHIL KLAY, *Redeployment*

"With a forest fire at our backs, Lampman's masterful story-telling compels us across Pacific Northwest wilderness and beyond—with human longing and the beating of birds' wings for company."

—CHARLIE J. STEPHENS,
A Wounded Deer Leaps Highest

"*The Origin of Ava* pins absolution and reinvention to faith in a hurt but resilient natural world. Children, like birds, are gorgeous creatures of Ava's planet, mirroring the past but gesturing toward the future—never fixed, not foregone."

—KARIN ANDERSON, *Things I Didn't Do*

"Lampman's prose crackles with wildfire and renewal. *The Origin of Ava* celebrates the people and places and myths that form us, hold us, and always welcome us home."

—MARTHA WILLIAMS,
The Community Library in Ketchum, ID

"An urgent and passionate portrait of the northern Idaho wilderness, its birdlife, and three of its human inhabitants, whose damaged lives intersect, revealing the redemptive power of nature, time, and chosen family."

—CAROL PRICE, BookPeople of Moscow

"*The Origin of Ava* is a captivating exploration of loss and renewal. Lampman weaves unforgettable characters into a narrative that celebrates the resilience of the human spirit."

—CHELSIA RICE, Montana Book Company

"Lampman has crafted a conversation between mythologies, landscapes, and continents, a novel that shows us the attainable grace beyond our deepest scars and the scars we inflict on each other and the natural world."

—*ROCHELLE SMITH,* University of Idaho Library

"*The Origin of Ava* is a poignant exploration of how deeply and surprisingly we are connected to the earth and to each other."

—ERICA NICOLE, Washington State University Library

PRAISE FOR **ANNIE LAMPMAN**

"A writer to watch."

—*PUBLISHERS WEEKLY*

"Lampman's prose has a haunting, poetic quality and a deep engagement with the natural world."

—*CRIMEREADS*

"With stunning, poetic language, Lampman weaves a remarkable novel full of wisdom and hope. Marvelous, metaphorical, and profound."

—BUDDY LEVY, *Labyrinth of Ice*

"I felt submerged in the lyrical writing, swept away by the undertows of desire, desperation, loss, and redemption."

—LESLEY KAGEN, *Every Now and Then*

THE ORIGIN OF AVA

THE ORIGIN OF AVA

A novel

Annie Lampman

TORREY HOUSE PRESS

Salt Lake City • Torrey

First Torrey House Press Edition, March 2026
Copyright © 2026 by Annie Lampman

Published by Torrey House Press
Salt Lake City, Utah
www.torreyhouse.org

International Standard Book Number: 979-8-89092-020-1
E-book ISBN: 979-8-89092-021-8
Library of Congress Control Number: 2024945516

Cover design by Kathleen Metcalf
Interior design by Eryon Shondffn Greenburg
Distributed to the trade by Consortium Book Sales and Distribution

Torrey House Press offices in Salt Lake City sit on the homelands of Ute, Goshute, Shoshone, and Paiute nations. Offices in Torrey are on the homelands of Southern Paiute, Ute, and Navajo nations.

*For a lost brother and father
who helped me learn how to fly.*

And the earth below smiled back in all its radiance. So
too the churning mass of the salty sea...
And the earth, full of roads leading every which way,
opened up under her.

—*Homeric Hymn for Demeter*
"The Abduction of Persephone"

AVA

Although the raven was hurt, Ava knew it trusted her.
She told herself this was just a matter of objective
ornithological observation, evidenced by the way the orphaned
fledgling tucked its beak into its own small warmth and closed
its eyes while cradled in her lap, dark downy ruff fluffed around
its head, hackles laid flat, newly-fledged flight feathers slack. But
she knew it was more than that. Something intuited, fraught
with wiggly subjectivity.

Trust went against an avian's innate survival instinct, especially when applied to a human like her. But this, too, Ava knew:
a creature's will to exist often went beyond the known into the
unknown.

Her own impetus for flight proved that. About to flee everything she'd worked her whole life to accomplish, to have, to be.
No matter the cost, no matter what—or who—might break in
the wake of her escape.

She let the injured raven nestle a moment longer, marveling
over the oil-slick kaleidoscope glinting from its black-feather
depths. The wonder of biological principles outside any human's
control.

Although she instructed her research students never to
name the wild birds brought into the university's Avian Rescue
& Rehabilitation Center, Ava had named this raven Persephone.

She reasoned Persephone was exceptional, personally / situationally / mythologically / genetically speaking. The anomalous white patch on her shoulder only added to her enchantment, this little messenger from the underworld.

The day after Ava had received news of the deaths, a burly wildland firefighter had found the raven fledgling wounded and immobilized in the North Fork Fire's blackened wreckage. He'd sped five hours from the backwoods to deliver the bird, wrapped in his yellow Nomex shirt, to Ava. His face etched in sorrow, he made her promise the raven would survive and be returned to the mountains and river, live the rest of its life wild and free.

He hadn't realized he was carrying a message to Ava herself. Like Odin's messenger ravens Huginn and Muninn. Like Raven of the Nimíipuu creation story, long-distance messenger of warning. Like the ravens associated with Apollo, god of prophecy. Birds of the abyss. Birds of the underworld. Birds who knew more than anyone would ever understand.

The university's lead avian veterinarian and vet-med program director, Dr. Ng, along with her gaggle of baby-vets-in-training, had come by to check Persephone over, granting her a good prognosis after their examinations and lab work, backing up what Ava had already diagnosed and treated.

"A few weeks of rest and good nutrition and she should be up and flying again in no time," Dr. Ng had said, patting Ava on the shoulder as if she were the one suffering from smoke inhalation and a broken wing, the one needing rehab. And perhaps she was. All of them fallen victim to the violence of this summer. A world gone up in flames. Hades come raging back to earth to claim his dead.

Everyone on campus seemed to know what had happened to Ava, although she hadn't told anyone but Sibley and Alfred. Colleagues receded, regarding her with a hushed pity that only enraged her and trapped her further within herself.

Every breath tasted like Claire's ashes, particles of her

drifting in the North Fork Fire's smoke. Ava choked and gagged. She couldn't unthink it. She could not attend to life's daily mundanities, much less concentrate on all the demands that once held her undivided attention. She was peripatetic as the thick brown smoke that enveloped them all.

The screeching hawks, falcons, owls, and eagles had finally fallen quiet in the raptor recovery barn next door, everyone tucked in for the night, the last of the caretakers gone home.

Ava was relieved to be alone, cloistered in the dark peace of avian sleep. She leaned her face close to Persephone's neck and breathed in her clean feather smell, murmured to her. It was how a raven pair bonded, dedicating themselves to each other for life—unlike Ava, preparing to leave a devoted mate behind.

Even as she recognized it, named it, she couldn't stop it—the press of grief and guilt and self-doubt and anger, drowning her.

She had no choice but to force herself up, fight for the surface.

She told herself that this was something she already knew how to do—take herself out of the equation. Analyze the data sets, the statistics and indicators. Battle the crushing surge and learn how to breathe again, exist in her own skin. Absolve herself, her father, her mother, her brother, Sibley, Claire—the whole fucked-up torched and burning world.

She slipped Persephone into the travel cage, settled her in the nest she'd fashioned out of soft cotton rags, and lowered the black cage shroud as if preparing for a funeral. Which she was.

Persephone rustled herself into repose. An inky blot of shadow, contained, for now.

Ava tried not to disturb the bird's balance as she locked the rehab room behind them.

◆

Campus was a ghost town this time of evening, empty paved paths like the branches of a dark river delta, bordered by towering brick buildings and trees black-sketched against sky. Starkly different than just a few hours before—noisy streams of students glad to escape the day's last classes, flocking to their favorite landing sites for night libations.

Plant debris cartwheeled along the sidewalks—heat-kill the ground crews hadn't been able to keep up with as temperatures surged past the one-hundred degree mark day after day, everything riven with heat and wildfire. The university had canceled classes several times already due to the hazardous AQI. A dark billow of choking particulates covered the Northwest, visible from space. A reminder of what they were up against, of what could be taken from them: even the air.

Out of habit, Ava glanced up to her third-floor office window on the corner of Hobbs Hall, the ancient bristlecone pine under it shaggy in shadow. The magpies had gone quiet in the gothic, bird-spiked eaves.

Packing up had taken no time at all: her coffee-stained Birds of North America mug washed and left in the break room for someone else to sip overcooked drip; student publications and dissertations filed; research books shelved; her vast collection of bird skeletons, nests, and feathers marked for donation to the university's animal museum. Her office door nameplate— Dr. Avanthe Estmund, PhD, Professor of Ornithology—now marked an empty office space.

Over a decade of research and teaching, the life she'd decided on at age seven, announcing to her great uncle Alfred that she was going to be a birder *and* an ornithologist *and* a professor *and* a researcher when she grew up. And she'd done just that, relentless in her pursuit.

Now here she was, fleeing. Abandoning her future. Abandoning Sibley.

She told herself there was more reason to go than stay. The Great National Brain Drain already well underway. The war on science, on academia. The goosestep march of federally slashed funding, programs, research, people. People like her, like Sibley, new targets of hate. Two women partnered against foes who only grew more numerous and robust each day.

She told herself Sibley would be better off without her, that she, Ava, was protecting Sibley from herself—Sibley's unbreakable sense of justice, her need to fight it out, to save what wasn't left to save. Ava had always been a realist, always had a gift for reading the signals, for knowing when it was time to jump ship well before anyone else perceived disaster bearing down.

This time, though, everyone could see calamity. There was nowhere else to look.

She tried to imagine the relief of arriving at Alfred's little beach casa in Puerto Cayo, breathing in coastal air nearly a hemisphere away from all the wildfires. But she knew being at the equator didn't mean being free from crisis. There could be no haven when she couldn't escape herself—or the warnings nature had been screaming for decades, come to fruition. Wildfire and intimate loss now forever coupled in her brain— permanent connections formed deep in the hippocampus, the amygdala, forging a new registry of peril.

◆

The day of the deaths, she'd been settled in her hot, sun-exposed office trying to prep for class. Instead, she'd refreshed the North Fork Fire's Inciweb page over and over, the steady tick of acreage ticking higher and higher: Size: 20,764 acres. Total Personnel: 79. Percent Contained: 0. Fuels Involved: mixed fir, hemlock, and cedar forming a thick continuous canopy with brushy understory on steep south-facing slopes. Location: west of the North Fork of the Clearwater River in North-Central Idaho on the Nez Perce-Clearwater National Forest.

Her sacred place, her home, burning.

According to data points measuring the distance from highways, airports, and towns, the remote North Fork country was the true middle of nowhere. But Ava didn't need data to tell her that. The largest, most unique interior rainforest in the world, the furthest inland temperate rainforest in North America, and the largest continuous wild forest in the lower forty-eight.

She'd fought to put the region on the map, even if she didn't want it to be "discovered." She knew how good a professor had to be to transcend the "local" stigma. To reverse generations of socioeconomic disadvantage by sheer determination. And she had. She'd published bird study after bird study, establishing a name—both for herself and the North Fork—in the worlds of academia and ornithology. She'd taught gifted grad students and even more gifted honors undergrads who'd published their work in esteemed scientific and literary journals, presented at international conferences, and won prestigious scholarships and grants that even many of the tenured faculty hadn't achieved. A generational baton pass—passions of birds and place.

She'd been rereading the North Fork Fire's "projected activity" and "planned actions" when the first phone call came, the dean's voice grave. "I know how closely you two were working together and what a promising and talented student Claire was. She would have made a difference in the world. She should have had a whole life ahead of her to do so…" and Ava had buckled to the floor under the sudden force of her anguish.

Just the day before, Claire had left Ava a voicemail, staticky from wherever she'd managed to get service on the fire line. She said the North Fork Fire had blown up, so she would be missing the first weeks of class, but she'd gathered great new bird data she couldn't wait to show Ava. Her tone, even with the bad connection, brimming with her typical exuberance. A brilliant, untamed young woman, unafraid of her own power and voice, embracing everything her strength and intellect promised, pushing herself so hard she didn't see what everyone else might have predicted: good things were bound to shatter.

◆

The second call came later that afternoon, this time from the Clearwater County Sheriff, a gravel-voiced man with local grammar. Without preamble, he told Ava that her father, Philip, had been found dead in his house. The cause of death appeared to be a gunshot wound, but it was too soon to say whether it was self-inflicted. They were waiting for the autopsy. "In the in between," he said, Ava should feel free to "make arrangements" so everything would be "set to go" with the funeral home.

As if they were discussing a bake sale. As if two back-to-back deaths, the out-of-control wildfire, and the hazardous fucking air were a regular part of everyday existence. Maybe, in his world, they were.

Ava sat stunned in her office's smoke-umbered light, an interior blur spreading up each limb until her lungs compressed, until her heart seized, until her brain ceased its neuron-firing. She felt choked out, burned alive, limbed, shot dead, finalized. Trapped in a surreal, liminal space where her father and Claire still existed, where life moved forward as usual while she struggled to make sense of what made no sense. Some kind of terrible cosmic curse, some kind of coincidence in timing and place, some kind of a warning notice from the universe translating loud and clear.

Enough to alter even the most meticulously plotted life plans. Enough to drive even the most devoted from their carefully woven nests.

◆

Persephone buckled in the back seat, Ava drove from campus, trying to take stock of the place she'd so loved—antidote for ignorance, racism, misogyny, sexism, homophobia, religious dogma. But everything was shrouded in smoke. Gray ashpit tendrils of smoldering stink reached around brick buildings like probing fingers, seeking to seize Ava next, wrap her throat in a stranglehold.

She told herself she wasn't panicking, wasn't plunging into a smoke-cloaked underworld where everyone would keep disappearing into the flames, one after another after another until none were left. That she was only trying to breathe, to escape smoke, death, failure. That fleeing was a matter of survival, whether Sibley or Alfred or anyone else could understand.

She didn't know how to grieve. Didn't know how to look her beloved in the eye and tell her how badly she was hurting. All she knew was what she'd studied for years, what she'd taught, what she'd written and published: enduring the pressures of the universe often required immediate and drastic action, no matter who or what you were. How that often meant creating distance between you and whatever threatened your wellbeing, your existence.

She had no real fight left—she had been drained of that. And if she froze, she would choke on smoke. There was no option but flight: wandering lost, head up, scanning the sky, trying to read the fleeting shape of a wing-born thing, understand the shape of shadow.

If that were even possible.

At the top of College Hill, the golden glow of fenestrated light from Sibley's upper-story apartment made Ava's heart speed. She parked next to Sibley's battered biodiesel pickup covered in save-the-world stickers. She turned off her car, engine ticking as she sat in the heat.

The fade of the wildfire sunset stained the sky tangerine, the hue of a flicker's flight feathers. "Dutch Orange" in *Werner's Nomenclature of Colours*, its related animal category the crest of the golden-crested wren; its vegetable category the seedpod of a spindle tree; its mineral category a streak of red orpiment.

All that vista. Unending light. All that time Ava and Sibley had spent together, loving each other, leaning into each other like another form of self. Ava had believed they were an unbreakable unit. Now, approaching Sibley felt like another form of failing.

Persephone rustled beneath her shroud as Ava hoisted the cage from the back seat. She tried to rearrange her face into something less funereal as she walked to the front door, repeating her favorite bird pairings under her breath, her mantra in times of distress: *flicker, dipper; nuthatch, chickadee; cat bird, canyon wren; mourning dove, meadowlark; bluebird, blackbird; osprey, raven.*

◆

The first bird Ava had learned to identify by both shape and sound was a raven. "Summer of the Raven" she and Alfred still called it. The start of everything. A two-decade bookending, beginning and ending with raven rescue.

Her parents in the throes of angry, unending divorce, seven-year-old Ava had stayed the summer with Uncle Alfred, who took her birding to keep her distracted.

It worked.

She was the first to spot the heap of black feathers lying alongside the roadway. As they pulled over, Alfred warned her that the bird was likely dead, struck by a vehicle. But when they approached, the raven lifted its head and hissed and spit like a furious cat.

Ava named him Midas—her father's penchant for Greek mythology already passed down to her—and devoted herself as an enthusiastic if clumsy bird rehab assistant. They took Midas along on their birding expeditions where Alfred pointed out the black unshorn silhouettes of wild ravens in the tops of conifers. He taught Ava how to mimic their guttural, echoing calls. The three of them—Ava, Alfred, and Midas—would caw along as the wild ravens flew overhead, looking down with cool remove.

A flock of three deranged ground dwellers longing for sky.

◆

Wan morning sun edged past the bedroom blinds and Ava buried her head under the comforter, avoiding what she hadn't had the guts yet to say. She burrowed further into the soft nest of Sibley's flannel sheets—always flannel, even in summer's stifling heat. Ava felt like Persephone, shrouded in the dark cage tucked in the bedroom's corner. A blanketing blackness that put everything on hold.

Ava and Sibley had picked out their bedroom's paint colors from *Werner's Nomenclature of Colours*, dissecting each minute variegation, holding up the book's tiny square patches to places on the walls, arguing between the closely matched "Ash Grey—Breast of long tailed Hen Titmouse," and "Smoke Grey—Breast of the Robin round the Red."

They would lie in bed, Ava twirling ropes of Sibley's thick hair around her fingers as Sibley read out loud. "'No. 9, Ash Grey, is the characteristic color of Werner's greys; he gives no description of its component parts; it is composed of snow white, with portions of smoke and French grey, and a very little yellowish grey and carmine red.'

"Whereas 'No. 10, Smoke Grey, is ash grey mixed with a little brown.' So, clearly," Sibley had insisted, pinning Ava and kissing her, "the characteristic color with carmine red wins over grey-brown."

Sibley's lips were also carmine. Ava had been powerless to demur.

◆

At least Ava hadn't grown weepy during this final night, lying tangled in Sibley's arms and legs.

Now Sibley was in the kitchen making coffee. Always the early riser. Always the one to get the morning fire going when they were out in the field. The smell of freshly lit pitch and tamarack smoke, of coffee percolating and bacon frying, her wake-up call.

Ava breathed in Sibley's soft-pillow musk. Ambrosia oil. Pachouli. Sandalwood. Rose. Earth-sweet and heady. Different than what you might expect looking at Sibley herself, her skin sleeved in tattoos and stainless steel piercings like a thorny exoskeleton, her thick pelt of hair uncontrollable. But the warrior persona couldn't hide her fine-boned clavicle shaped like bird wings; slender shoulder blades articulating over a knobbed spine; delicately tapered fingers, so overt in their femininity.

The Sibley Guide to Birds Ava called her, the name of her favorite field guide, battered now after twenty-five years of referencing. Sibley called Ava *Blackbird,* or simply *Bird.* When they'd found each other, it was like recovering a lost twin. As if they'd been born together into another sphere and didn't belong to the earthbound, but instead belonged to the air.

Ava tried to memorize Sibley's smell, hold it a moment longer.

"Coffee's ready," Sibley called.

Sibley's footsteps approached the bedroom, then there she was, wild and disheveled and fierce and beautiful, everything Ava had wanted before she ever knew she wanted it.

"I thought you were in a big hurry to get Persephone over to Alfred's for the rest of her rehabbing?" A hint of questioning awareness.

Sibley's intuitiveness, coupled with her unwavering intellect and passion, were the qualities Ava admired most about her. Ava herself went out of her way to use logic—or anything else available—to avoid conflict, to smooth the way, but then again there was nothing logical about fleeing to Ecuador. A migration path drawing her into the sky nearly two hundred years after Darwin's expedition.

Sibley had tried to argue her out of it, insisting Ava needed to let go of her pain and anger and guilt. But Ava didn't know how to let these things go when so much was already gone.

She pushed the covers off her face and swiped her hair out of her eyes, but everything still looked filtered through a grayscale lens—the bedroom walls in their tones of smoke and ash. It felt as if the whole world were preparing for the worst, or the worst had already happened. Everything some version of broken.

Even if Ava was about to do more breaking.

Tired of waiting, Sibley sat down on the bed with an exaggerated sigh and shoved a hot mug into Ava's hand, then plumped a pillow against the headboard. She leaned back and stretched her legs out on top of the comforter, holding Ava tight. There was nowhere to set her coffee, the mattress shoved up against the wall on her side.

"I finally got a reply about the new field project," Sibley said. "The department gave tentative approval pending fiscal year. With the newest round of budget cuts, who knows. But I thought I'd reserve the equipment, get ready to go."

Sibley sounded cheerful, the way she always was with field work on the horizon, especially as close to their hearts as this: countering the logging destruction and clearcuts that had spread outward from Headquarters, threatening the North Fork's virgin forests and waters. Along with the wildfires.

Leaving Sibley to the North Fork project was not just betraying their professional plans; it felt like abandonment of Ava's child self. Summers spent on the banks of the river. A forest refugia, a riparian sanctuary, a coastal disjunct community. Its vascular plant species found only in Oregon and Washington's coastal rainforests: thickets of red alder, western hemlock, western red cedar, understories of maidenhair and sword fern, Rocky Mountain maple, buckthorn, new species of earthworms, terrestrial beetles, and macro-invertebrate communities.

All her most beloved birds.

When she was young, she'd memorized scientific avian names in batches of hundreds, reciting her favorites aloud—a Latinate chant people would stop to listen to, clapping along in beat: *Colaptes auratus, Cinclus mexicanus, Sitta canadensis, Poecile atricapillus, Dumetella carolinensis, Catherpes mexicanus, Zenaida macroura, Sturnella neglecta, Sialia mexicana, Agelaius phoeniceus, Pandion haliaetus, Corvus corax.*

Flicker, dipper, nuthatch, chickadee, cat bird, canyon wren, mourning dove, meadowlark, bluebird, blackbird, osprey, raven.

At the North Fork, her father had taught her how to swim deep currents; how to make a fire out of nothing more than a bit of pitch, cedar bark, and flint; how to listen to the water talk as she body-floated through frothing rapids to the uninhabited white-sand beaches of the other side, thick with towering cedars, ferns, and wildflowers.

Fairyland, they'd called it. The Woods-Fairy Forest. Her father told her story after story about its magical inhabitants. And it *was* magic—its earth enchantment always calling her home, so intertwined with her she didn't know how she would unravel herself no matter her pending absence, no matter what her father had said about her misplaced priorities, no matter how estranged they had become from one another before he was suddenly gone for good.

Ava tried not to picture him as they'd found him, sitting in his recliner with its view of his beloved mountains, his pistol at rest in his lap, an empty whiskey bottle tucked at his side. The mess he'd made of his life.

Like Daedalus, he had tried to craft wings for himself and his two children to escape imprisonment, even if Ava had been the only one to fly. But, like Icarus, she was skimming too close to the sun, everything crashing down in wreck and ruin.

She struggled to sit up to eye level with Sibley. To be direct.

"Sibley," she started, stumbling over the ponderousness of her tone.

"Ava," Sibley mocked, glancing over with her little half-crooked smile. Eyes wary.

Ava came out with it. "I can't go."

She looked at Sibley, tried to take a mental snapshot of this, of them, lying in bed, together. Sibley with her wild mane and botanical tattoos. Sibley with her delicate bones and soft skin. Sibley who'd always been there for Ava, fearlessly attacking life's injustices.

Sibley's voice like glass: "What do you mean you can't go?"

Ava tried to take her hand, but Sibley pulled away. The betrayal in her eyes marking the moment forever. Shards raining down.

"I submitted my leave of absence paperwork. I leave for Cayo today."

Sibley turned to stare at the blind window. Cascading anger. Silence.

"I'm so sorry, Sib."

Ava fought the urge to reach out again. What that might precipitate. The grief inside her threatening to break like a dam.

Sibley wouldn't look at her. She sat on the bed a moment longer before abruptly standing up. Her hands balled into fists at her side, ready for a fight as always, her jaw clenching and unclenching, molars grinding.

"So that's it then?" she said, throwing her arms wide. "Don't give a fuck about everything you're leaving behind, don't give a fuck about me?"

"Of course I do!" Ava said, trying to escape the quicksand of flannel and memory foam. Their twin imprints molded in.

Sibley dropped her arms. "Stay then. We'll figure it out together. We always do. Or I'll take a leave of absence, come with you."

Ava gave up trying to get out of bed. "I can't let you wreck your whole life because of me. There's too much riding on your research—your tenure, this new project, the North Fork."

"Oh, I see. But it's totally fine for *you* to destroy everything." Sibley's sarcasm heavy as the ash-cloaked air.

"None of this is fine," Ava said.

When Ava had learned the scientific term "chemotaxis," she'd loved the idea of it—a molecular attraction where even the simplest, single-celled organisms were pulled by powers they could fight but not defeat. But now it was just another metaphor for wrenching futility.

Sibley stared at her, her beautiful Modigliani features taut. *Girl in Bedroom. Girl in Umber. Girl in Grief and Anger.*

"You know, it was rare what we had. Two people loving each other that much, caring so much about the world. We were a fucking force of nature. Too bad you can't see that. Too bad you're so messed up in the head, giving up like this, walking away without even putting up a fight. Fuck you, Ava. Fuck. You. I hope you have fun finding yourself—whatever there's left to find."

Sibley strode out and slammed the apartment door before peeling out of the driveway in her rattly pickup.

The cupboard's pots and pans and glasses chimed. Then silence settled in deep.

In her shrouded cage, Persephone seemed to be holding herself as still and breathless as Ava.

So this was over too. Survival instinct just another version of forfeiture.

EZRA

After ten years locked up, Ezra thought he'd put the curse behind him. There were days, weeks even, when he no longer heard the sizzle of hair under a flame's slight touch, no longer woke from nightmares of walls and windows burning.

But wasn't that always how it happened? Right when he thought he'd made peace, thought he was better, moving on with life, that's when memory would hit him square in the face again: *What do you think of me now?*

He closed his eyes and tried to breathe through his nose into his lower stomach. That's what the self-help books said to do when the past came flooding back. Breathe deep. Exhale. Count. He braced his shoulder against the prison van's window, his stomach churning as the driver took another corner too sharply, rushing the crew to the newest fire. The nausea always came on as they started climbing above the valley. The road curved like a snake winding up the mountainside, banking vehicles toward cliff edges, trying to throw them off its back.

Several years ago, the prison had an opening on the labor crew, so Ezra had signed up. The work did him good. Distraction from the dark reaches of his mind. But then the depths of the decade-long drought hit—a succession of blistering years accumulating into the worst wildfire conditions anyone had ever seen—and they converted the crew into a wildland fire unit. When Ezra balked, the guards shrugged their shoulders, said take it or leave it. And he gladly would have left it, chosen to stay in his cell forever instead of facing flames again, but for his window's southern exposure, sun bearing down, burning him alive just as surely as fire.

Maybe it was the universe's way of saying he needed to face it. He'd been reading books about healing from trauma, and they said you could never move on if you didn't deal with the past. *No healing without dealing.* And he needed to move on.

With his release date at the end of summer and a good safety record, he'd been appointed the inmate wildland fire crew boss. In reality he was nothing more than an indentured servant. An expendable U.S. felon. Once he was out, he was leaving this country for good.

By the end of spring, grass fractured underfoot. The Clearwater River—usually visible from the prison yard—had slipped out of sight, its rocky banks chalked and exposed. The Clearwater valley was a cauldron of shimmering heatwaves. It took one storm to ignite it all. The air like a furnace, heat like murder, a theatrical set born on sweltering air. *Fire Threat Stage I, Stage II, Stage III.* Fourth of July fireworks just a prelude to the main show—torched trees that sparked and popped like explosions, flames hundreds of feet tall. A smoking curtain call with millions more drought-parched acres to go.

Spotter planes flew from dawn to dusk, calling in one blaze after another. The calls for the inmate fire crew came fast. One trip after the next until it was routine: the fire call, the marathon drive, the unending smoke, sweat, and char—Ezra's long-familiar nightmares.

The driver took another corner too fast and the inmates lurched sideways in their seats. Ezra clenched his fists. The books said to think of something light to replace the darkness, something good, right now. Be positive in the present.

He breathed in deeply, recited Shakespeare's Sonnet 111:

"O, for my sake do you with Fortune chide,
The guilty goddess of my harmful deeds,
That did not better for my life provide…"

He tried to steady himself with its lilting language, its sure rhythms, but instead he thought about his brother Timothy as he so often did—the only true goodness he'd known in his life. Memories that only led into the dark. A flame's slight touch.

Working to relax his shoulder tension, he released and refilled his lungs, but the only "present" thing to concentrate on was the sour stale-smoke stench of his crew in the van's oven heat.

The North Fork Fire was burning in the steep Bitterroot Mountains off the North Fork of the Clearwater River's ice-green whitewater, banks studded with ancient cedars, maiden-hair and sword ferns, white-sand beaches, and moss-covered rocks. From the Forest Service work center, you could walk out the back door and fly fish for trophy cutthroat as you drank morning coffee on the beach. If you weren't a prisoner, that is. There was no other human habitation until Superior, Montana. Nothing but wild high country, untrammeled. Ezra dreamed of living in those mountains, like the 1800s miner Billy Rhodes, finding his freedom where no one else ventured.

◆

Ezra unfurled his fists to catch a rare sweet memory, a pol-ished, pocket-sized rock—even if recollection wasn't exactly being "positive in the present." He was a child, tubing the St. Joe River's lazy flow, face underwater, eyes wide open. He saw trout nesting against rocks, whipping river silt into a cloud as his shadowed silhouette caught them dozing. Fingerlings nosed and nibbled the bubbles on his arm, the smooth flick of their bodies through water, an effortless glide. A whole world going about its business underneath him, his presence real only in shadow as he spun without weight or direction, cast loose and drifting.

But then, like always, it became the two of them—Ezra and Timothy—like a tape circling back. Brothers along the Joe playing pirate, playing Huck Finn, playing search and rescue, performing heroic feats. Spinning on the tire suspended from a weeping willow, water below them like a promise. Timothy's blonde head whipped back from the centrifugal-force, wispy hair in his eyes, willow branches brushing their faces, hands gripping the twisted ropes until they unraveled, kicking them free. The two of them—Timothy four, Ezra six—lying side by side in tall grass, listening to crickets chirring, dreaming of floating so far away they couldn't be found.

Long days in his cell—his fellow monkeys howling, smashing against their bars—Ezra studied the library's gilded copy of Shakespeare's sonnets and a book of art, both long overdue. He returned to Bosch's painting, *The Ship of Fools*, over and over, examining every detail, trying to find hidden meaning in its brush strokes. Bosch captured people in their folly: a man vomiting over the side of the ship, drunks naked and imperiled in the water, even a monk and a nun caught in foolhardiness. *Eat! Drink! Be Merry!* Floating to nowhere, the scene was even more grim and foreboding than Hogarth's *Gin Lane*, whose streets were filled with corpses, whose happily drunken mother let her baby tumble from her lap to its death.

"Wine is a mocker, strong drink a brawler, and whoever is led astray by it is not wise." That proverb he remembered himself. His father stumbling home drunk again, paycheck long spent, his mother weeping and begging as his father raged into her. During school recitation, the nuns taught them that verse and a few others he remembered. "Be sober-minded; be watchful. Your adversary the devil prowls around like a roaring lion, seeking whom to devour."

He'd wondered how they knew—Sister Gonzaga, Sister Thelonious. Their eyes on his in pity, in warning. How they'd known it was him the lion sought. He'd thought his father's rage was a secret. Once, when it was really bad, when all their father could find was a chain to remind the boys and their mother of their sins, there had been talk of someone from the church "taking them in."

Their mother would have none of it. She told Sister Gonzaga to mind her own meddling business. Said, "Let they who've not sinned throw the first stone."

But the stones of their father's sins buried them all.

At the end, his father had abandoned them for a month or more—that's why Ezra wanted so badly to help his mother and Timothy. Build a fire to keep Timothy cozy while he slept. Make the house cozy when their mother returned from her night shift. Build a fire. A six-year-old's faith: if he could do this one thing, he could right all wrongs. They could start again. Their father would come back sober and penitent, clean the logging-equipment grease from the folds in his rough mechanic hands, and pull Ezra and Timothy into his lap. Their mother would bake bread, humming, and they would all sit and eat, and they would be warm and full. They would be happy.

The kindling took easy. The curtains even easier. Flames crawled up the wall, licking the fray, climbing hungrily for more, gobbling faded roses and wallpaper pansies, moving impatiently to the ceiling, framing, roof.

He'd called until his voice went hoarse, his cries like the bullfrogs he and Timothy hunted along the Joe's marshy banks. But Timothy didn't come out of the bedroom, didn't come out of the house. By the time the neighbors came running, it was devoured.

While Ezra watched, the smoke turned toward him, opened its mouth and roared.

◆

Just before Headquarters, Idaho—a defunct outpost in the middle of backwoods and razed mountains, a few rickety shacks remaining of the early logging boomtown, the last "civilization" until Montana—the prison van met up with the lead crew from Timber Protective. The van followed their red crew cabs out to the North Fork Fire. All fire entities had been called in: federal, state, private, prison.

Ezra stared out the window as they bounced over water bars, potholes, ruts, and tank traps. It was a tunnel of green—woods so thick, the trees so close together that the fire was burning through the crowns hundreds of feet from the ground, held aloft by air. He focused on the view straight ahead, breathing slowly in and out, in and out, trying to hold himself steady, to ready himself for the action.

◆

Ten years ago, eighteen and high on heroin, Ezra had been driving too fast through the dark. At first, the man walking along the roadside was just a blur through the windshield. Then Ezra recognized him. A quick stutter like the thrum of a woodland grouse in his throat, and then in his chest. His father, after all those years.

Ezra turned the steering wheel toward the man and punched his foot to the floor. Engine roaring, tires spinning and catching, the car seemed to hover a second before impact. Shoulder gravel crunched beneath the tires like broken glass.

The man's pale face flashed bright with surprise in the headlights.

He wasn't Ezra's father. He was a drunk out-of-work logger who looked like Ezra. Like his father. What they'd all become.

◆

At the bottom of the burn, the inmates unloaded and geared up. Ezra's stomach was steadied by the smells of oil and chainsaw gas, smoke and char, talcum dirt and weedy heat. Behind it all, the wild fragrance of green, unburned primeval forest.

He balanced a chainsaw over his shoulder, his crew carrying an assortment of tools. The Forest Service Incident Commander directed the inmate crew to the lower west end, the local Forest Service fire crew above them. Conditions were windy, hot, dry. But not just that—it was eerie, menacing. The dark sky felt like a warning. Smoke hung like a tattered funeral shroud over torching trees. Heat was as thick and choking as the smoke, air become dust. Everything brimmed with threat.

His crew began digging their line. The Forest Service crew above were all black-smeared, looked as burned as the trees. Ezra was surprised to see a girl on the crew—long blonde hair in two thick braids down her back—heaving away with the rest of them. She stopped to right her hard hat and glanced down at Ezra and his men. She gave a quick wave and smile. A happy picnic host. Everyone else kept their heads down, attending to business.

It was a bad burn already, but then the wind gained speed. Three hours into sawing and digging line, the burned-out snags started falling, dislodging boulders that barreled down the slope like god-sized cannonballs. At one point Ezra ordered his crew to shelter behind any still-standing green tree and stay put. There was no way to work without getting crushed.

In the mayhem, the fire jumped the line and the Timber Protective crew lost their heads, calling in bucket and fire-retardant drops, misdirecting everything in the smoke.

Ezra knew to maintain radio silence. The inmate unit was the lowest in the fire hierarchy. Even if they hadn't been, this was no time for discussion. It was time to keep your head down and watch your back. But every now and then, as work resumed, Ezra looked up and saw the girl, her shoulders heaving, her Pulaski bouncing back from the hard-baked ground like it was rubberized. She swung the tool over her head with everything she had, her feet planted wide apart, her braids whipping with her efforts, going at it as if she alone would stop the fire.

When Ezra's men finally caught up with the Forest Service crew, it was late afternoon. They all took a break, set their saws down, pulled out canteens and granola bars. The girl wandered over and sat down next to Ezra. "Claire Barnes, at your service." She flashed a dazzling grin and bubble-smacked a wad of gum as she held her gloved hand out.

"Ezra Kittredge," he said, surprised by her iron grip, as if he hadn't watched her swing that Pulaski all day.

"Nice to meet you, Ezra Kittredge," she said, pumping his hand before she pulled out a smashed sandwich. She worked her bubblegum into a tidy purple ball with her front teeth before taking it out of her mouth and placing it carefully on her sandwich bag. She took a bite of PB&J as she flopped backward into bear grass. She chewed and talked at the same time, swiping wisps of hair and ash stuck in her eyelashes, her forehead and temples smeared with soot. Told Ezra her older brother worked on a Missoula fire crew. Discussed the fire conditions—how they were worse here than anything in Montana. Complained about her schoolwork piling up and her crew calling her a bird nerd.

Ezra wanted to tell her to conserve her energy, so many poorly paid hours ahead, so much fire still to fight. When Claire finished her sandwich, she popped the ashy gum back in her mouth. She grinned at Ezra as she gave him a high five. "Hey fire bro, we're in this together," even though they were worlds apart—a hardened prisoner and former heroin addict convicted of vehicular manslaughter, a gregarious and plucky co-ed studying river birds.

◆

When the smokejumpers showed up, the man in charge, Hemingway Maclean, hiked the fire line to assess the fire's trajectory and conditions, then make his recommendation to the Incident Commander. The fire had jumped another section and was burning heavy into virgin forest. Trees were still falling and boulders still rolling, almost rhythmic by that point: the thumping heave of Pulaskis splitting the dirt open like a wound, the shuddering whoosh and earthshaking thud of another tree, the rattling thunder of dislodged boulders.

Maclean told them they should leave; it wasn't safe. He was writing a report detailing the conditions, the organizational and operational problems, the mismanagement. An unacceptable level of hazard. Ezra wasn't surprised the smokejumpers wouldn't commit personnel. Who would? Well, the prison would, and it wasn't Ezra's job to question. He told his crew to keep their heads down; they wouldn't stop until someone in charge directed them to. It wasn't their fire to call.

After the smokejumper's report, he expected Claire's Forest Service crew to pack up, but they stayed on too. They were young, wanted to prove themselves. From the fire line above, Claire leaned on her Pulaski and grinned down at Ezra. Smudged and disheveled, she fist-pumped, yelled, *"Oh Yeah! Fuck Montana!"*

Everyone hooted.

The remaining crews battled on, side by side, through rippling heat and smoke. Chainsaws spat oily wood into peach-colored confetti on dark-churned dirt that quickly dried to dust. Hoses strung out like white intestines across the hillside. Cedar trees burned from the inside out, punky heartwood consumed, outer shells left standing.

By evening, the firefighters bore the marks of the battle: reverse raccoon masks gleaming out of blackened faces, singed-off eyelashes, boots baked stiff, saw slashes in their leather toes. Yellow Nomex shirts drenched with sweat, green Nomex pants crusted brown. The fetid smell of the burn, of smoke and charred wood, overwhelming.

Claire was glassy-eyed, looked like she'd been rolled in an ash pit—even her light blonde hair black with soot and dirt. Ezra gave her his extra canteen and last packet of Kool-Aid. Told her it wasn't his business, but she looked like she could use a rest. She nodded and sat on a clump of beargrass. Ezra sat with her, directed his crew to continue up the hill.

She drank her Kool-Aid and pushed hair out of her eyes, smiled at him despite her obvious exhaustion. Said she couldn't wait to rub *this* fire in her big bro's face. Everything still coated with the simple sweetness of sibling rivalry. Who got the biggest slice of pie.

You would have thought that after Timothy, Ezra would never have struck a match, never thumbed a lighter to flame. But he couldn't get enough. All those lost, dark years, burning everything down. He even tried to burn himself, light his flesh like a candle, inked flames into his skin. He'd wanted to die in flames, go straight to the hell the nuns warned of. A way of going home.

Booze, drugs, fire, fights, what was the difference? Sister Gonzaga had said it over and over. If he didn't watch out, the world would eat him alive and spit out his bones. Destiny a curse in the blood, a cruel kiss.

But he was here now, he reminded himself. Fighting flames, cauterizing the past. His coming release glimmered like a waterborne mirage, promising a new life—the one he'd dreamed of as a teen. Ecuador, the Galapagos, beach after beach, surf break after break, until he became one with the sea. Back then, it had just been about the surfing, but for the last decade locked up, it had become much more. A quest to be fully alive again. A life transformed by water instead of fire.

In his cell, he'd read and reread *On the Origin of Species*, as fascinated by the finches as Darwin had been. If small birds had figured it out, so could he. Adaptation. Evolution. Survival. And Ecuador's lax extradition enforcement was, of course, appealing.

Ezra closed his eyes, ran through his preplanned route again, everything familiar yet vague as a recurring dream: parole check-in, parole check-out, bus from Bumfuck Idaho to the Port of Seattle, 90 West, I-5 North, exit left on Madison Street, right on Alaskan Way, Pier 46 on the left past the skybridge. There was the exit, there were the docks, there was the container ship, there was the Pacific, there was South America, there was freedom.

Ten years of waiting, day after day after day, until his mind traced the route even in sleep, tireless as the riderless barrel-racing horse he'd once seen walking a dusty arena on its own: first barrel, turn; second barrel, turn; last barrel, turn; straight home to the finish. Begin again.

◆

Next to him, Claire was talking about how she couldn't wait to get back to the work center and go swimming, dive in the North Fork and wash off all the dirt and sweat and soot. She said she could fall asleep floating on her back, that she'd once accidentally dozed off and floated down some rapids, waking to whitewater and a flotilla of confused mergansers.

Ezra smiled, committing this moment to memory. A small, beautiful thing.

Both were still sitting when Ezra heard it. Almost a whistle—all that air rushing through torched needles. He knew it was coming fast. He lunged on instinct, but Claire did not.

She had taken her hard hat off to tuck loose hair back underneath it—not that it would have done any good, the force of an uprooted and flaming hundred-fifty-foot grand fir whooshing past Ezra almost gently, catching him on the backs of his legs, its heavy branches pinning him momentarily.

It buried Claire so deep they had to saw their way to her. Dozens of feet of flat-needled burning branches. A smell like Christmas. Like hundreds of smoldering campfires. Ezra sawed and pulled limbs so frantically that the crews forced him to stop, get out of the way, said he'd be burned too. But he kept trying to dive in through the branches.

They bucked the trunk off her body in the blackness of early morning, lit by orange smoke and flashing headlamps. The hell the nuns had foretold.

As weak daylight broke, they maneuvered Claire's incinerated form in a sling down to the ambulance that had come from four hours away, sirens screaming even though there was no rush. No call for haste or announcement. Only mourning.

Authorities pulled all the crews as the fire rushed on into Montana and British Columbia. Hemingway Maclean filed his report. National news outlets picked up the story of a young, promising female wildland firefighter and local honors undergrad. Beloved, destined for great things, the first fatality of the season.

There would be an investigation. There would likely be charges, lawsuits. But other than a few police interviews—the inmate crew suspended pending conclusions—Ezra was removed from it all. He sat in his cell, sun boring down like punishment, remembering the fragrant greens of cedars and ferns, the clear silver river rushing over slick stone. A soot-covered girl with a wide smile and a wad of purple bubblegum.

GREER

"Come on Greer Grade, give it your best shot." Reggie taunted, his arms held wide. His sneaker toes nearly touched the gym's center court line, flirting with being DQ-ed. He'd caught everyone else's throws, also as usual, so Greer was the final threat.

Everyone knew she had been born on the stupid Greer Grade with its crazy S corners that made her sick as a dog, that her mom had popped her out in the back seat on the way to the hospital. Greer hated it when people called her the name of a road, but she hated her real name, too. *Greer Groff.* Like an old sick dog barking.

She wished she had a beautiful, adventurous name like Amelia or Isabella or Sacagawea, although she didn't mind the chant Juan and the rest of her teammates had taken up from the sidelines: *Grr-eer, Grr-eer, Grr-eer!* It made her sound tough, even if she didn't stand a chance against Reggie, a foot taller than anybody else in the fourth grade. His muscled arms were twice as big as her scrawny colt legs.

"You gonna throw that ball or not?" Reggie mocked, eager to take his victory lap, flexing and kissing his biceps as he ran.

She shook her head, gripping the smallest dodgeball of Pierce Elementary's assortment at her side, acting like she was giving up. She turned her unprotected left side to Reggie as she walked toward her sidelined team. Sure enough, he couldn't resist the bait. He wound up his hardest power heave, but she sprang into action, diving across the polished gym floor as she threw. Her ball nailed Reggie right in the guts. She skid-dodged his rocket ball that smacked into the wall, ricocheting with enough force to take out skinny Joe Morris a second time.

Her team erupted into wild cheers, Juan screaming as he ran to her, jumping with his fists in the air like a deranged kangaroo.

Across the line, Reggie stood dumbfounded. He hadn't lost a game since the start of school. He won last year's tournament too, before he'd grown even taller over summer break. Both teams lined up to shake hands but Reggie was in such a huff that Mrs. Smith, their PE teacher, pulled him to the side to lecture him about being a sore loser. Fat tears streamed down his red face like slugs.

Big fat baby, Greer wanted to call, using the sneering voice of her mom's drunken tirades. But Juan would be disappointed in her if she did. Juan's whole family was nicer than anybody Greer had ever been around. When she'd started hanging out at their house—his family in Headquarters for the tree-planting season—Greer was confused by their politeness, *pleases* and *thank yous* and *I love yous* volleyed back and forth like a gentle badminton game.

It'd taken Greer a long time to pick up even a few of Juan's good manners. Mrs. Cedeño rewarded her with tall glasses of fresh-squeezed lemonade and spicy quesadillas that Greer tried not to gulp down like a starving dog.

Juan gave her a little elbow in the ribs, smiling sideways, as they walked to their last class. She grinned back, knowing what it meant. They would recount the victory, frame by frame, second by second, on the long bus ride home. Just the thought of it satisfied Greer—that and the extra helpings she hoped to score from Mrs. Cedeño, as kind to Greer as she was to her own much nicer kids.

She wished the Cedeños would just adopt her, even if Greer's mom and her boyfriend, Rory, were still around. With three younger sisters, Juan already had plenty of siblings, but he didn't seem to mind adding Greer to the mix. He shrugged off teasing, even when Reggie called him a homo because his best friend was a girl. *Greer the Queer* Reggie's favorite name for her, along with *Meth Baby*. But if Greer got angry, Juan reminded her: *Water off a duck's back*. She liked the image of cute yellow ducklings floating and flapping in the water, although mallards were the only ducks she'd ever seen and Rory shot every one he spotted.

First in line for the bus, Greer yelled "Yeessss!" and did a fist pump when she saw Lonnie wasn't driving. Today was her day. She'd even scored cinnamon cookies from Juan's lunch. She wolfed one down as she ran down the aisle to her seat.

"No running," the old lady substitute driver barked, but Greer could tell she didn't really care. She kept her eyes in front of her instead of roving in the big mirror over the driver's seat, like Lonnie the Creep with his leering moon face. Girls dodged his hands when he reached to pat their behinds as they got on or off the bus.

Greer avoided Rory the same way. At first he'd seemed nice—he bought her a porcelain doll she was afraid to play with and an itchy lace dress she never wore. But then, like all her mom's boyfriends, he turned out to be a perv. Now he came in her room each night to "tuck her in," his hands slithering under the covers. Last week she'd caught him standing outside her bedroom window trying to watch her get dressed, a pile of cigarette butts heaped on the ground.

Her mom acted like Greer was trying to steal Rory from her. When he was around, she was extra mean to Greer, saying Greer was going to be a zit-faced flat-chested fat-ass. That she stunk like her dirty little beaner friend and his tree-planter family. It'd become a game by now, Rory stepping in, playing nice guy. "Oh now, Cynthia, you don't mean that, Greer's a good kid." He smiled and winked at Greer like they had a pact.

"Our little secret," he whispered in her ear at night, his breath hot.

On the bus, Juan joined Greer in the back seat by the emergency door, where they got to sit now since all the older kids had left Headquarters—most people gone except a few families that included the Cedeños, and Greer's mom who bartended at the Timber Inn in Pierce. Rory worked at the Jaype plywood mill halfway between Pierce and Headquarters. Greer always checked to see if his pickup was there when the bus drove past, so she knew whether to go home or hide until she could go to the Cedeños' for dinner. Rory got more pissed off than her mom when Greer didn't come home on time.

After early stops outside of Pierce, Greer and Juan settled in for the longest part of the bus ride—trees out the windows and time to talk. Pretty much the best part of her day—other than visiting Mr. Estmund and his pack llamas.

Mr. Estmund had told Greer to call him Philip, said he was "no Mister Rogers, never was," but the Cedeños had trained her good. Now Greer called grown-ups mister or missus like they were in a '90s TV show. Mr. Estmund looked the part, handsome but shaky and tottery as he sipped from his fumy coffee mug. Her mom called him an "alkie," but Mr. Estmund was one of the most interesting people Greer had ever met. He didn't treat her like some stupid kid. He talked to her like she already knew everything about life, which, mostly, it felt like she did. All the other kids were like stupid babies. Even Juan sometimes, with his super nice mom and dad and three little adorable sisters.

Juan and Greer did their superstitious knock on the bus window as they dropped down 57—the steep, winding grade near the Timber Protective fire camp. Last year Lonnie had wrecked them into a logging truck and they'd almost gone off the edge, the bus's front tires dangling in space. Greer's face had smacked into the side of Juan's head; she got a black eye and fat lip. He got a bite mark on his ear. The EMTs told her she had a concussion and needed to stay in bed with no lights for a few days, but her mom was working swing shifts so Greer hid at Mr. Estmund's pasture, staying in his barn that smelled like sweet hay.

The llamas had enjoyed the company. They hung out with her instead of walking the fence as usual, looking for a way out. They hummed, flicked their ears at her, sniffed her shoes and knees, even lay next to her to chew their cud. She brought them apples and fresh Timothy grass, laughing as they plucked it from her hands, their long lips tickling her palms.

◆

Greer had helped Mr. Estmund repair fences that spring. Kelly and Yavell were expert escape artists, breaking out and running into the woods whenever they could, or, worse, running alongside the highway where log truck drivers blasted their horns and called them in on CBs to the main Headquarters logging office. The office people hollered through a loudspeaker that boomed all over town: "Llamas on the loose. Repeat. Llamas on the loose," instead of calling Mr. Estmund on the phone like normal people.

Whenever Greer heard the loudspeaker llama-escape alert, she dropped whatever she was doing, grabbed lead ropes and halters, and climbed into Mr. Estmund's old pickup with him to round up the llamas. She felt like she was in a rodeo, like she was an old western ranch hand lassoing llamas and hanging on to their long, fuzzy necks for dear life. It was pretty much the best thing in the world—besides hanging out with Juan and his family.

◆

"Did you *see* his face," Juan was saying, talking about Reggie the giant crybaby.

"*Wwwaaaa*—I want my *mommy*," Greer whined, mocking Reggie's tears while Juan was in the mood to gloat. Of course Greer always felt like crying and calling out for her mom whenever Rory came into her room, but she pushed that thought out of her mind. Juan and Greer rubbed their fists on their cheeks as they fake cried and then fake sucked their thumbs, laughing into fits of real tears until they had to bend over to catch their breath.

"You two were in rare form today," the substitute driver lady said as she let them off in Headquarters, smiling with her craggy horse face and stained horse teeth. They burst out laughing again after she pulled away. Now that Greer was on a roll and Juan wasn't disapproving, she started mocking the driver lady, too—even though she was pretty nice.

But then Greer saw Rory's truck at the house. She'd forgotten to check when they drove past the mill. Her mother's car was gone; that morning she'd said she needed to go score some more "logger's candy," acting like Greer didn't know what that meant. Rory had winked at Greer, said, "Looks like it'll be just you and me tonight, kid," and Greer's skin had crawled. Somehow she'd let a good day at school erase the dread.

"You coming?" Juan asked, stopping on the first set of stairs that led up to the Circle—all the houses left in town, except Mr. Estmund's place down by the fire pond. *Best spot in town,* he always said, even though the mosquitoes and biting flies hatched thick there and everyone thought he was a freaky hermit weirdo.

"I've got to help Mr. Estmund with the llamas," Greer lied. "I'll catch you later."

Juan scrunched his eyes. "Okay, but my mom made torta tres leches, and you know how much my little sisters can eat, so you don't want to be late!"

"Tell those three little piggies to stay away from my cake," Greer said, although thinking about the Three Little Pigs dampened her mood even more. They lost their home time after time, stranded outside, Big Bad Wolf lurking. Greer acted like she was too old for the bedtime stories Mrs. Cedeño read to Juan's sisters, but she made sure to sit close by and secretly follow along. She'd never had anyone read to her, but she kept a flashlight handy for night reading after her mom and Rory passed out.

Ash had started falling like dirty snow, and the smoke from the big North Fork Fire made it seem like they were in a winter storm, even though it was the end of summer. Greer sang *Ring around the rosies / Pocket full of posies / Ashes, ashes / We all fall down*, making sure to stand where Rory couldn't see her from the house. From the top of the last stairs, Juan looked back once more. "Don't be late," he called, cupping his hands to his mouth.

"Ha! You couldn't keep me away from that cake if you tried," Greer yelled back, even though it wasn't true. She planned to stay hidden all night.

◆

She hurried to the rickety bridge over the creek at the back of the pasture. Mrs. Cedeño didn't allow Juan to hang out anymore at Greer's house or even at the llama pasture. First it was because of Rory, but then Mr. Estmund ran his car into the creek right in town and some loggers winched him out. Mrs. Cedeño didn't want her son around a drunk, even a nice one. But Greer didn't mind having the pasture to herself. Enough hideouts to dodge anyone who might come along.

She stashed her backpack in the barn, where she'd rearranged bales of alfalfa and Timothy grass to make her secret hideout—a sweet-smelling prickly hay cave full of her favorite things. Bits of fool's gold Mr. Estmund had taught her how to pan out of the creek like the old-time miner Billy Rhodes; a raven skull with its giant eye sockets and black beak; ancient green bottles, rusty cans, and square nails she'd unearthed. She kept her Mr. Estmund interview tapes squirrelled away in there too, safe and dry in a zippered baggie.

She hadn't told anyone she'd kept up the fourth grade interview project long after Mr. Rears went on to a new unit. Doing the assignment was how Greer had become friends with Mr. Estmund in the first place. The teacher asked students to interview a veteran before the Veteran's Day assembly, so Greer and Juan had partnered up like usual. Mr. Estmund was the only veteran left in Headquarters, so they'd hiked down to his house to ask him. He was all jumpy and sketched out about it but he said yes.

They'd heard crazy stories about him—how he'd killed somebody and was hiding out, how he ate nothing but canned beans, how he made a coat out of chipmunk hides, how his fingernails were as long as a witch's and he never bathed. He turned out to be sort of disappointingly normal, but he told Greer and Juan cool stories. His house smelled like stew and fresh bread. His fingernails were short and clean.

After that, they went to his house every day after school. Greer used her mom's old tape recorder to record his stories (only a few of them about war) until Mrs. Cedeño said they had enough and it was time they stopped pestering the poor man. Greer knew that wasn't the reason. She knew it was because Mr. Estmund's words were often slurred, as if they'd recorded him at low speed. That he drove drunk. She let Juan think that she had stopped going to visit him too.

That spring and summer, she'd helped Mr. Estmund train the llamas, making them "kush" on command, taking them on long day hikes with loaded packs so they would be in shape for the long trips Mr. Estmund planned but never took. He'd bought the llamas after he'd broken his collarbone and couldn't carry a backpack. He made all their pack equipment using leather, sheepskin, canvas, oak, and old wax-coated cardboard dynamite boxes. They'd tried everything out on the llamas again and again, tightening this strap and that, making adjustments.

The llamas hummed and moaned and rolled their eyes, picking up one foot and then the other when something pinched or pulled. When they grew exasperated they would lay their ears back flat and hum in a new threatening pitch. They lifted their noses and tightened their lips and gurgle-burped wads of stinking cud from their impossibly long throats, letting loose on whoever was in spitting range.

Greer had learned to dodge their spitballs just as she'd learned to decipher their humming. Kelly's was high-pitched and questioning, Yavell's deep and vibrating. Their humming, along with their ear position and spitting, was how they communicated, different when they were happy or tired, curious or worried, consoling one another or fighting. Their voices had become as familiar now as her own, and she would often hum back, trying to enter their world as they had entered hers. Everything about them was strange and mysterious: their lushly-lashed eyes; their long giraffe necks; their thick fuzzy wool; their flicking tails; their swiveling ears; their soft-padded hooves; their dirty matted knees; their gurgling-throat fermented-cud breath; their long, expressive lips.

On their hikes, she led Kelly while Mr. Estmund led Yavell. Kelly was a small, gentle white and black fellow and her favorite although Yavell was prettier, tall and fluffy brown and white, with black super-long curled eyelashes even though he was a boy. They were always happy to get out on the trails, all humming cheerfully together. She and Mr. Estmund would laugh when Kelly got stalks of headed-out Timothy grass between his lips, his lower buckteeth jutting out, transforming him into a hilarious cartoon-hick llama.

Greer grabbed a granola bar from her hay-cave cache of food, water jugs, tarps, ropes, and trail maps. She'd learned from

Mr. Estmund to always be prepared for whatever might come. She wandered around the pasture as she ate her not-so-great dinner, looking for the llamas. She found Kelly at the old apple tree. Yavell was patrolling the back corner where the fence wire sagged no matter how many times Greer helped Mr. Estmund fix it. She ran at Yavell with a stick, shooing him away before he could escape, then headed to the pasture's frog pond—her favorite place of all.

The frogs recognized her now. They hardly even bothered to jump when they saw her coming. She'd named each of them—Striper, Blossom, Cordelia, Spotty, Leaper, and Lulu, easily telling them apart by their color variations. Her teachers all said she had excellent observation skills.

Greer had watched every day as the eggs developed from black specks to quivering pollywogs encased in clear jelly. When they hatched and started swimming around the cold ditch water with their cheerful black heads propelled by tiny whiptails, Greer was as proud as if they were her own babies. When they grew legs and arms and their tails shrank away—when they turned into adorable miniatures of their parents—she thought she might die of joy. She'd stayed at the pond each night until dark, guarding them until they grew large.

Once, before most of the other kids moved away—Headquarters dropping from two full school busses down to one with just a handful of riders—she'd gone to the other frog pond, down past the old log landing. It was horrible: all the frogs were slaughtered, skewered on sharpened sticks. She still wanted to hunt down the boys who did it and skewer them too.

Why did people in this town love to kill things? Garbage bins overflowed with elk and deer heads each fall, dull eyes looking at Greer every time she took out the trash. Dead cougars, black bears, and wolves were tossed into pickup beds, people gathering around like conquering heroes. Each fall, during hunting season, Mr. Estmund tied florescent flagging tape around the llamas so some stupid hunter didn't shoot them in the pasture.

Suddenly she didn't feel like catching frogs. She wanted to hide out in her hay cave and listen to some of the stories Mr. Estmund let her record. Rory was probably fuming, wondering where she was as evening fell, waiting to yell at her. And "tuck her in."

Mr. Estmund's stories about his daughter and son, Ava and Adonis, might help her think about something else. She had listened to them over and over, wearing down the recorder's batteries. Today she picked the Raven tape.

◆

"So, tell me all you know about ravens," Greer's voice started, a little squawky.

"Well, it all begins with earthworms," Mr. Estmund had said. He'd sat back in his chair and looked out the window as he always did when he got talking. "When Ava was little, she was so afraid of worms that I finally dug up the fattest one I could find, popped it in my mouth, chewed it up, and swallowed it. Told Ava that if worms were good enough for birds, they were good enough for people.

"After that, she turned into a bird *and* a worm lover. Didn't play a bassoon for earthworms or convert a billiards room into a sanctuary for them like Darwin did, but she gathered worms that got stranded on roads and parking lots and put them back to soil. Populated our garden. When she was just seven, she helped raise an injured raven named Midas and he ate worms out of her hands. And then she became a bird expert and a professor—an ornithologist—and studied ravens along with all the other birds that live here."

"Ravens and crows are the same family, right?" Greer asked on the tape, proud of the research she'd done at school to prepare.

"Corvidae, yes," Mr. Estmund said, falling into his serious teaching voice Greer liked so well. "Which includes ravens, crows, magpies, rooks, jackdaws, jays, treepies, choughs, and nutcrackers. The common raven, *Corvus corax,* is often confused with the common crow, *Corvus brachyrhynchos,* but I would argue it is an easy distinction to make just by size alone, not to mention their calls, social structures, and habitat preferences."

"Where do ravens like to live?"

"They're largely forest creatures, living in boreal, conifer, and deciduous forests, but also in the tundra, prairies, and human-inhabited areas. They prefer large trees for nesting and protect up to ten square kilometers with their breeding partner, staying with the same mate until death."

"What do they like to eat?" she asked, ticking through her handwritten questions.

"Arthropods, small mammals, amphibians, reptiles, birds and their eggs, berries, carrion, grains, buds, plants, human and livestock food…the better question would be what *don't* ravens eat. They're very adaptable creatures."

Greer liked to think she, too, was a very adaptable creature.

"So, they're smart?"

"Oh, yes, they're very, very smart. The avian brain is not celebrated or appreciated as much as it should be, especially corvids. We are talking about a mental capacity that exceeds or matches nearly any titan of the animal kingdom. Ravens have more brain cells, neurons, in their pallia—the structured cortex in the cerebrum—than mammals do and have human-level intelligence in certain behaviors. For example, self-awareness in mirror tests, using tools, and planning for future events and tasks—previously thought to be only human and ape capabilities. And when it comes to puzzle solving or tool acquisition and use, you won't find any creature more advanced."

Mr. Estmund sounded like a proud parent bragging about his gifted child.

Greer loved it when he spoke about her the same way.

"I learned in school that ravens recognize human faces, friend or enemy," she said.

"Yes, episodic memory, which we once believed only humans and other primates have," Mr. Estmund replied.

She remembered him circling his hands as he spoke, his face animated.

"They hold funerals for their dead and hold grudges against other ravens that cheat or are unfair to others in the social group. They plan for the future and barter. They are better at planning future trades than orangutans, bonobos, and chimpanzees, and match apes at planning ahead and using tools, even though they don't need tools to gather food in the wild.

"They gesture to communicate, pointing with their beaks, and they play games like hide and seek. They are extremely acrobatic and do rolls and somersaults in the air, and often soar wingtip to wingtip, swooping together in unison, tumbling through the sky. They have even been witnessed flying upside down for more than a half mile."

"Do you know any other stories about ravens?" Greer asked. Mr. Estmund was one of the best storytellers ever, no matter what kind of story he decided to tell.

"Well, Indigenous Peoples of the Pacific Northwest regard Raven as trickster with high intelligence, and a keeper of powerful medicine, bringing fire to people by stealing it from the sun, and stealing salmon to drop them in rivers all over the world. One of the seminal Nimíipuu creation stories features Raven, who has the gift of warning and carrying messages over long distances."

"Do you know any other raven facts?" Greer asked, wrapping up her interview just as Mr. Rears had taught them to.

"Well, they are the largest songbird, although most people didn't think of them as songbirds. They sing soft warbling songs to their mates and preen each other's feathers while they make 'comfort sounds.' They mimic human voices often better than parrots, as well as other animal and bird calls and sounds—like a toilet flushing or a car starting. Their beaks are threaded with cells that can detect vibrations, like remote sensing, like echolocation. And their feathers aren't really black. They're blue, green, violet, pink, gold. They are magical, mythological creatures, just like some children are magical, mythological creatures."

He'd grinned and patted the top of Greer's head as she pressed STOP, just as she did now.

◆

After she'd recorded the Raven Interview, she put her raven skull over the door in her hay cave to stand guard, keep her from harm. She named it Icarus. She liked to think that she and the skull raven were part of Mr. Estmund's family, like Ava and Adonis. In her head, she'd named them all the Raven Family, herself an integral member.

She stood up now and brushed off the hay, deciding she would ask Mr. Estmund to tell her one of his river stories, when he and Ava swam across rapids to where forest fairies lived. He and Ava had even spotted one once, darting through the ferns before it disappeared into the ancient cedars he said were thousands of years old—growing when Homer wrote the Iliad and the Odyssey, which Greer had never heard of. So he told her it was when Moses was alive. He said the cedars were like giants. Maidenhair ferns and flowers named queen's cup, lady slipper, fairy bell, fawn lily, wood nymph grew under them—names that gave Greer shivers of delight. She dreamed of living in the cedar forests like the fairies and dryads.

But when Greer got to Mr. Estmund's house, he was in one of his quiet, sad moods. He didn't want to talk. She sat with the tape recorder running anyway, tried to ask good lead questions about his adventures with Ava, but Mr. Estmund only grumbled.

Usually he gave her something good to eat or drink, but tonight he stayed slumped in his chair, refilling his coffee cup from the bottle he kept tucked there, his hands shakier than usual.

"Are you okay, Mr. Estmund?" she finally asked.

He looked at her with such sad eyes it made her want to cry. She didn't know what else to do, so she pulled the wool blanket off the back of the couch and laid it on his lap.

"Do you want something to eat? Some water?" she asked.

"She won't come here anymore," Mr. Estmund said.

Greer didn't know who he was talking about.

"Told me I needed to get help. AA." He laughed, but it wasn't the happy kind. "I told her she was the one who needed help. Working herself to death. Forgetting that real life is happening right now. Not seeing what she's losing, what she's already lost.

"*I* remember who she wanted to be. She wanted to live at the river when she grew up, speak its language, learn its secret fairy-land magic. But where is she now? Head buried in her studies, in her data and reports."

He glanced at Greer, his voice suddenly steady. "That's life's truest secret, Greer. Pay attention to everything nature says. You've got to listen to nature if you want to know anything about yourself or this earth—breathing its air, drinking its water, eating its plants and its creatures. Nothing else can teach you what you need to know about real things. You must learn to hear it. To see it. To taste it. To smell it. To feel it. To know it. To be it. Only then will you know what it means to be real and alive."

He stopped and glanced out the window, like he did when-ever he told a story. Greer looked out too, thinking how she would try harder to listen to what nature was saying, and how if she did—

They saw Rory at the same time, his dark bulk crossing the wobbly footbridge nobody ever used but her, coming toward Mr. Estmund's house fast and angry.

Coming for her.

She knew to run before Mr. Estmund told her to. Knew where to go and how to get there undetected, fleeing out the back and through the pasture. When she reached her hay cave, she knew to pull bales down to disguise the opening as Rory pounded on Mr. Estmund's front door.

From her shelter she could hear Rory's angry voice.

"You fucking little whore you better not be in there with that kike lech or I'll fucking kill you both…"

She clutched her knees to her chest, quivering so hard her teeth rattled. Her fingernails dug into her palms and her pants were wet where she'd peed herself, the smell like animal musk. Like terror.

A moment of silence and then a gunshot, unmistakable, the echoing report so loud it surrounded her. The percussion tamped her eardrums. She tipped over as if she'd been hit.

She wrapped herself into a ball on the hay-covered ground and sobbed until she choked.

◆

The rest she'd recall as if she were watching another girl, not quite her, moving from the barn to the house. Fleeing. Seeing what no child should ever see.

She watched herself stand before Mr. Estmund slumped in his chair. Blood. The tape recorder whirred where it fell, hidden by the blanket slipped from his lap. She picked them up like up a baby in swaddling. She pressed STOP.

She caught the llamas in the dark, fit their harnesses and gear, loaded the packs with the supplies and tools Mr. Estmund had taught her she'd need. She clutched the raven's skull in her hand for protection as she led the llamas into the night.

Greer saw the girl-who-was-Greer reach the trailhead hidden in the trees' enfolding blackness, sense the contours in the dark, and orient herself toward the North Fork.

AVA

Ava gripped the steering wheel, her gaze on the horizon. One slip of emotion and her resolve would crumble—and there was no way to go back. The damage was done. The future she'd believed in was torched with everything else in this fire-cursed summer.

To steady herself, she counted birds: three rough-legged hawks, *Buteo lagopus;* two sharp-shinned hawks, *Accipiter striatus*; a Swainson's hawk, *Buteo swainsoni*; a murder of crows, *Corvus brachyrhynchos*. A small conspiracy of ravens, *Corvus corax*.

The Palouse Prairie's gusty thermal updrafts and rolling fields of wheat, lentils, and canola made a heady raptor paradise brimming with quarry: mice, voles, moles, weasels, squirrels, rabbits, snakes, songbirds. Ava told her students that on any given day they could spot a dozen raptors from the highway. From the Latin *rapere*: To seize, snatch, grab, take away. Harris's hawks, Cooper's hawks, Swainson's hawks, rough-legged hawks, ferruginous hawks, sharp-shinned hawks, red-tailed hawks, northern/American goshawks, northern harriers, prairie falcons, American kestrels, northern hawk owl, great horned owls, great grey owl, prairie owl, western screech-owls, burrowing owls, bald eagles. Not to mention all the migratory raptors, and with them, the resident corvids—crows and ravens and magpies that raucously harassed the birds of prey, stealing hard-won kills, dismantling carefully laid nests, and scaring them away from their own boisterous corvid broods.

At a stoplight, a starling, *Sturnus vulgaris*, landed atop a power pole and sang his rendition of a dozen songs copied from other birds more melodically gifted, although Ava conceded his meadowlark imitation was solid—that watery trill of empty prairie.

Ava, already spinning through time, was transported back to the loneliness of her early childhood on the Fraser Prairie. *Sturnella neglecta.* The universe had sung her fate long ago.

◆

When Ava's mother conceived her, Ava's father felt urgent about "going back to the land." They drove from Washington's bustling west side until they chanced upon the camas and wild rose expanses of Idaho's Weippe Prairie. They fell in love with it.

Perched above the Clearwater River, the Weippe Prairie was the ancestral home of the Nez Perce people, where they lived abundantly on berries, camas bulbs, salmon and elk. Ava's father taught her that the Weippe Nez Perce saved the Corps of Discovery—Lewis and Clark—from certain death, feeding and clothing them, nursing them back from exhaustion and illness, teaching them the lay of the land. Without this friendship, the explorers never would have made the last and cruelest leg to the Pacific.

Ava's parents rented a primitive log farmhouse on the prairie surrounded by sky. With no running water except what ran from the roof to the cistern, they trotted to an outhouse thirty yards out back and bathed in a salvaged clawfoot tub in the kitchen next to the wood cookstove where they heated water and bucket-filled the tub.

They had good garden space, chickens, peonies, and a giant

ponderosa that swayed in the wind, scenting the air with its butterscotch bark. It was exactly how Ava's father had always dreamed of living—where they could grow and put up food, where they could have elbow room and unending views. Where they could be the kind of family he'd always wanted.

But of course the reality of it impeded on the dream.

Her father loved to tell Ava's birth story. How she'd shot from Fiona's loins, sailing off the delivery table and into the air. How the midwife barely caught her by one slick tiny ankle, and he'd known right then his little girl would charge headlong into life, doing everything she was meant to do, being all she was meant to be. *A real go-getter,* he always said. *A girl who's going to fly.*

Her mother weighted the origin story with a somber detail: an identical twin, undeveloped and undetected until after Ava's delivery. Ava had often wondered who she might have become with a mirror companion. Had her twin made it into the world with her—accompanying her on her lonely childhood journey, connected in that way only those who share a womb can be, developing together every step of the way, making decisions together, watching each other's backs—what different life might she have led? Her unrelenting loneliness and introspection had likely begun with that early elemental loss, shaping all else that was to come.

Long limbs, umber eyes, dark hair—Ava's maternal heritage was immediately evident, ancient Ashkenazi DNA linking one woman to the next, lineage traceable to a primeval bottleneck event. Some unknown catastrophe had left only four founder women, passing themselves through the ages to Ava. "A daughter of royal blood," her mother always said, although Ava never saw anything royal about her life. Except birds.

It wasn't until she'd entered the university that she learned the long history of atheist scientist Jews like her, questioning the world, setting about to find the universe's possible answers.

The best and truest answer had been Sibley.

Normally this time of year, Sibley and Ava would be making weekly trips to the Saturday farmers market, sampling the hottest peppers and funkiest fruit, choosing a new book from BookPeople. They would be petting passing dogs and greeting friends before helping Alfred harvest his copious garden, taking bushels of extra produce to the ornithology break room on Monday mornings, scavengers from surrounding departments swooping in for the bounty.

◆

Near the airport parking lot, a flock of American goldfinches, *Spinus tristis,* and lesser goldfinches, *Spinus psaltria,* flitted around a weedy ditch full of native sunflowers, hammering their wedged beaks into the ready feast of seed.

Ava told her memorizing-weary undergrads that at least Latinate nomenclature applied the same rules to everything and everybody instead of the exceptionalism so often evident in common names—like the two local species of goldfinches—*American* and *lesser.* Claire had embraced the Latin names with gusto and delight, appreciating their beauty and cadence. Ava could still hear Claire's voice, a clarion. What kind of ornithologist she would have become. A friend, a collaborator, a sister scientist.

◆

Open prairie rolled in an undulating expanse under the plane's wings, the sky orange above thick wildfire haze (No. 81, Deep Reddish Orange / Gold Fish lustre abstracted / Scarlet Leadington Apple). Trapped smoke created a citrus-colored sunset. When she was a child, Ava loved seeing things from the air—the earth new and strange from the perspective of height.

The plane banked over Orofino, the state prison below glinting in the strange sunlight.

Oro-fino: fine gold, her father had taught her as they drove through the river valley town on their way to Headquarters— the regional names mapping the 1800s goldrush, or the logging rush that quickly followed.

Her father's favorite mountain man stories paid tribute to the Ridgerunner, who'd haunted the North Fork in the mid-1900s in life and beyond; and Billy Rhodes, a legendary nine-teenth-century goldminer, a Black man. Place names across the wilds of the North Fork's Idaho-Montana Bitterroot Mountains alluded to his remarkable life.

Her father had taught Ava how to pan for gold like Billy Rhodes, goading her on with visions of a "deep vein." The most they got were pans of mica and silt. Fool's gold, like her father's life. Dregs of lost promise. His body, awaiting autopsy and cre-mation, about to become silt.

◆

Ava had considered contacting her mother about Philip's death—not that Ava had a simple way to do that. As far as she knew, her mother was still in the no-tech, ultra-religious cult she'd joined twenty years ago, abandoning Ava, moving on to produce a host of half-siblings Ava had never met, who likely didn't know Ava existed.

Darkness falling, the plane reached altitude and Ava sat back in her seat, waiting for Houston—a visit with Adonis at the Huntsville prison to deliver the news of their father's death. A heavy unspoken weight strung the distance between brother and sister, pendulous and tipping.

Ava hadn't met Adonis until the Summer of the Raven—her paternal half-brother from Texas, eleven years older. After his high school graduation, he came to Idaho to finally meet his "baby sister." As soon as Ava saw him, she worshipped him, this tall, blonde, curly-haired, copper-skinned brother she'd had all along—but also had not.

They were so different at a first glance that nobody would guess they were siblings—until catching the identical cant of leg and jaw and shoulder blade. Until hearing them laugh the same laugh, even though he was an adult man and she was a little girl.

That summer with Adonis was burnished in Ava's memory. Holding his hand as they walked downtown to buy ice cream cones; clinging to his neck like a monkey as he did pull-ups from a tree in the backyard; sitting on his lap, both sweet-talking Midas the raven. Adonis had been so gentle, so strong, so self-possessed. He loved to make her laugh with his jumping biceps, with his uncanny ability to mimic voices and sounds and people, with his animated, expressive face. He would swing her up on his shoulders, and from that dizzying height she owned the world. They owned the world together.

They released Midas the morning before Adonis returned to Texas. The scene was cinematic—Adonis with Midas on his forearm, a golden god and his dark talisman. Adonis tossed his arm into the air and Midas took flight, black wings stretched wide, Adonis and Ava running and calling encouragement as Midas flew low, confused by sudden freedom. But then, with a few strong wingbeats, Midas lifted into forest and disappeared.

Ava sat down and cried. Adonis sat and cried with her. It seemed like the end of magic.

Adonis returned to Texas and within months transformed into a junkie who traded sex for drugs. A prominent congressman picked him up from a street corner one night and the next morning Adonis used a stolen pistol to deliver two close-range shots to the back of the congressman's head. He took the man's I.D., went to the bank, and tried to make a sizable withdrawal. The police swarmed in and arrested him, the news helicopters circled. The new D.A. was eager to make his Texas law-and-order name prosecuting a flashy, high-visibility capital murder case.

During the trial, the defense told the court what Adonis hadn't been able to spill. He'd spent the night before the murder hogtied and raped by the congressman, just as he'd spent three days restrained and raped as a ten-year-old out at hunting camp by a family "friend." In a state hungry for executions, the revelation had, for better or worse, softened the sentence to two consecutive life terms, no chance for parole.

Only once before had Ava flown to visit Adonis, right after his conviction. Eleven years old, she'd been shocked by his transformation—hollow face and sunken eyes, body covered in death-head tattoos effacing the ephemeral golden brother. Sitting at a bare round table with a guard nearby, they made distressing small talk. But then he opened up, warm, sharing his plans. He would join the Merchant Marines and move to South America. Fish for his supper, live free and easy.

Even at eleven, Ava understood that Adonis would never be free again.

Before the guards took him back, he squeezed Ava's hands across the table, made her promise she would forever guard and follow her heart, always stay true to herself, never let herself be captured.

◆

Houston's lights blinked in the void ahead. The pilot's disembodied voice announced approach as the seatbelt alert chimed. Ava imagined Adonis in his prison below, waiting for what would never come.

As Ava rolled her carry-on out of the airport's security zone, she spotted Beth right away. Tall, big-boned, and buxom—a ship with a mast—Beth cut through crowds like she was parting the sea. She swept Ava up in a full body embrace, her scent just as Ava remembered from two decades ago: gardenia and Marlboros.

"Look at you," Beth said, pulling back. "Pretty as a picture. Little Ava, all grown up. Ya'll need to come down from Idaho and visit your Texas cousin more often!"

"I planned to come sooner, but—"

"If the plan don't work, change the plan."

Ava smiled. "Yes, something like that."

"You're here now, that's all that matters," Beth drawled. She commandeered Ava's bag and rolled it clacking behind her as she plowed through the mob. Ava stuck close until they reached Beth's white and gold Cadillac, gleaming in its premium parking space. Ava was relieved to be led and ordered, at least for now.

Beth sped down the freeway, windows down as she smoked and filled Ava in on twenty years of news. Warm air buffeting, Houston came back to her—downtown skyscrapers, the awe of being in such a large city—as a child, her first journey out of the Pacific Northwest. The turgid air felt like a solid physical entity. Her first cardinals, their bright red bodies miraculous. A teal-headed pigeon lying dead at the front door, victim of fire ants.

Ava imagined Ecuador's impact would be similar—the wonder of parrots with beaks strong enough to snap human bones, even the little lime-colored parrotlets able to carve chunks of flesh from a fingertip in one quick nip. Ravens relied on cleverness rather than force, which is why Ava would always love them best. But maybe it was time to appreciate another tactic.

When Beth pulled into the Woodlands—trees and shrubs taking over the city's detritus—a great horned owl swooped low in front of the windshield, illuminated in the headlights before vanishing like an apparition. Beth swerved and cussed.

"Goddamned owl gives me a heart attack every damn time.

I swear it just waits until it sees me to do a fly-by. It likes to give me a start. Trying to kill me."

Ava laughed. She could imagine the owl's nightly flight path deep in the heart of the fourth-largest city in the nation. She'd always been awed by animal abilities to adapt to messy human development. Peregrine falcons proliferated in NYC high-rises. Coyotes and cougars stalked LA streets. Black bears bellied up to porch rails like they were ordering drinks, sipping nectar from hummingbird feeders, leaving them intact for refills.

Beth pulled into her air-conditioned three-car garage. She'd worked her way up from kennel cleaner to operating her own high-end pet boarding facility. Over the years, she'd sought Ava's advice, mostly on how to deal with problem parrots.

Ava put her luggage in the bedroom Beth ushered her to, pillows laid with chocolates, scented candles burning on the dresser. Ava thought of Persephone, adjusting to her new temporary home with Alfred. One more step until freedom. But from there it was only a short jump to thinking about Sibley, so Ava went out and lifted a glass to Beth's toast. "To cousins, to reunions, to running away from it all."

She could see it would be a late night. Her head was buzzing and shorting as if she'd been shocked. She sat outside with Beth in the warm, humid night. Sounds of the city. Beth lit a post-dinner cigarette—a ritual Ava envied a little, that effortless flick and flare of a lighter, the sweetly acrid smell of burning tobacco.

"I'm so sorry Uncle Philip went out that way," Beth said behind the red glow of her Marlboro, the Texas sky a black expanse over their heads. "I thought he would live forever, wild nature man that he was. Cousin Donnie will be crushed. He worshipped your dad."

The rush of secondhand smoke spun Ava's head. She felt like a messenger from the underworld, come to deliver sorrow. Her father had been absent years before his death. She never made the three-hour drive from the university to visit him in Head-quarters. He and Adonis hadn't made contact in over a decade. But this was different. Now their father was truly gone.

Packing up her things for storage, she'd found photos from the Summer of the Raven. Adonis and Midas and little-girl Ava perched on a porch rail, hanging fuchsia blooming behind them, Midas's feathers glossy in the sun. Adonis and Ava mid-stride, her hip at his knee, her head at his chest, both with the same long legs in cutoffs. Both holding an ice-cream cone in their right hands, their elbows and chins and shoulders and necks and knees and feet the same cant. Genetic repetitions of one another.

Of Philip.

"Bright and early, then?" Beth asked, stubbing out her butt. "The prison likes to make things as much a pain-in-the-ass as possible. You brought long-sleeved shirts and pants? They've been turning visitors away for 'clothing violations.' Goddamned Nazis make you dress like a nun. What's a little cleavage ever hurt?"

She gave her ample breasts a shake.

Ava smiled. "I think I'm prepared," she said, though she was anything but.

EZRA

From Seattle it was simple: the port, the gulls, then nothing but sunbaked metal, oiled rope, engine roar, water. The Pacific a wide empty highway south.

That's when Ezra finally let himself look—really look—for the first time in ten years. Standing in place, dripping mop in hand, portside on a small cargo ship (its name, the *Valiant Endurance,* a stretch), eyes on the water. The reality of one day following another and another toward endless days ahead, open as ocean.

At first, as the crew made their way out into the shipping lanes, Ezra was had been sure the Coast Guard would come roaring at any moment, horns blaring, lights flashing. Take him back into custody, return him to his cell forever. But now, despite the radios, despite the GPS, despite the filed route plans and crew manifests, locating one quiet parole fugitive surrounded by thousands of miles of water seemed unlikely. Impossible. The ship a gray speck bobbing in a silver sea. The vastness arrested him with its raw, disinterested power. The movement of a whole planet beneath them.

So many years on guard. So much vigilance. Any time he'd let his mind wander, lost his foothold, the monkeys howled in, sensing vulnerability like vibration. A scent.

He'd learned to sleep tuned in, to incorporate exhaustion,

because the consequences of relaxing, even for a minute, were too brutal to risk. But even after all the years of fear and fatigue, planning each step to release and freedom, he hadn't imagined how firmly this great expanse of water would hold him. He was captured by it. Overcome.

◆

"Ezra Kittredge?"

"Yes, Your Honor."

"Mr. Kittredge. Do you understand your rights?"

"Yes, Sir. Yes, Your Honor. Yes. I understand."

The right to run, to escape, to live life my own way.

The right to leave the world behind and all that I've ever lost.

He understood perfectly. Fire and loss, fire and loss. Ending and beginning...

Everything began at a precipice, at the jumping off point.

He'd made the leap. There was no going back. Ever.

◆

He heard footsteps behind him. He tore his eyes from the water, turned back to the deck.

"What are you doing, waiting for the fucking shrimp buffet?" Tiny (who was not) glared from behind the predominance of his stomach, his rankness a cloud. He pointed a stub of a finger in Ezra's face. "This ain't a freeloader cruise, it's a working ride, so fucking get to work, con."

The breeze kicked up and Tiny's odor enveloped Ezra, a full-body embrace. That was all it took. Ezra's stomach turned sail, churning like the swells slapping against the ship's hundred-ton push. If they'd been on land, Ezra would have gotten in Tiny's face, said, *What's that, shitface?* Would have planted a fist in the ample padding below his sternum and altered each plane of his features. But instead, Ezra stumbled over and gripped the railing, his knuckles white, his stomach roiling.

Tiny narrowed his eyes further. "One call's all I have to make, and you can stare at white walls all you fucking want." He turned and lumbered away, his smell hovering like roadkill.

Ezra held out until Tiny was out of view before hurling watery vomit. He watched it spread like mist against the side of the ship. When there was nothing left to bring forth, he straightened and wiped his mouth with the back of his hand. He re-wet his mop in the bucket and concentrated on the slippery lines of his strokes. The mop head splayed against the deck, fraying out like a woman's wild hair. He tried to ground himself by reciting Sonnet 65:

> Since brass, nor stone, nor earth, nor boundless sea
> But sad mortality o'ersways their power,
> How with this rage shall beauty hold a plea…

When he finished the side deck, he wiped the sweat from his face. Breathed salt air. Calmed. Work did him good, always had. Set his mind toward liberation.

He'd known that when his parole finally came, he wouldn't stay put even though the courts and their flunkies told him he must. To wait around for what? Some mistake, coincidence, fluke? That's all it would take for him to be back in. Who would accept those terms? Who would accept such an existence? A lifetime was already spent and over. He wouldn't give another.

He dumped his bucket water over the side, watched as it atomized. Sweat soaked his torso. He longed to jump overboard, swim, clear his head, straighten his stomach, but the waterline was fifty feet down and he knew the ship wouldn't stop for him to climb back up. Tiny was right. Ezra had been lucky to get on at all. He'd stay on to safe harbor.

He'd spent years studying shipping terminology and routes,

preparing himself for the sea, but he was no sailor. Expendable as a paper boat. Who couldn't manage a mop and dirty dishes? Who couldn't scrub toilets and mirrors, peel potatoes and chop onions? He wished he could float his way to the Galapagos Islands without interacting with anybody. Safer for everyone. The few passengers on board—the young couple with crosses around their necks, the three old women with swollen feet and ridiculous hats—would likely share his sentiments if they were privy to his rap sheet. That would wreck their sleep, knowing a man who ruined everything he touched was changing their bedding, refreshing their towels, mopping out their bathrooms, peeling their spuds.

The air was damp. The breeze blew droplets on his cheeks. He put his face to it, took a long breath before rolling his bucket behind him into the maze of multi-colored towers. Shipping containers were stacked like a giant's toy blocks, worn green and red paint. Faded lettering and clanking chains. Inside were rich men's cars, speedboats, motorcycles. Luxury items enroute to pollute another shore with fouled desires.

Ezra had limited his desires to some food in his stomach, some clothes on his back, some shelter over his head. No extravagance. No excess. Was this a strange gift of imprisonment? Life crystallized.

He stopped between rows 12 and 13, leaned back against a container, absorbing the heat radiating from its metal side. He tipped his face to the sun, cupped his hand around a cigarette and lit up, inhaling deeply. Smoking wasn't allowed on the ship, but that didn't stop anyone. He'd seen butts crumpled under the containers. He took another pull, flicking the ash to his feet.

The sun was a round blot haloed in the sky's pale wash. An expanse that matched the sea. What wasn't possible in such space? What limits could hold tenure in such vastness?

◆

While Tiny was still making his rounds, Ezra hoped to trot to the messroom closet without seeing anyone, refresh his cleaning supplies, and get back to work. But no such luck. He'd picked the worst possible time—the passengers and most of the crew were gathered at the dining tables. He'd forgotten the lunch schedule.

The captain, Vic, clapped Ezra hard on the back and said, "Easy, buddy."

Ezra wished he'd stayed up top longer, Tiny or no Tiny. He knew how fast things could turn with a big man who liked to be boss. He was surprised the captain was mingling with the passengers at this time of day, but then again, one look at the missionary wife was enough to explain.

"You met everyone?" The captain pointed from left to right with his thick ropey arm. "Mary, Penny, and Grace. And the Talberts, Chadwick and Angela."

"Chad and Angie," Chad corrected, clearing his voice as he rose from his seat. He was a small man, nearly bald even though he was probably only in his late twenties. Ezra's age. Chad would likely be potbellied and atrophied by the time he reached mid-thirties. One of the early-married religious. How the hell did he score a woman like Angela?

The captain tried to smile but it came off more as a sneer. "Yeah, a lot of people don't go by their names on the manifest. Take *Easy* here for instance." He grabbed Ezra by the back of the neck, fingers twitching for a ball and bruise. The captain gave Ezra a hearty shake and bared his teeth. "You need any-thing, you let him know. Garbage picked up, toilet scrubbed, anything."

Angie seemed interested. "Nice to meet you," she said, standing up to offer her hand, looking Ezra in the eye longer than a Christian wife should. She was nearly his height, six feet. Big brown eyes. Thick, wavy brown hair. Long legs. A body curved to turn heads.

Chad leaned past her, gave a brief nod and limply shook Ezra's hand, letting go too fast.

It made Ezra flinch, how thin and vulnerable people allowed themselves to be. How easily they gave themselves away. He'd seen enough of these two to know all he wanted to know. Plenty of people like them circulated through the prison system, peddling salvation like a drug.

But Angie wasn't done. "What kind of name is 'Easy'?" she asked, still standing, her shapely eyebrows arched.

"That's what I want to know," the chattiest of the old women said with what once must have been a coy smile. She turned to her friends, stage whispering, "This is the one I was telling you about. I told him I could use some of whatever he was selling."

Penny slapped her on her leg. "Stop it, Mary. You're embarrassing the poor kid. Look at him blush."

Ezra wasn't embarrassed. Nor was he a kid, and he wasn't poor, at least in the sense the old woman meant it. "A nickname," he said. "Short for Ezra."

(*Teachers, counselors, principals, wardens, captains: "Easy now. Easy there…"*)

"Not a name you'd forget," Angie said. She sat down with her husband. "Would you like to join us?" She looked at Ezra, something in her expression more complex than he could read.

"Just getting more supplies," Ezra blurted.

"Next time then," Chad said, taking a bite. "Can't beat these sandwiches."

Angie regarded Ezra. "Yes, another time perhaps," she said, and now Ezra thought her dark eyes were saying *help me, help me, help me.*

Timothy's hair whipping out from the tire swing's twirling force, suspended above the dark flat flow of the St. Joe. Out-of-work logger walking the roadside, his face turning toward Ezra's headlights in acceptance and defeat. Mother in her hospice bed holding his hand in her thin, papery palm. Claire sitting on bear grass talking about swimming cold water, the burning tree coming. Help me, help me, help me...

He backed away, gripping the mop handle.

"You must come around and regale us with your swash-buckling stories *E-Z*," Mary chattered, obtuse. "I'm sure you have some good ones."

"Is this your first trip to Ecuador?" Penny asked. "It's our third. Gets better each time."

Re-incarceration—a term like a terrible version of reincarnation...

"First and only," he said, sweating.

◆

In the dankness of the supply closet, the vibration of the engine in the ship's bowels reverberated through the beams and rivets, a thudding roar. Ezra rinsed his brushes and mop, trying to work methodically, settle his pulse, calm his harsh breath. Shut out Angie's pleading, liquid eyes.

He took a circuitous route toward his cabin. The ship was a maze he had yet to fully learn—decks, stairs, berths, and holds. He heard someone coming, the steps light and quick. He crushed his freshly lit cigarette underfoot, toeing it under the dunnage.

Domingo, the boatswain on watch, gave Ezra a quick nod. "You enjoying the ride?"

He was slight but wiry, spring-loaded. Not someone to ignore.

Ezra glanced out at the choppy gray expanse of sea. "So much water."

Domingo laughed. "So much fuckin' water. You ever been up Iceberg Alley? Coldest route I ever shipped. Had to run double watches to keep up with the bergs. It's their birthing ground and fuck if they don't look like giant water babies, all smooth-skinned and blue."

For some reason Ezra pictured the whip-thin racing dogs he'd glimpsed the first foggy morning on the ship, emerging from one of the floor-level containers.

Domingo smoked thoughtfully. "Ecuador's beaches now, mmhm." He shook his head and smiled. "Sunset, good waves, warm enough to swim naked. Kind of water I like." He flicked his cigarette in the air, the red of its burning ember tracing down to the water. "Manta," he held his hand up to his heart and gazed skyward in reverence. "Manta's got all the action, if you know what I mean. You'll be wanting some, no?" He hit Ezra on the arm. "Finest ass there is."

Ezra watched the horizon fade to yellow then gray. Imagined opening his arms to the world again, accepting its gifts. "I was planning on heading further south, finding a little beach town to stay a bit, then the Galapagos."

The name rolled in his mouth.

He'd read everything he could about Ecuador, plotted the ways he might lose himself. He memorized photographs of straw-hatted men with ancient, wrinkled faces, leading burros hauling cut poles from the forests; colorful parrots flocking in the tops of trees; beaches and blue waters dotted with boats of varying shades of teal, the names and likenesses of saints painted on their hulls to bless their catch.

Domingo nodded with appreciation. "Yeah man, you never know what you might find if you don't go looking for it. You've got to live whatever makes you happy, that's what I say. 'Be happy, don't worry.' Me and Bob Marley. Me and my baby mama, Dahiana. Can't wait to get back to her, mmhm."

Whatever makes you happy.

A little boy brought back from the flames? A drunk out-of-work logger walking a road into the night, finding his way home? A bright, bird-loving firefighter girl floating in cold green river waters?

THE ORIGIN OF AVA

When Ezra got back to his berth, he found a glossy pamphlet wedged into his door, its front cover demanding, "Have You Thought About Your Future?" above a photo of a man contemplating a starry night sky. A sticky note with a scrawled message: "Didn't suppose you'd be in yet but stopped by anyway. We'd love to talk when you get a chance. Our best, Chad and Angie." With the wide, sensuous cursive, it was obvious who'd written it.

Ezra sat on his bunk and read the pamphlet. The world was crumbling and "Man" was facing certain demise unless he found The One True Way. Didn't these people ever doubt their god's inviolability as grand puppeteer? Didn't they realize there was nothing beyond this one life? There was no help. But people like Chad and Angie would just keep preaching, believing, keep trying to make people live "right" forever and ever amen, never taking responsibility for their own fates or actions.

He threw the pamphlet in the garbage.

In his cramped shower, he focused on the cascade of warm water and lather of soap and shaving with a four-blade razor—luxuries that still felt like dreaming. He toweled off and lay on his bed, the sea lightly rocking. He tried not to think about Angie as the engine lulled him groggy. He needed to keep his head straight, his eyes open. Nine days—a little over a week—and this leg would be done. How hard could that be after five thousand, one hundred and thirty-four days?

He kept his green Army-surplus rucksack packed and ready.

Follow the Malecón, find your way. Go south.

◆

He'd always understood the ways of water—streams, creeks, rivers, lakes, the Pacific with its rolls and swells, its unbroken flats that looked like silver-blue glass, its white-capped waves that slapped now against the ship's metal hull. He'd tried to prepare himself to be at sea, imagined the wind overhead, dark clouds bunching, slanting rain and angry waves—but so far it'd just been a push through flat waters.

Out his port window the sky was striated—high cirrus clouds streaked behind a sinking sun, burnished as an August wildfire moon.

The first time he'd been to the coast—his mother taking him and Timothy—he'd watched the sunset in horror, certain he was witnessing the end of the world. As the sun was extinguished by the sea, he could hear it sizzling, steam rising as it cooled into a dead blue disc sinking forever into dark. Ezra had wailed and cried despite his mother's reassurance. He stayed awake through the night with a terrible knowing: humans would never see the light of day again. When the morning sky started growing light, when the birds cheered, when the sun peeked over the horizon, triumphant, five-year-old Ezra woke Timothy with cries of joy.

What a disaster they'd averted!

Outside his window, the sun's smooth curve touched down on the flat Pacific. A whisper of meeting, a sensuous first touch. A lipping.

Darkness came fast, the ship's rhythmic push through water thrumming beneath him.

A sigh born upon the waves. The humid air scented with his own sweat.

It was a thing he'd almost forgotten—the dark earthy recesses of your own senses inhabiting you. No different from an animal, but he already knew that. Men driven by things they couldn't name yet knew by taste, smell, sound, sight, touch. Flashes of pure colorless light, so bright they could hold you, if only for a brief moment, aloft.

GREER

The fire Greer built was smoky. Damp branches and punky tinder.

On hands and knees, squinting, she blew on the miniature teepee. Mr. Estmund had taught her that teepees made the best campfire structure, lichen and bark and amber globs of pitch tucked inside. She blew until the flames grew from yellow babies to licking orange-and-blue monsters, open-mouthed and greedy.

She fed them sticks until the teepee collapsed into a red bed of coals and glowing ash. Then she perched a can of chili and a pan full of creek mussels over a crosshatch of thick branches. The flames ate the chili label and blackened the can, though it took forever for the beans to steam and the mussels to boil.

Living in the mountains was so much harder than Greer had expected: opening cans with the janky can opener, finding dry firewood, staying warm, boiling water, eating enough to satisfy her hungry stomach but not enough to use up the rations.

Hiking each day was the easy part, even with bloody blisters on her ankles and feet, even if she didn't know where she was or how much longer she had to go to make it to the river. She kept losing track of time, of days. It felt both like forever and just yesterday since she'd run away.

The llamas moaned their complaints from the trees where

she'd tied them. Only Sirius seemed unaffected by day after day of walking, so relentlessly cheerful it wore off on Greer.

"Goofy galumphus," Greer said, ruffling Sirius's ears as she sat begging, her long pink tongue dripping drool. Sirius licked Greer's face and eyelids until Greer buried her head in the soft ruff, inhaling the good, clean leather smell of her coat.

Greer didn't how Sirius had found them, except that's just how Sirius was. "Too smart for her own good," Mr. Estmund always said. Sirius was the only good thing that came with Rory—a floppy-eared shepherd pup he'd brought Greer's mom as a present. Greer's mom had named Sirius after the dog star—a good name for once—and Greer adored her. Her ears were like velvet, her tail a whapping bough, her oversize feet with paw pads that smelled like soil and musk. Greer couldn't resist sniffing them sometimes, tickling their sprouts of long hobbit toe-hair until Sirius donkey-kicked.

The first night of running away, Greer had heard a noise on the trail and turned to see a dark shadow rushing up behind the llamas. She panicked, thinking it was a wolf about to leap on the llamas' haunches and sink its teeth into their necks. She pictured blood dripping off glinting canine teeth, the wolf's growling, hackled crouch before it sprang to rip out Greer's neck. Blood spurting like a geyser. But instead of a bloodthirsty wolf, Sirius had appeared, whining and nuzzling Greer's hand. The llamas hummed a new pitch as they leaned down to touch noses with Sirius.

Happy as they all were, Greer had another moment of panic as she imagined Rory tracking them from Mr. Estmund's pasture, Sirius run ahead of him in warning. But there had been nothing but trees and darkness and the quiet rustlings of things in the woods.

Sirius stayed close by Greer as they hiked, gaining distance from Headquarters and Rory. The llamas hummed behind, Kelly first and Yavell last, just like Mr. Estmund had taught. They'd hiked through that first night and the next day. They hiked until Greer couldn't hike anymore. They would keep hiking, every day, until they reached the North Fork and could make a home for themselves, little family of runaways.

Greer wished Juan was with them. She imagined him sitting alone on their favorite bus seat or next to her empty desk wondering where she'd gone. She imagined tests and assignments and activities. It was like a ghost of her was still there, going about each regular day even as she walked deeper into wilderness.

She wondered if her mother missed her, feared for her safety. Even though her mother was probably long gone now—run off with Rory, hiding "underground" from the cops like she always did, changing her job, address, phone number. "A tumbling-tumbleweed," as she said.

Finally the chili was bubbling and the mussel shells had slit open. Greer used a wadded sock to grab the can and the pan out of the fire. She dumped half the chili and mussels on the ground for Sirius before slurping up her own half. The beans were half cold and half scalding, the mussels tasted like bland gritty fish, but they were better than the freeze-dried stroganoff she'd eaten the first night.

"Beans, beans, the musical fruit / the more you eat, the more you toot / the more you toot, the happier you feel / so eat beans for every meal," Greer chanted to Sirius. Mr. Estmund's ditty. Greer missed him so bad her eyes stung.

She petted Sirius and watched the fire spark and hiss as darkness descended. The forest was different at night—a whole new world of busy life. She tried to attend to every detail, every sense, just as Mr. Estmund had instructed. Listen closely to each noise, sniff out each smell, feel each touch, see each thing, taste each flavor. And with Sirius there, Greer felt braver, more capable. Mr. Estmund had called them "Wolfpack sisters."

Greer had often hid Sirius in the hay cave, protecting her

from her mom's or Rory's rages. Sirius was a good dog, never mean or disobedient, but she was a convenient body to kick or hit with kindling when Greer's mom or Rory were in the mood to fight. To take the blows that might have gone to Greer.

"Not ever again," she said out loud. Sirius tilted her head.

Somewhere in the trees an animal called low and deep, reverberating through the dark. Greer stroked Sirius's fur as she hummed the lullaby Mrs. Cedeño had sung to Juan's little sisters: "Flowers are closed and lambs are sleeping / Stars are up, the moon is peeping / While the birds are silence keeping / Sleep, my baby, fall a-sleeping..."

◆

Listening for noises in the dark, watching stars blink and streak overhead, unable to sleep, Greer took the recorder from Kelly's pannier and put in one of her favorite tapes of Mr. Estmund's North Fork stories. But when she hit PLAY and Mr. Estmund's voice came through the little speaker, deep and resonant, right there next to her, she had to hit STOP.

Greer thought how far she might have to go, how many days and nights, unknown weather, unfamiliar trails. She remembered the battery was low. But she was alone and needed to hear a strong and loving voice. She decided to listen just long enough for comfort, enough to remember the story herself, in her own way, once Mr. Estmund's voice gave her the beginning.

It took several shuddery breaths before she could turn the recorder on again.

Mr. Estmund's voice sounded like wind in the trees, carrying her along, telling a story of Sacagawea, Watkuweis, and York.

"They climbed forever upward, leaving the rivers behind—the Lochsa, the Selway, the Clearwater. Each

step higher into the mountains thrummed Sacagawea's heart. She hummed the coming home song quietly, first in Hidatsa and then in Shoshone, vibrating it into Baptiste's body slung tight to her own, his fists grasping her hair, his breath wet on her neck, his lungs breathing with her lungs, his blood coursing with her blood. A song of mourning and loss but also joy. A lullaby Sacagawea's Lemhi-Shoshone mother had sung to her along the Salmon River, its waters always rushing by, gray and blue, before the time of loss, before she'd been stolen away by a white man, one of his many wives."

Greer stopped the voice. She put the little recorder against herself, inside her jacket, to preserve the battery. She wrapped herself tighter in her sleeping bag. Sirius snuggled beside her, radiating warmth.

Greer whispered to Sirius, "Sacagawea knew the land and wasn't afraid. She sang songs of her people, their pain and glory. Ancestors, mosquitoes, journeys, having babies."

Sirius seemed interested enough for Greer to keep going.

"Watkuweis was an old woman who had traveled her whole life, but not always because she wanted to. She had been stolen, too, and had lived among many kinds of people. Now she wanted to return to her first home, her own people. She protected the white explorers from attack when they were most vulnerable. She showed them the ways of the prairies and mountains. She knew Sacagawea's song, too, and sang with her."

Sirius breathed steady and slow against Greer.

Greer said, "In the village, the women were perplexed by York, who did not look like the other explorers. Didn't look like their own people, either. They took him to the stream to wash him clean, scrubbed and scrubbed, but his skin stayed dark and then they understood that he was made after the ravens, and so they cherished him..."

Sirius jerked in her sleep, made a little sleep-bark, and settled again.

Greer wrapped around her warmth and fell asleep dreaming of mountain and river crossings, of Sacagawea, Watkuweis, and York, singing their songs of freedom.

♦

She woke to the whine of a chainsaw. She jumped up and looked around wildly, but there were only the llamas munching grass in morning light. And Sirius, who was listening too.

Sound had a strange way of carrying in the woods. One of the first dark nights, a woman's bloody-murder scream had awakened Greer, raised the hair on the back of her neck. She shook in terror, unable to sleep, body tuned to high alert. The next morning she'd found cougar tracks pressed into the mud along a nearby stream. Fresh scat. Mr. Estmund had told her mountain lions could scream. Now she knew firsthand. Straight from a horror movie.

The chainsaw revved and then when silent. Greer could make out voices—little kids squealing, the deep rumble of a man's laugh punctuated by a woman's high-pitched hoot. A family. It'd been long enough since Greer had heard human voices that they sounded strange—noisy animals that didn't know how to be in the woods. But she couldn't help her curiosity. The children's happy voices drew her.

She left Kelly and Yavell tied by the cold campfire and made Sirius heel close to her. They slunk through the trees, moving like furtive foxes, careful to not snap any sticks. And luckily when they emerged, they were on high ground overlooking a small clearing off a sharply-banked skid road. A family of five sat on a pickup's tailgate, drinking from steaming mugs.

The smell of coffee and hot chocolate wafted up. Greer lifted her head and sniffed the air like a wild beast, her stomach growling so loudly she pressed her hand against it, worried they would hear. But they were too busy with each other to notice a girl and a dog in the brush.

The three little boys jumped down and tussled over something in the dirt. The mom and dad leaned against each other, grinning over their children's antics. They gave each other a kiss and the little boys hollered in disgust. They ran circles around the truck, chasing each other, the biggest holding up an insect, going after his younger brothers with it until they turned on him. The littlest picked up a stick.

The mother jumped down and took it from him, her scolding voice gentle. She confiscated the insect and the boys followed her as she carefully returned it to the grass. The dad sluiced his leftover coffee into the dust and then bent over his chainsaw to file the chain. Back and forth, back and forth, little zimmings against the chain's teeth.

◆

Mr. Estmund had given Greer money for every load of firewood she helped him transport and stack in the woodshed. It made her love the smell of saw gas, tree fungus, and fresh woodchips. Wielding his chainsaw, Mr. Estmund explained back-cutting, wedging, how to avoid rainbowing. He taught her firewood species—the tall spires of live trees, the way a good tamarack snag is barkless and straight as an arrow, how to distinguish punky, unwanted white fir from long-burning red fir.

She learned to curse red fir splinters, to make kindling out of white pine, to revere the way a good tamarack log could burn all day and cast even heat. *Use the Humboldt cut to fell. Look out for leans and twists. Look out for widowmakers, barber chairing, pinched chains. Watch the top, watch your back. Never underestimate the ways a tree might fool you.*

Even though he'd been doing it his whole life, Mr. Estmund

was a nervous tree faller—"feller" he always corrected her. He made Greer stay in his running pickup, ready to back up fast if the snag he was felling twisted toward the road. She watched closely, her head craned, following the tree's slow shiver and tip, trying to judge how far it would come.

Sometimes the snags landed up cutbanks, or worse, broke and rolled off the road into thistle and knapweed. Mr. Estmund used the truck as a skidder then, pulling and jerking until the truck threatened to come apart, until the busted-up log length was back on the road, covered in talcum powder dust, studded with fern bits and shredded thimbleberry leaves.

The real work started then. Greer measured and marked with a kindling length and axe, the steady roaring whine of the chainsaw pursuing her as Mr. Estmund cut rounds and the apricot-colored chips flew like confetti. Then he worked the peavey, digging its one-toothed jaw in, leaning his weight until the log rolled belly up so he could finish the cuts, firewood rounds separating with each chainsaw upstroke. Greer tipped the rounds upright, readying them for splitting—Mr. Estmund's hardest work. The sweat dripped off his nose and chin as he took position and swung—big arcing heaves, the woodblocks cracking like gunshots as they split apart. Greer would dart in and gather each split piece, re-righting the rounds as he set up his next swing.

Scattered heaps of sawdust and split wood littering the road, Mr. Estmund resting in the shade, it was Greer's turn to show off her strength and speed. She was designated stacker—no slouch of a position. The stacker worked the truck after carrying the split wood from the road. The stacker was responsible for fitting all the pieces for transport. Tight against the flatbed's bang board and side racks, Greer stacked neat rows of split wood, each chunk like a puzzle piece. No leaning or tipping on her watch. She took pride in the way she could fill even the smallest gaps with pieces of kindling.

They drove home in the low growl of granny gear, firewood heaped high in the back, brakes squeaking as Mr. Estmund puffed on his pipe. Sweet tobacco smoke trailed out the open windows. When they got home, Mr. Estmund backed into the woodshed by the llama barn and Greer stood in the bed of the truck to put pieces one by one into his outstretched hands. He stacked higher than his head, as high as he could reach, row after row, until the shed was full except for a narrow passage to let him shimmy out.

Mr. Estmund's woodshed took eight cords, transferred from places with names like Dull Axe, Thunder Saddle, Scofield, and Scurvy. Enough to make sure he could make it through another winter, the wood his only fuel. Eight months of continuous burning, the cast iron stove radiating sure heat. He said stoking the stove was like brushing teeth, like meals of the day, like sleep and waking.

◆

Now Greer watched the mother gather the boys and walk them down the road while the father approached the snag Greer had already picked for him: a tall tamarack as big around as three people standing together. Enough firewood to fill their truck and high-sided trailer. Greer's spot was a safe distance away, so she made herself comfortable to enjoy the show. The dad started the chainsaw in one pull, revving it high before making his back-cut. Then he pounded wedges, the sharp whack of the back of the axe echoing.

Another quick pull, the chainsaw roared back to life, aggressive and throaty—this man sure of himself as he made the final cut. The top of the snag waved then tipped as he hollered "Tiiimber!" The snag whistled through the air and smashed down on the road, broken limbs flying, dust billowing. The tree lay like a broken spine in the dirt, stretched along the tracks in the road—a perfect felling.

The little boys hooted and waved their arms. They ran to their dad in exuberant glee, jumping around him like puppies. He tousled their hair, and they bent to gather bright bits of lichen knocked from the thick trunk, holding them up like trophies. Greer expected the dad to get right to work sawing rounds, but instead he sat on the tailgate and drank water as the mom marked the tree, fired up the chainsaw, and cut with equal skill.

The little boys wrestled and roughhoused on the other side of the truck—the side closest to Greer. Neither of the parents saw when all three lost their footing, the loose dirt on the edge of the steep cutbank sloughing beneath them. Scrabbling and tumbling, they disappeared into the brushy ravine.

Before Greer could stop her, Sirius leaped and charged down from their lookout, barking so loudly that it carried over the deafening chainsaw. The dad jumped down from the truck as the mom stopped sawing. They looked for their kids, ready to shield them from a crazy dog, but Sirius ran to the bank, barking her most impressive rescue bark. She stared down, signaling, and the parents scrambled, hollering for their kids who were wailing below, hidden in thick brush.

Greer stumble-ran down to the clearing, calling, "They fell, they fell!" until she was breathless. Sirius barked as she plunged toward the kids. The parents looked so surprised at the sight of a wild girl coming out of the woods that it would have been funny if it weren't for the crying children. It didn't take long for the mom and dad to reach them and haul them out, their faces dirty and streaked with tears and snot, bloody scratches on their arms and cheeks.

They set the boys in a row on the tailgate.

Greer called Sirius to her as the mom wet a handkerchief to wash the boys' faces, kissing their wounds, shushing their wails as she checked their limbs and eyes and bellies for further damage. The dad got out a first-aid kit and bandaged their cuts.

The sniffling kids stared at Greer and Sirius as if they were aliens from Mars.

"Who she, Daddy?" the middle boy finally asked, snuffing. His eyelashes glistened with tears, angry welts rising where he'd been slashed by branches.

The parents turned to Greer like they'd forgotten she was there.

"Well, I don't know, son," the dad said. "Why don't you ask her?"

"Who are you?" the oldest boy asked, bashful. He held his hand down cautiously for Sirius. She licked it and then moved on to the other outstretched hands.

"I'm...Cordelia," Greer said. "That's Sirius. We saw you fall."

The mom squatted down to pet Sirius. She smiled at Greer. "Thank you for alerting us, Cordelia and Sirius," she said. "Are you with your parents?"

She stood up. Looked Greer over.

Greer backed into the grass to hide her feet, blood seeping up her dirty socks where her sneakers had chafed. She nodded. "They're just out hiking. I didn't want to go with them this morning, so me and Sirius...um...stayed in camp. We heard your chainsaw."

"Well, these three knuckleheads owe you a big thank you," the dad said. "Can you tell Cordelia and Sirius thank you?"

The boys chimed in chorus, "Thank you Cordelia and Sirius." Except it sounded more like Cordy and Cheery when the youngest one said it.

"Let's see," the mom said, rooting around in a bag to pull out a handful of mini chocolate bars that she divided among each boy. "Why don't you offer Cordelia some of your treats as a thank you gift—wouldn't that be nice?" she asked. The boys looked hesitant, but after the dad lifted them one by one off the tailgate and gave them a little nudge, they wiped their noses, walked over to Greer, and solemnly presented the chocolate bars.

"Thank you," Greer said.

Chocolate and caramel. She could barely keep herself from ripping them open, right there, and devouring them.

"I'm sure we have something Sirius would like, too," the mom said, pulling out a hunk of jerky that Sirius eyed with such intensity that they all laughed. "Looks like the ticket." She tossed it to Sirius, who snatched the jerky out of the air and wolfed it down in one gulp.

"She didn't even chewwww," the littlest boy marveled, his eyes wide.

Greer worried they would see how hungry she and Sirius were, but the mom was fussing over the little boys again, smoothing their hair and giving them hugs. Greer wished she would hug her too. She knew she should leave before they could ask more questions. She knew the story of parents gone hiking without her sounded fishy. She hoped the family wasn't from nearby, where people might know she was missing.

"Welp, I better go back to our camp," she said, backing away.

"Are you sure you don't want to stay here with us until your parents get back?" the dad asked, concerned.

"Yes, I'd hate for you to get lost out here," the mom said. "It's big wilderness for a little girl to be all alone in, although you do have good, watchful company." She patted Sirius's head and Sirius leaned against her leg, panting happily.

"My parents just went a little ways. They're probably already back, making breakfast. Me and Sirius better go before they start worrying about us."

The mom and dad didn't look convinced as Greer called Sirius to her and started backtracking, taking a different route so they wouldn't know where she was headed.

"You be careful, now," the mom called out. The little boys waved and said, "Thank you Cordy and Cheery," their voices like chiming bells.

Greer smiled and waved back before scurrying into the trees, breaking into a run as soon as she was out of sight. She floundered in the undergrowth, losing her way, just as the mother had warned. Greer feared for Kelly and Yavell, but Sirius found a trail. Greer was breathless, even crying a little, by the time she reached the llamas. They batted their eyelashes and hummed in greeting.

She rolled the rocks away from the dead campfire, threw the charred wood into the trees, and kicked dirt over the ash, trying to hide her tracks. She tied up her bedroll and reloaded the packs.

The llamas flattened their ears and hummed less pleasantly as she strapped on their saddles, cinching with such haste that she pulled clumps of their hair. Yavell spit before she had time to dodge it. A big stinking wad dripped down her arm. She grimaced as she swiped a fir branch to clean it off.

She led them to the trail and picked up speed, the candy bars melting in her pocket. She peeled one open and ate it as they hiked, looking behind her, half expecting to see the dad or mom running up, catching her alone without any parents. Without anyone at all.

The chocolate melted in her mouth and covered her fingers when she broke off a chunk for Sirius. Mr. Estmund always said chocolate was bad for dogs.

"A little bit shouldn't hurt," Greer murmured, letting Sirius lick it from her fingers.

She thought of the family sawing their firewood into rounds, then splitting, loading, and stacking. Going back home nestled together in their pickup's cab, the dad driving, the mom singing lullabies and stroking the little boys' hair as they fell asleep on their parents' laps, warm and cozy and loved.

AVA

The drive to Huntsville with Beth helped settle Ava's nerves. It'd been so long since she'd seen Adonis; in her mind, he'd remained suspended in time and space, unchanged since she was eleven years old. But he'd been living his life, too. Incarceration didn't mean an escape from age and lived experience. Adonis would not be the man his half-sister remembered from nearly two decades ago.

She didn't know who Adonis was now any more than she had then. A middle-aged man who'd married and divorced while in prison. A brother who'd lost friends, made enemies, taken college classes, and spent decades battling a legal system that didn't care who he was or who he thought he could become.

She knew a few things. He'd contracted hepatitis C and now required constant treatments to keep his body from succumbing to cirrhosis. He'd slit the throat of an inmate who'd led a gang rape against him, putting the man in the infirmary to be resuscitated four times, earning Adonis another life sentence.

They'd written to each other in fits and starts, a small family history captured in word and licked stamp, each letter a record of being. Ava had kept them all, had them with her still.

...Things are way thingy here. Nice and cool and calm and peaceful. Summer has FINALLY decamped and taken her sultry sweaty stinky sticky underdrawers with her, thank the godz. It's so sad. I so LOVED summer in the world, and now I dread and fear and loathe her. I imagine we can come to terms and reach some kind of reconciliation after I get out, but for now we are sworn enemies. N-E-Wayz…it's been a good long minute hasn't it? I wish life would have twisted a bit differently and allowed me to experience more directly, first-hand, you and your life. Regret is about the most useless thing ever, but I REALLY regret not being actively involved in ya'll's mix. But whatever, that's my fault and my problem.

…Okey Dokey, I'm back. My cellie came in so I skedaddled. I try real hard to keep the time I spend in a concrete box with an adult male down to a bare minimum, like only when I have to! This one here is the cellie from hell, there's absolutely ZERO common ground. He smoked crack for 16 years straight prior to comin' to prison and it SHOWS! Promise me, little sister, that you'll never smoke crack, that stuff will melt your brains, 4 REAL! …Anyway, it's hotter than the seventh level of hell, but it's always that hot so no biggie. It'll be over in 6 or 7 weeks, so I guess I've got this summer kicked in the keister. I really can't understand why anyone would live in Texas, especially in summer. To each his own, I s'pose. I myself intend to seek to a place that has more variation in its climes than "real hot" and "not quite as hot as real hot"!

…It's a lazy hazy gray and dazey Sunday morning now and I happen to have a couple of spare moments to holler atcha. You're a frequent flyer on my mental air-line. I love you baby gurl! And I admire the life you've made for yourself, and am <u>SO</u> proud of you for your accomplishments! I get a tingly feeling of excited anticipation when I think of the potential that your future holds. Hey I know it's pretty lame, but I gotta get my kicks <u>somewhere</u>! My personal prospects are somewhat less than spectacular, so I'll settle for a vicarious 'ooomph' outta <u>yours</u>!

...I really <u>really</u> HATE how my bull-shit self-induced circumstances impact on the emotions of my circle of loved ones. I <u>SO</u> very wish I had stayed up yonder with you last time I was there. I would have at <u>least</u> been another presence in a house consisting of you and <u>TWO</u> coo-coo for co-co puffs characters in your mom and our dad. You survived it and turned out <u>WELL</u> but maybe I could have decompressed it a bit. H.Q. is only a ghost-town occupied by the living, its only virtue pristine wilderness and <u>that</u> being sacrificed on the altar of human greed. I swear, humans are just a cancer. Oops, sorry, little bit of personal pessimism squirted out, my bad! I just took an environmental science class, the world is headed to a <u>real</u> not-good place, courtesy of human-beings, and nobody seems to give a fig! Ignorance <u>IS</u> bliss baby gurl, knowledge can be bitter.

...I'm in the day-room now, it's sparsely populated and as quiet as it gets, later on it'll be crunked up and roaring like a beast but during this brief window it is calm and quiet. I decided to come down here 'cuz my cellie makes Oscar the Grouch look like Mr. Happy on Prozac; my cellie doesn't do wakin' up in the morning well at <u>all</u>, so here I am to refrain from having to give him an attitude adjustment and a reality check early in the morning. And you know, I wanna talk to you about our Dad. I'm thinkin' you know him as well as anyone does, and better than most. I don't really know him, ya know? And lately he's been the recipient of some bad press from everyone, even my mom, and she's NEV-ER really been one to run him down. He was her first love, her first lover and the father of her child and she's always harbored a place in her heart for him. But his reported actions and antics and expressions have me concerned. I'm seeing him in an unflattering light, and seeing the things I most dislike about myself in Him. But I'm far removed from the mix, so have no true experience and exposure, so I'm asking YOU, who I feel can give me an honest, SANE and accurate take on the old man, WHAT'S UP WITH THE OLD MAN? Can ya tell me? I don't even know the status of ya'll's relationship, though from your tone in letters, you are at least a little amiable towards him. That's what gave me the idea to ask you, along with the picture you sent of you with him on the North Fork. You were a itty-bitty girl in that picture and are now a fully grown woman. So help me if you would, help me understand him better. It might help me understand myself, for although he didn't raise me I'm still of him and he therefore HAS to exert some kind of influence, right? But whatever, no biggie either way, just if ya feel like foolin' with it, y'know?

Ava couldn't remember exactly what she'd written in reply. What had she told Adonis about their father? About the life he'd come to lead?

It was too late for ruminations on genetics and culpability. For finding a key to unlock all that came before, hinting toward future.

As Beth would say, *It is what it is. What's done is done.*

◆

The drive was green and bright with sun and Beth smoked contemplatively with all the windows down, both comfortable in their silence. But when they arrived at the red-brick sprawl of the prison, Ava felt her pulse beating in the tips of her fingers. The building was menacing, a monstrous being exhaling the vapors of entrapment. When she visited Adonis for the first time, she'd been too proud to admit how terrified she was—flushed hot with fear. It wasn't much different now.

Beth drove into vehicle security then stopped to open the doors, trunk, and glovebox for the guards and their drug dogs. Once cleared, Beth and Ava walked through corridors of razor wire fences, stopping to get scanned through three layers of locked-gate security before finally arriving at a guard station where they got matched, approved, and signed in.

They were marshalled into a waiting room with all the other visitors.

When the inmates were allowed in, the guards opened the doors and ushered in the visitors. Suddenly there he was: Adonis, tall and gaunt but still beautiful, his blonde curls shaved off, his eyes encased in wrinkles, his sharp jawline and cheekbones outlined by his grin.

"Baby girl," he said, and Ava melted into him.

Hugging him felt like hugging a taller, thinner version of their father—a genetic recognition so profound it shook her emotions loose in a torrent. Beth handed her tissues to blot her wet face as they sat at their designated table, Adonis on one side, Beth and Ava on the other.

Adonis gripped Ava's hands, his long fingers tremulous as he traced the lines of her thumbs. People at the surrounding tables did the same, grabbing onto each other as if rescuing a drowning swimmer.

"Sweet little Ava," Adonis said, studying her so intently that she had to break her gaze. Overcome by emotions, she fought the urge to pull away, to hide. All of it too much, tinged with communal desperation.

"How have you been?" she asked. Vapid. A coward bringing bad news to a brother who'd had more of that than anyone should.

"Just look at you," Adonis said, squeezing her hands tight as he shook his head and grinned. "My little sister, the professor. Smart and pretty enough to knock anyone's socks right off. I couldn't be more proud of you, little Ava, little raven girl, all grown up. A real-life bird woman," he said, smiling wide. "Flying down here to see your no-good triflin' brother…"

"What's left of me," she said, before she caught herself.

"Tell me everything. I wanna know it all, everything about you and your wonderful life—all the birds, all the mountains and trees, all the trouble you've been makin'."

When she hesitated, Beth jumped in. "Hey, I just got the new boarding suite finished up—an African savannah theme. Some people just can't get enough giraffes and elephants."

"Sounds just like somewhere I'd like to be—grass blowin', elephants trumpetin'," Adonis said. "But I wanna hear about Idaho. What have you and the birds been up to, Ms. Ava? And how about your gal, Sibley? You two up to your same old tricks, huntin' down trespassers in the North Fork wilds?"

Beth stood up. "I'll catch you next month, Cousin Donnie, you handsome devil." She winked at the guards and shook her chest at them as she left, daring them to intervene.

"So tell me, little sis—how are you doing, for real?" Adonis stroked Ava's fingers.

She felt like she had a rock lodged in her throat. She focused on the veins in Adonis's hands, the pattern of his fingers and thumbs and tendons. Soft whoosh of air-conditioning overhead, the clash of voices, the rattling of the vending machines, the clank of change all the visitors had brought to feed into them.

They brought little paper bowls full of naked candy bars and unbagged cheese puffs, cans of sweating soda back to their tables. Junk food meant to soothe cravings that could never be satisfied.

"Philip is dead," she finally managed, the peal of someone's laughter cresting over them. "He shot himself in his living room. I wanted to tell you in person."

Adonis stared at her before slowly shaking his head. The pulse in his fingers accelerated her own.

"The old man's gone?" he said, his voice disbelieving. His eyes a pooling reflection. "The old man's really gone?"

"There's a scheduled autopsy and Alfred will pick up the ashes when it's done."

"You came all this way to tell me?"

"No, not entirely," she said, hesitating.

"What?" Adonis demanded.

The five-minute warning light went off. Everyone glanced up in unison at the white prison clock.

"I'm on my way to Ecuador. I had to get away. I took a leave of absence."

"Ecuador?" Adonis was incredulous, his voice too loud. Sodden tissues balled up on their table.

"Alfred has a little place in Puerto Cayo—"

"Wait a minute. For how long?" Adonis leaned toward her. The guards shot warning looks their way. Adonis lowered his voice. "I mean, I hear you, little sis, I hear you, but fuck me, this is all a lot to take in." He shook his head emphatically.

"I know. I'm sorry," she said, wooden.

"I can't stand the thought of you jeopardizing everything you worked your whole life for because of our dad." The disgust and anger made his voice resonant. "Fuck Philip. Fuck that. You've got to live your life, Ava. You've *got* to. Promise me you'll do that? *Promise* me you'll keep living your life fully and happily and with someone, not alone. You're all I've got left."

"Yes," she said without conviction, gripping Adonis's hands. A guard appeared, knocking on their tabletop with thick knuckles. *Time's up.*

The guards stood at attention as the visitors exchanged final hugs with their inmates—their fathers, sons, brothers, husbands. Friends. Everything so abrupt Ava felt like crying out.

Adonis's body was so thin under her arms. More frail than he let on. A broken-winged bird in a cage. She watched them take him away, shackling his bony wrists to his ankles before they led him shuffling back.

◆

She pushed herself into sunlight, gulping for air.

There was Beth in her Caddy, patting Ava's back, saying, "There, there, darlin'. Sorrow is knowledge and the tree of knowledge is also the tree of life."

In her own mix-and-match way, Beth wasn't wrong.

Trees filled with birds who already knew the long way from the underworld to the sun.

EZRA

Ezra arrived in the kitchen three minutes late. Joel, quartermaster and cook, glanced up as he cracked eggs into a heap of bloody hamburger, massaging in ketchup, cracker crumbs, black pepper, and garlic powder with his bare hands.

"Glad you could make it, Sailor," Joel said, egg yolks and pink meat squeezing up between his hairy fingers.

"Sorry I was late, Sir," Ezra said, swallowing bile. He went directly to the cutting board and knife Joel pointed at, chopping tidy rows of onion, breathing fumes hard through his nose.

All those hours lying on his bunk reading books on seafaring, Ezra had imagined a team of leathery rough-and-tumble seamen directing his trip south. But Joel was soft as dough, pouched belly and a fuzz of hair on his shoulders, fingers, back, and chest. Everything about him was white and orange and slightly furred. It felt ridiculous to call him sir.

Before Ezra had gotten out, his cellie had looked at all Ezra's seafaring books, laughed and said, "Ah, yes, it's important to study up on semen."

Semen Joel.

Joel motioned with his chin toward Ezra's arms. "You ever feel like you're on fire?"

Ezra had noticed Joel's side-eyes at his tattoos—assessing the flames and skulls, the screaming heads with fire coming out their eyes. Prison tats, special-made from Ezra's nightmares.

"No," Ezra lied. Even beyond prison, he couldn't wake himself from dreams of fire consuming everything and everybody but him, left intact to watch.

"Huh. Well, I hear it hurts worse than people let on," Joel said. "I was thinking of one here," he said motioning with his meat-covered hand to his shoulder. "A ship anchor, maybe a meat cleaver."

He laughed nervously. "It doesn't hurt *that* much, does it?" he asked, kneading the heap of meat.

"Nah, it's not that bad," Ezra said, splitting another onion in half. Joel was one of those people who needed to be lied to.

Joel scrutinized Ezra's arms like an art critic. "Do you have any low-key ones? I mean those flames and heads are killer, but I think they'd scare my girlfriend."

Probably more like his mom, Ezra thought. Joel was in his thirties, but tender-faced as a pimply fourteen-year-old. Given, the *Valiant Endurance* was one of the few container ships of its age and size in the Port of Seattle, the crew representatively smaller than on the bigger vessels, but Ezra had expected a more impressive set. Vic as Captain. Tiny as Chief. Joel as Steward. Himself as mop-and-onion guy. A ship of fools.

People on the outside seemed so young, so soft, underbellies exposed. It made Ezra feel ancient, his young body an illusion housing a hardened kernel of a soul. He'd spent most of his youth looking forward to death—seeking out blankness. He'd envied the ones who found it.

"An anchor, that's a good one," Ezra said, as if tats were accessories like belts or cufflinks. Sometimes he wished he could take them back, his history broadcast every time he exposed his skin.

Joel squished the onions into the burger and then deployed an oversized wooden spatula to smooth the meat mass into a pan. "You don't think an anchor is too overdone, too common?"

He wiped his hands on his filthy apron.

"Seems fitting to me," Ezra said. "You are a licensed semen after all."

"Hells yeah," Joel said, missing the joke. He flexed his flabby bicep. He lifted his eyebrows. "Hey, we should go in together, next stop, Manta!" He peered at Ezra's arms. "You got room for a few more there—some more color or something."

"Yeah, sure," Ezra said, knowing Joel wouldn't last the first minute of a needle gun pulsing into his tender flesh. He wished the pain would have stopped him.

He dumped out a bag of potatoes, their dank earthiness reassuring. As he peeled, Ezra thought of the dogs. What this ship might be transporting. The vessel was small enough to skirt the checks, escape notice. Ezra wasn't the only one hoping to fly under the radar. Probably every person riding this tub was trying to get away with something.

Joel worked beside Ezra, likely picturing the anchor tattoo he'd never get, impressing the girlfriend he didn't have. "So, you met the other passengers?" he asked, and Ezra knew exactly where he was going. "That Angie—maybe I'll get converted after all."

Joel lifted his eyebrows. "I mean, did you see those tits?" He whistled as he jiggled his hairy meat hands in front of his chest. "Now that's the kind of religion I'm talking about."

Ezra peeled another potato. "I thought you had a girlfriend."

"Well, yeah, but a guy can look. I mean, we don't get much to look at out here. You think I'm bad, you ought to hear the other guys. Probably jacking off every ten minutes over her."

"She's married. She's a Jehovah's Witness." Ezra was suddenly weary. An old man giving a lecture.

What did Angie want with those *help me* eyes? To bring him to Jesus? She'd been wrong to think he was a nice guy, to think she could talk to him like she understood. Like she knew anything about him.

Joel held up his hands, a scolded child. "Hey, I'm just admiring the landscape."

He worked a moment in silence, then cocked his head at Ezra. "Didn't Tiny get you on?"

Ezra knew it would come—the need to explain himself.

"We have a common acquaintance," Ezra said.

"What's that make you then?" Joel asked.

"Nothing. Nobody."

"Well, Nobody, if you could cube up them spuds, I'd be much obliged," Joel said, maybe more savvy than he let on.

Ezra picked up a big knife. For the potatoes. "So what's this boat carrying?" he asked, watching Joel's face for clues.

"Household goods mostly—furniture, pots and pans, the comforts of home. You know. Personal shipping is a good business these days. Retirees from Canada and the States looking to stretch their Social Security. You've heard the talk I'm sure, Ecuador the new expat darling. Cheap—that's what it comes down to."

But Joel's eyes said it all. He knew something. They all did. Except maybe Chad and Angie. And Ezra. Ezra considered the slender racing dogs hidden in some low, dark corner of the ship, housed in a container, sniffing the stifled air, muscles twitching in anticipation. Ready to put their feet to land. Ready to run.

He glanced at Joel and almost said more, but let it drop.

◆

Meal prep done, Ezra filled a cart with linens, towels, and cleaning supplies, then checked again for his keys. When Tiny had first shown him around, pointing out his duties, Ezra hadn't been able to focus on anything but the ring of keys in his hands. The wonder of locking and unlocking doors. In and out at will. Gatekeeper.

Joel covered the captain's quarters and his own, but Ezra had the rest—three double-occupancy passenger cabins, two single crew cabins. The passenger rooms opened to the main deck, all in a row—two rooms for the retirees, one for the Talberts.

Ezra knocked, hesitating outside Grace and Penny's door even though they knew to vacate during his scheduled cleaning. He opened the door and pulled the cart in behind him, cleaned the room and went on to Mary's. Ezra looked for signs as he worked, something to tell him what these women were up to. But other than a few clothes and toiletries, a dog-eared novel and a blank writing pad, the tiny room was empty.

He replaced tidily hung towels, scrubbed clean toilets, Windexed spotless mirrors, ran the vacuum over dirt-free carpet, replaced full toilet paper rolls. He double checked his work and locked up. Nothing to reveal what these apparently innocuous women were up to. Gambling rings? Breeding aristocracies? Expat dog-racing retirement plan?

Ezra opened the Talberts' door cautiously. Their bed was made. He picked up their pillows, sniffing to discern which was Angie's. In the bathroom, he looked in the cabinet and found a flowered makeup bag. Tubs of lotions. He saw discarded panties behind the door. He sniffed them too, held them to his face—so small, nothing but lace scrap. He left them folded in the bathroom on top of fresh towels and washcloths so she'd know what she showed him.

Tiny's room was strewn with chip bags, candy bar plastic, pop cans, plates of half-eaten food forbidden in the cabins. Ezra rolled the garbage bin with gloved hands. Tiny must have forgotten Ezra wasn't just the cleaner; he was also cook's assistant. In the joint, everyone was extra polite and cautious with the servers and cooks. It was a matter of common sense. Everyone knew what someone like Ezra could do to their food—food a glutton like Tiny shoveled in without thought.

As Ezra scrubbed Tiny's shit-splattered toilet he imagined Tiny masticating on scabs, spit, piss—whatever substances, bodily or otherwise, Ezra might feel like feeding him. Before he was done with the toilet, Ezra opened the cabinet and sure enough, there was Tiny's frayed toothbrush. Ezra ran the bristles around the toilet's inner rim, rinsed it in the toilet bowl just enough to lose the brown, then shook it off and put it back in the cabinet.

Everyone left things out—a photo, a book, a stack of magazines or newspapers. Clues that revealed them, which was why Ezra kept his space empty. As he pulled his cart into the last cabin—Domingo's—a gruff voice yelled, "Goddammit, what the fuck you want?"

Ezra jerked back, knocking the cart into the door.

"Goddamn it. Fuck me. Quiet the hell down," the voice commanded. Too rote to be human. Around the partition, a domed cage hung, a compact grey parrot perched inside. His blunted tail was bright red, his charcoal beak hooked and dangerous, legs and feet scaly as a dinosaur's.

The bird tilted its neck and examined Ezra with one yellow eye, pupil pinning in and out. Reaching a conclusion, it fluffed a collar of feathers and tucked one foot up. It had assessed him, judged him, and found him wanting.

Oh well.

Keeping an eye on the parrot, Ezra ran the vacuum, avoiding the seed scattered under the cage. Finally, he edged the vacuum toward the bird. Other than slicking its neck feathers down, the parrot didn't react.

When Ezra finished and turned the vacuum off, the bird cocked his head and squinted his eye at him again. Ezra felt a wash of empathy. He knew what it was like—locked away, everything beyond reach, door operated by a genie—open, close, open, close. Someone else deciding when you might take flight, stretch your wings. When you would not.

"You a smart bird?" Ezra asked, leaning in.

The bird cocked its head, lifted one foot, then the other,

pacing in place.

"Yeah, I can tell you're smart. You know what's going on. I bet you know all the secrets. The dogs? The ship's cat. Fucking Noah's Ark around here. All we need is a dove and a raven. The raven did the hard work, you know. Flying back and forth until all the water dried up."

The parrot turned on its perch and shook itself. A cloud of feather dust puffed and settled. It picked up its foot and cleaned one of its sharp-nailed toes.

Ezra was starting to think the parrot had taken a liking to him—all that feather fluffing and cleaning. He leaned in closer. "Nice bird," he said, in his rusty sweet-talking voice. "What do you say, pretty bird? Polly want a cracker?"

Coy, slant-eyed, the parrot regarded Ezra. It cocked its head, met his eye, and then spoke three perfectly enunciated words in a woman's soft, coquettish voice.

"Pants on fire," it said, bobbing its head and chortling as Ezra went cold.

◆

Ezra paused at the door to get a grip before entering the mess room.

Mary's perpetual voice: "I said, 'Maeve, you've got no choice—jump!' and by God, she did, she took a flying leap, and you should have seen the splash she made, skirts billowing around her, arms flappin'. That dog of mine didn't know what to do. Just stood on the dock looking amazed. By the time Roger pulled him off, poor Maeve was so waterlogged she was fixing to sink—"

Mary pulled her hat down and made a face, laughing. "You should have seen them trying to pull her out. A whale in petticoats."

Everyone was chortling as Ezra appeared.

"Look who the cat dragged in," Mary said. "Mr. E-Z. Ain't he a sight for sore eyes?"

Mary, Penny, and Grace sat on one side of a long table, Chad and Angie opposite. Chad sneezed four times in quick succession and held a hand up in apology. "Allergies," he said, sniffing.

"Probably from the cat," Penny said. "Worst creatures for allergies."

Angie handed Chad a napkin, solicitous as he pinched it to his nose.

It took Ezra a few trips back and forth to deliver the food—stainless steel bins of meatloaf, mashed potatoes, gravy, hot rolls, and corn in the warming trays. Sliced apples, cheese and green grapes on the side. A pot of coffee.

The passengers stood in line cafeteria style.

"Anyway, there are lots of hungry dogs in Ecuador," Grace said to Angie. "You could adopt a new dog—have one on each continent." She sniffed. "Plenty of them need a home, that's for sure. The first time we went down, I thought Grace here was going to stay for good, she was so worried about all the mongrels."

She shuddered. "You should have seen their skin."

"They just had mange."

"They had everything," Mary said. "I can't believe you actually touched them."

"Well, they deserve care," Grace said, "no matter how bad off they are. No matter they aren't one of your precious purebreds."

"Well, what can I say. I like purebreds, plain and simple. Dogs that run fast, dogs that make money."

Penny patted Grace's hand. Eyed Ezra. "That's right, Gracie, everything deserves a little love, no matter its past."

Chad put a roll on his plate. Sniffed again.

Mary put a finger to her chin. "You a dog person or a cat person E-Z? No, let me guess. I'm going to say feline."

When Ezra didn't correct her, she beamed. "That's what

I thought. I told Gracie she better look out or she'll be one of those crazy old cat ladies. Worse, a bird lady. She had these noisy, unsanitary finches for years."

"Finches aren't unsanitary," Grace said.

Penny looked to the ceiling and sighed.

"Just wait until you see the parrots they keep in cages on the streets, then you'll know what I mean," Mary said, mostly addressing Ezra. "Eating rotten fruit, half their feathers gone, sickly as they come. Dogs, cats, birds, it's all the same down there. Unless they're still in the wild and meant to be, then it's different."

"What about Domingo's bird?" Grace said. "He seems pretty content to me."

"Filthy thing. He says it's trained. I say it's a health hazard. Heard of the bird flu? It'd be just the one to carry it," Mary said.

"What is it, a parrot?" Angie asked.

"African Grey. He says he's had it for ten years and it'll live to be sixty. Creepy. Those beady eyes." Mary shuddered. "Domingo knows to keep it away from me. You better watch out for it, E-Z, when you're cleaning. It doesn't take to strangers. Took a chunk out of someone's ear once, I heard."

"Too late," Ezra said. "Doc and I already met."

Doc. A cartoon name but there was nothing cartoonish about him. Those eyes indeed.

Mary said, "I told you that bird was a hazard."

"What happened?" Grace asked.

"I thought for a minute he liked me." Ezra shrugged, although he was still shaken. The parrot calling him out for what he was. Skin displaying the flames of his own personal hell.

"They say parrots are a good judge of character," Mary said, "but I only trust dogs."

Beneath her cartoon exterior, there was nothing cartoonish about Mary, either. She eyed Ezra shrewdly. He turned his back.

Penny said, "They don't get much smarter than an African

Grey—they're as intelligent as a human five-year-old. They don't just mimic our language but make meaning out of it too."

Liar, liar.

◆

Joel pushed through the kitchen doors with another hot pan, motioning for Ezra to eat. Ezra spooned potatoes onto his plate; he knew they hadn't passed through Joel's meaty hands. Of course, he'd just come from a place with Ziplocs full of greasy coins circulated among vending machines, guards, and visitors. He pictured the snacks arranged between him and the ex-cellie who'd come for a final visit—little plastic bowls filled with wrapperless candy bars, pre-filled peanut butter crackers, pieces of jerky and processed cheese. Washed down with sodas.

Ezra bucked up.

He sat down with Joel just as Tiny filled his plate, gravy sludging over the sides. When Ezra tore his eyes away from that carnage, he saw Angie was looking at him. She dropped her eyes. He wondered if she'd found her underwear.

Domingo joined them as Joel forked in a big bite of meatloaf. "Well?" Joel asked Ezra. "What's the verdict?"

"It's good," Ezra said, lying. He took a bite, washing it down with a slug of coffee.

Joel smiled wide. "Save room for the apple pie," he said to the whole room. The trio of ladies clapped in delight and Joel tipped his head to them.

"So where are you headed from Manta?" Penny asked the missionaries.

Ezra quieted his chewing to listen.

"Oh, we'll travel around," Angie said, dabbing her mouth. She sat very straight, legs crossed. She placed the napkin back on her lap and smoothed it.

"First we'll go north to Quito, Cuenca, then down to Guayaquil or the coast," Chad said.

"Wherever we're needed," Angie added.

"How about you?" Chad asked. Both so polite, so proper. P.R. training—that's all it was. Rehearsed holiness. Consider the panties.

Mary waved her hand. "Wherever the wind blows us, right friends?"

"You ladies are free spirits," Domingo said, grinning. "You'll do just fine in Ecuador."

"We just have to stay away from all those filthy street animals."

"Aw, you'll be fine, Domingo laughed. "What's the saying? What don't kill you is good for you."

"What doesn't kill you makes you stronger," Chad corrected.

Domingo grinned. "Well then, Our lady of Ecuador will make you fucking superman."

Joel gave Domingo a look and Domingo said, "Oh shit, sorry man." He looked at Chad and Angie. "I forgot you was missionaries and all."

"We're just here to give people the Word. We feel called to serve," Chad said.

Domingo nodded seriously. "Bless those who've sinned," he said and crossed himself.

Mary gestured at Ezra's arms, said, "Looks like you need lots of blessing."

Angie met Ezra's eyes briefly. A cool, pitying look. No *help me* in it.

"All of us need blessing," Chad said. "We are all infected and impure with sin. When we display our righteous deeds, they are nothing but filthy rags. Like autumn leaves, we wither and fall, and our sins sweep us away like the wind. Isaiah 64:6."

That shut everyone up a minute.

"We would love to have you for tonight's reading," Chad ventured, still looking at Ezra.

"Oh you don't want us. We're a bunch of reprobates," Mary cackled. "Drink, smoke, gamble." She winked at Ezra. "Like Mr. Domingo said, we're free spirits."

"Christ did not send us to baptize but to preach the gospel, not with words of eloquent wisdom, lest the cross of Christ be emptied of its power. First Corinthians 1:17."

"Oh very good," Mary said, clapping irreverently.

Penny gave her a warning look.

"Yes, yes," Mary said. "What about you E-Z? You religious? You don't look it, but nowadays one never knows.."

"Catholic."

Domingo crossed himself again. "A brother," he said, grinning. "I knew it."

Joel pushed his chair back and took his plate. "Time for pie," he announced.

"We hope you'll come by our cabin to talk, Ezra. You're welcome anytime," Chad said.

"Yes," Angie said, her big brown eyes pinning him. "Please come by."

◆

Ezra excused himself and went back to the kitchen for dish duty. He broke a plate into shards in the soapy water. He reached in to fish them out, but Joel came over frowning, told Ezra to take it easy.

"You'll have to drain the sink," Joel said. "There's gonna be little pieces in there."

"Hey man, I know just what you need," Domingo said, coming in and leaning against the doorframe, addressing Ezra.

Joel threw his dish towel over his shoulder and glared at Domingo. "No deckies in my kitchen."

Domingo gave him a salute. "Hang loose, man." A flick of metal behind his eyes. Joel should know to be careful.

Domingo nodded toward Ezra. "Hey, man," he said. "I got some fine-ass weed. Communion. All the heavenly delights. Shit, I could quote you scripture if it'd make you feel better. I saw how much you liked that."

"I like this better," Ezra said, taking a long toke. Right there, in the kitchen, as Joel gaped.

Domingo clapped Ezra on the shoulder. "It's all good, man. It's all good. Let me show you what Our Lady of Ecuador is made of."

AVA

Ava kept still, her limbs at awkward angles—one elbow cocked out, the other braced against a root serving as a tripod, both hands gripping her birding binoculars.

She didn't dare readjust. Didn't dare move her left knee off whatever sharp thing it was planted on. She'd waited her whole life to see a male paradise tanager in the wild, *Tangara chilensis*, gaudy in his polychromatic array, singing brightly for his mate. The feathers of his "Auricula Purple" throat stood out and the centerline of his "Verditer Blue" chest expanded with his warbling. The lime green and black and bright red of his head and back flashed as he flitted up and down the branch. Colors so saturated, even Werner hadn't fully captured them.

When she risked a shallow breath and blinked, he was gone.

Scanning the brush, she waited a moment before answering her body's complaints. She tucked the binoculars in her shirt, arched her stiff back, and massaged her sore knee. A quick afternoon rainstorm had left the forest dense and verdant, glowing with refracted light—Jipijapa's jungle-like flora and fauna so unlike Puerto Cayo's desert coast, only a half hour away.

Alfred's little Cayo casa was only two streets back from the beach's crashing waves. Near enough for Ava to hear and smell the Pacific but miss the ocean breeze. The house was stuffy with heat, buzzing with tiny voracious mosquitos that fit through even the smallest-gauged window screen. Ava wished Alfred had bought one of Cayo's beachfront places instead, but how could she complain? Staying on Ecuador's coast for free. The only cost? The life she knew.

Alfred had seen her off from the tiny local airport. Handed her a brown package, said, "A little travel gift from me."

A four-inch-thick brick of a book, *The Birds of Ecuador*—a glossy catalogue of all the South American equatorial birds Ava had dreamed of viewing but had been too busy to seek. Hundreds of birds she needed to see, hear, understand.

She and Sibley had planned on taking summers abroad, ticking off life-list birds one country at a time, but work, funding, and research intervened. Ava tried not to think of Sibley continuing without her. Tried not to think of anything but equatorial birds.

After the boarding announcement, Alfred had hugged her, then gripped her shoulders and looked her in the eye. "Don't you worry. We'll get Persephone back to the North Fork and flying again. But you can stay, you know. It's not too late. You've worked so hard for what you have. You and Sibley have been together so long. Time has a way of healing."

That precipitous loss of oxygen…

Ava's consuming wish had been to live year-round on the North Fork, studying its birds, surviving and sustained by its wildness. When she was a child, she'd begged her father to take her there, day after day, so she might memorize every tree and rock and bend of rapid, each osprey's stick nest, each wren's brushy hideout, each dipper's favorite fishing shallows. Each raven's favorite calling perch.

◆

She stumbled back down the birding trail, stubbing her already blackened toes. That was the price of looking at sky, scanning dark shapes in the canopy—flitting shadows, a fleeting shuffle of feathers. It still astonished her how many people walked—city or rainforest—never looking up, never seeing the flapping and fluttering and flickering aerial beings.

She supposed not even the foot-watchers could miss the magnificent frigate birds that soared overhead like giant black kites. *Fregata magnificens,* also known as "frigate petrel" and "man o'war," grew a wingspan up to eight feet. It was one of the world's fastest birds, reaching speeds of nearly 100 miles per hour. A pterodactyl bird, "magnificent" part of its common name, fitting its enormity and gliding fork-tailed grace. The males pumped their dramatic red-balloon throats like bellows for their mates.

All flash and dash, Sibley would have said.

How much more it all could be with Sibley.

It was what Adonis had intuited, holding Ava's hands and making her promise not to live her life alone. His instincts were true. Every time Ava saw a new thing in this astonishing place, she found herself turning to tell Sibley, who because of Ava was not there.

Sibley wouldn't likely be alone for long. How could she be? Somebody so beautiful and brilliant, so full of fight. When Ava pictured Sibley with someone else—someone without so many fresh failings, without an overdeveloped urge to flee, who deserved everything Sibley had to give—she wanted to sink into the damp earth. Bury herself.

Two black vultures, *Coragyps atratus,* circled lazy loops overhead.

Ava had seen more black vultures so far than any other Ecuadorian avian species—as common here as the American robins, *Turdus migratorius,* that flocked into the Pacific Northwest with early spring snows to gorge on winter-fermented mountain ash berries and chokecherries. Except instead of berries, the vultures sought rotting carrion.

◆

When her flight from Houston descended into Quito, Ava had spotted her first new species: a flock of grey-breasted martins, *Progne chalybea,* veering away from the roaring jet. A luxurious flight, a hard-jounced landing, and a whole new world opened up. Ecuador in shining glory. She'd made her way through the bustling press and sweat of customs, out to Quito's winding streets to take it in—the sensations of a place she'd flown to like a migrating bird. She'd only had a moment before she had to catch her flight to Manta, and from there the taxi to Puerto Cayo: empty stretches of Ecuadorian coastline, magnificent frigate bird families soaring overhead, rows of little wooden turquoise fishing boats heaped with nets. The sea was a silver-gray expanse stretching forever, so different from the moody Pacific Northwest. "Pearl Grey. Backs of black headed and Kittiwake Gulls." The ocean taken flight.

The taxi driver had stopped at a roadside cabana, and Ava ate hot greasy empanadas a tiny, wrinkled woman cooked up in the dark, cicadas calling in the warm humid air. The ocean crashed in the distance, the smell of salt, the planet's watery breath on her skin. Everything so sensual, like being kissed for the first time, fondled by the air and sea.

Then she was standing in front of the casa's slatted entry gate, Alfred's low-slung house with its royal blue trim, thatched roof, and tiled front porch strung with hammocks, enclosed by a low concrete wall. In that moment she understood that her flight instinct might be something beyond mere cowardice. That being-ness meant always looking for home, but also yearning for its replacement. Cycles of migration—the familiar suddenly altered and realigned. Permutations. Possibilities.

◆

In Cayo, they called her *La Chica de Aves*. The Bird Girl. People shook their heads and laughed at her—neck craned, binoculars glued to her face, stumbling as she tried to see everything airborne, aloft. She'd point excitedly and whoever was close by would look up and nod, saying the Spanish name too quickly for her to repeat. But she tried, good student that she was, scribbling on her expanding life list, paging through the book Alfred gave her.

A crew of teenaged boys liked to talk to her at the beach when she went to watch the sunset. They tried out their halting English and she practiced her halting Spanish and all of them would laugh as they mimed along together.

The boys held their dented surfboards as they awaited the mercurial waves that curled in each afternoon. Ava showed them pictures in her field guide. They pointed out the birds they knew. She showed them the birds on her dream list: the blue-footed booby, *Sula nebouxii*; the Andean cock-of-the-rock, *Rupicola peruvianus*; the green honeycreeper, *Chlorophanes spiza*; the hoatzin, *Opisthocomus hoazin*; the jabiru, *Jabiru mycteria*; the paradise tanager, *Tangara chilensis*. And all the wild parrots flying free and raucous.

She'd memorized her Ecuadorian life list species so far in order of their appearance: grey-breasted martins, black turkey vultures, magnificent frigate birds, brown pelicans, pacific parrotlets, ground doves, eared doves, scrub blackbirds, guanay shags, snowy egrets, sooty-crowned flycatchers, shiny cowbirds, southern yellow grosbeaks, house wrens, long-tailed mockingbirds, northern crested-caracaras, cattle egrets. The coastal desert birds were as drab as the landscape, unlike the Amazon species, technicolored in feather, foot, and beak. Ava intended to see them all, traveling Ecuador from rainforest to sea and back. And again.

Alfred called often, keeping Ava updated on Persephone's recovery. He said she was the most brilliant bird he'd ever known, that she had high human-like intelligence, that she was already more than he'd suspected she would become. She could open her cage door by using a stick as a lock pick. She knew where the tastiest treats were stashed in the kitchen and how to coax Alfred to retrieve them. She called other birds to her garden window for her own entertainment.

Ava wasn't surprised. Persephone possessed a supernatural comprehension well beyond human reach. Now that she wasn't limiting her thought to the logic of science (more frequent now that she lived beyond her professor role), Ava let herself reclaim the terminologies of myth and fairy tale. Her father's language. Some truths could be expressed in no other way; plain and simple, Persephone embodied the wisdom of the underworld.

Alfred sent a video of Persephone, already larger and fuller-bodied than when Ava had left. She was vocalizing little *gruauk, gruauk* sounds, content, her feathers fluffed. She bobbed her head and chortled, lifting one foot and then the other, then climbed up to her cage perch to clean her beak, swiping it assiduously along the branch like she was sharpening a knife on a whetstone. Her black-bead eyes seemed coy, as if she wanted to say, *You humans. When will you learn? Life is life is life is life.*

Persephone was going to be just fine.

Ava kept telling herself that the same would be true for herself.

◆

From the Jipijapa birding trail, she caught the late bus back to Cayo and as usual it careened down the narrow, winding road at breakneck speeds, passing slow-moving trucks on blind corners, leaning sharply sideways. Ava clutched the armrest. The mounted TVs blared soft porn as loaded trucks and speeding cars and whole families on one motorcycle passed each other blindly, honking and swerving as they made their own center lane.

She wondered how many people died on the roads each year. Billboards displayed grisly images—people with black eyes, bloody faces, and mangled bodies. The lettering warned something she couldn't translate, although the images said enough. Riding these roads was a deadly proposition.

When the bus returned her to Cayo at 3:30, the evening's candied gloaming glinted on the water—time on the equator unrelenting: twelve hours of daylight, twelve hours of dark. So unlike the Pacific Northwest's long summer days—dark at 10:30 p.m., sunup at 4:30 a.m. She welcomed the early dark here, evening a kind of morning, the world stirring to life after the sweltering sunlight.

Before she knew better, Ava had taken long beach walks in the midday heat, marveling that she had paradise to herself. Beaches were deserted, roads empty, cabanas closed for the afternoon. But then she'd gotten heat exhaustion so severe that she had to lie for days on Alfred's woven couch under the gusting ceiling fan. Migraines and nausea held her motionless. Now she followed the local schedule—out only at the crack of dawn, or after sunset.

◆

She decided to run down to the beach for a swim before going inside Alfred's stuffy casa. At the uninhabited end of the beach, hidden behind a steep drop, she shed her sweaty clothes, stripping down to bare skin.

A pair of dogs ran the stretch of flat shoreline as they did every day—a black male and a brown-spotted female, taking their nightly constitutional. The eared and croaking doves called to each other as the cicadas filled the air with their evening chorus, so loud and buzzing and high-pitched that when it suddenly stopped—a predator spotted perhaps, some danger unseen to Ava—it seemed the world had paused.

Other than the dog couple, the beach was empty but strewn with garbage: cigarette butts, bottles, plastic bits, shoes with no mates, a toothbrush. The palms and hibiscus beyond were illuminated by a single dim streetlight. The distant row of cabanas, with their plastic chairs and tablecloths, clanked with hanging shells. The air was soft, sticky, and smoky—warm as the ocean water Ava waded into, the sun resting on the horizon like an orange ball adrift on the sea.

She welcomed the sting of saltwater in her eyes and nose, rose to the flat foaming expanses between the waves, swells every fifteen seconds. The pull lifted from her shoulders to her chin, receded to her hips. Ava turned slowly to take it all in, as her father had taught her: teal egg-shaped rocks glowing in evening light; the pattern of plowed beach raked with heavy tire print; dry, raw cliffs, studded with brush. Moto taxis roared up and down the Malecón. Wooden fishing boats lined up on the beach. *Anita Elizabeth*, *Moby Dick II*. Fine dust pricked her eyes. Tiny lizards scampered the sand as geckos chirped in the grass.

The Pacific's bubbling evanescence held her aloft as she floated on her back, her arms extended like wings, the magnificent frigate birds flying low and long over her head as the sun sank beneath the sea.

When she waded back to shore and dried herself off, she thought a hump in the sand was another scrap of garbage. But then she realized it was what she'd come to Ecuador hoping to see. There on Cayo's beach, with the lovey ultra-marine webbed feet associated with wild Galapagos Islands (not stray dogs and trash, shacky cabanas and moto taxis), was a blue-footed booby, *Sula nebouxii.* But it was weak and struggling. Its movements caught the attention of a small, mottled dog who trotted toward the bird, eyeing it with hungry interest.

Ava jogged to the booby's side before the dog could, expecting the bird to bolt to the sea or air, but it couldn't right itself.

Couldn't get its feet underneath. She knew that as marine birds, boobies spent very little time on land. When they did, it was for breeding or training the little ones with their signature high-stepping moves. She was sorry that the first one she saw was in distress, attracting predators.

Running to it along the crest of a swale hidden behind the beach, she spotted another and another. And another. A dozen blue-footed booby carcasses strewn like a child's stuffed animal collection, their blue feet and legs standing out like bits of colored plastic.

Crouching, Ava lay her shirt over the still-living booby, expecting a struggle as she tucked its wings to its body and scooped it up, but it was limp in her arms. She walked with it to Alfred's casa, waves crashing in the dark behind her. An iguana the size of a crocodile walked slowly across the neighbors' roof peak. Something dead and rotting wafted from the windrow of brush and garbage banked against a broken fence.

The booby rested so still in her arms she feared it had succumbed, but when she got in the gate and laid it on the shaded tile porch, it opened its sunken eyes. Pale lice scampered out from beneath its feathers before diving under again. She knew they needed a live host just as much as she hoped for a live bird.

This bird. This bird she broke her own rule for, again, giving it a name: Bluebell. Suddenly, everything channeled into this one ailing booby, gravity and sorrow pinning them earthbound. But all she could do was offer Bluebell sardines and fresh water, shelter it in a dark hidden spot in the yard, away from dogs and vultures. Bluebell lay still, blue, webbed feet spread wide under sagging beak and serpentine neck, hollowed eyes closed.

Suspended and swaying in the hammock above Bluebell, Ava slept and dreamed they were sheltered together in a wind-blown nest.

She woke early to the sounds of the next-door family bathing and washing laundry in their backyard cistern. She got up to the wafting stink of her dirty dishes left overnight in the sink and damp towels gone sour on the clothesline, her water cooler rattling empty, the fish vendor rolling his cart along the street yelling "Camaron, calamar!" as a pregnant woman passed by, a passel of children crying after her. Fresh mosquito bites welted Ava's exposed skin. Strange blue-black house wasps hovered silently overhead.

She faced what she knew had been coming: Bluebell a gray unmoving hump in the shaded corner, lines of ants threaded over body and beak, streaming over those fantastical blue-water feet. Ava dug a deep hole and buried Bluebell in the backyard, the sun a miasma of hazed heat.

EZRA

Domingo's homemade liquor was a thick, potent moonshine made with honey and starfruit. Mixed with marijuana, Ezra felt as though he were sailing. Then he remembered he *was* sailing—well, riding an outdated cargo ship with a cast of eccentrics. He laughed so hard at this deep insight he fell down the stairs, landing in a heap on the passenger deck. He tried to sit upright, thinking he could hear Doc the parrot laughing derisively above him.

Whenever Ezra visited Domingo's berth, Doc climbed outside his cage and sat on its dome top, coolly watching them smoke and drink. Domingo had demonstrated Doc's gentleness by petting the feathers at the back of his neck, Doc lowering his head for him. But it wasn't Doc's rumored ferocity that kept Ezra cautious. It was the knowingness in his yellow eyes.

This time Ezra had remembered to roll down his shirtsleeves. He covered every bit of skin he could, but when Doc had tilted his head and pinned his eye at him, Ezra felt stripped bare. Doc hadn't said much—just preened his feathers, fake-coughed at the smoke, and called himself a good bird a time or two. Still, Ezra kept his eye on him.

Now, semi-upright on the passenger deck, Ezra heard a door open and close and looked up at Angie's legs, a hundred miles long.

111

"It's beautiful, isn't it?" Angie said, stopping appropriately to gaze at the sea before coming to where he sat.

Ezra, reeling on moonshine, felt caught in a moment he hadn't planned on sharing.

"I love watching the sunset," she said, shivering, though it wasn't cold. She folded her arms against her chest. "I love this part most—the anticipation, the excitement. Everything so... possible." She glanced at him. "You know what I mean?"

Was that what he was? Excited?

"The first time we came down, Chad was so sick. I didn't think he was going to make it. But he recovered. We all did. You will too," she said. "Just give yourself time."

She looked at Ezra with the proselytizer's pensive and patient concern.

What kind of recovery did she think he needed? She was the one who needed something. Trying to save the world while she was crying for help.

Ezra motioned with his hand up, unsteadily, said, "A woman's face, with nature's own hand painted..."

"Is that Shakespeare?" Angie asked, frowning.

"Hast thou, the master-mistress of my passion;
A woman's gentle heart, but not acquainted..."

Ezra struggled to pull himself up to better recite the rest of Sonnet 20. She bent to help him, her hair falling around her face.

Ezra said, "With shifting change, as is false woman's fashion."

"Are you okay?" she asked. So serious, so solicitous, her fingers brushing against his arm. Ezra gazed, then reached up and tried to touch her hair, but she pulled back, swept it behind her shoulder. Too sanctified for his touch.

"You," he said thickly, grinning at her. "You." He pointed a wobbly finger.

"Oh. You're drunk," she said flatly.

That set him off again, the hilarity of it all: Doc and Domingo, Joel and his burger and pies, Tiny and Captain Vic-the-Prick, the three old ladies, and *Angie and Chad*.

She stood up. "I guess you know what you're doing. Goodnight."

He said, "Wait. Don't go!" but that set him off again—calling out to her so absurd he couldn't stop, fits of laughter so hard he almost choked.

He heard the door shut behind her and wondered what Angie would say to Chad in their little berth with panties on the floor. *Oh, it was nothing,* her hands at her sides. *Just a stray dog.* Then Ezra remembered he was on a ship. All the dogs were in Ecuador—except the ones that weren't. Except the ones they were smuggling. He laughed until it hurt.

◆

He woke to licking. His first thought was of the racing dogs, but the tongue was sandpaper, rasping against his unshaven cheek. The ship's mangy cat purred and headbutted his face, already on those kinds of terms.

Wincing, Ezra eased himself upright. Each lurch of his stomach told him there was as much sea inside of him as there was below. Whitecaps broke and formed, broke and formed.

He crawled toward his cabin, the deck alternately light and dark—overly bright fluorescents strung like landing lights. He wanted to invite the cat along, but what would he say? "Here kitty, kitty, kitty?" Too frivolous for either of them, and anyway, what cat worth its title ever deigned to come when called?

He wanted to stop for a smoke but he needed to get to his cabin, no matter how his guts complained. Otherwise he might pitch overboard. It took an eternity to get to his door, and then he half fell, half crawled inside his room. The cat followed him in and jumped up on the dresser.

He pushed the door shut with his foot and lay on the floor.

The ship moved underneath him, engines rumbling. The loose liquid feeling of his guts. Ezra put his hands out to anchor himself, but it was too late—the room rotated like a carnival ride. Cat, bed, door, cat, bed, door. He pressed his arm over his eyes, but that made it worse.

He crawled to the bathroom for a cold washcloth and pressed it against his face, breathing through its wet cleanness. He brought it back to the bed with him, laying it on his forehead like a mother's cool hand pressing down—something from a long-ago dream. Something from a world that had once made sense.

Outside the window, the sky was black, and he was glad for night—the last on the Ship of Fools. The so-very *Valiant Endurance*.

It was time for something better than endurance. It was time for a life made new.

AVA

She sat under the blowing ceiling fan and called Alfred again. She needed to hear his voice, needed to hear about Persephone there in the sunny kitchen, watching from her perch as garden birds came and went. She imagined the two of them, avian pied pipers, summoning all the winged beings.

Ava pictured Alfred planning his camping trip to the North Fork, packing Persephone along with him, "to remind her of home," he said. Sibley would be there, too, keeping up the good fight to keep the river wild and protected. But Alfred didn't answer, his recorded voice tinny and distant. Ava hung up without leaving a message, knowing her own voice would quaver and only make Alfred worry.

Lying on the couch in the dark, she felt nauseated and fevered, her body pulsing with electrical pain. This time it had nothing to do with heat or sun, with dehydration or exertion. She fell into fevered sleep, dreamed of lines of ants staking her down and carrying her to Hades.

The phone rang and she startled up, sweating in panic, looking frantically at her limbs, trying to locate the source of their binding. She answered, expecting Alfred, already relieved to talk to him.

Instead, Sibley's familiar, euphonious voice.

"Hello? Bird? Are you there?"

Ava's brain wouldn't work. *There* was a dark, distant, and unexplored realm. Sibley's voice came from the future, from the past, from a place that couldn't exist. Ava slowly bobbed from one shadowy planet to the next.

The still-thinking part of Ava's brain told her clearly that she wasn't thinking clearly. A panic attack. A fugue-like state. She couldn't break the bonds of Lilliput. She was very ill.

"Ava, listen, if you're there, please don't hang up," Sibley pleaded, her words clearer now, her breath in Ava's ear. "Please, Ava, are you there? Please, say something if you can hear me—"

"I'm here." Heart pounding in her throat, heat flushing along her limbs.

"*Here, here, here, here, here…*"

No gravity, no form.

"Oh, thank God. I didn't know if I'd catch you. Alfred gave me his house number. Please don't be mad. I made him. I went to his house. I met his girlfriend, Willow. When did *that* happen and how did we not know about it?"

We.

Sibley breathed in and out, in and out, a deep-sea diver.

"I'm so sorry, Ava. You've been through so much. I shouldn't have stormed out on you. It was reactive. I was angry. I didn't want to lose you. It felt like you were pushing me and everyone else away. I so badly wanted *us* to stay *us*."

Breath in and out, in and out. "I didn't—I *don't*—want to lose you. We belong together. I know you believe that. We have too much together to let go."

"Yes…" Ava said, her voice coming from farther and farther away.

She was shivering, her teeth chattered, the house was suddenly freezing, winter blowing in, her bones ice, her skin clammy and sheened.

"I want you back, I want us back," Sibley said, her voice breaking. "Ava, please, just come back. I miss you so much.

Please, please, just come back."

The water cooler clanked and rattled with ice, the fans blowing arctic air.

"I'm…no good." Ava heard her own broken words breaking through brokenness. Pulverizing, sharp-edged glass.

"Please, let me come to you. I'll leave right now—I can be there tomorrow. At least just let me be there with you."

Hard breath in and out. In and out.

"Ava, are you okay? You don't sound okay…"

Okay, okay, okay, okay, okay …

She couldn't stop staring at her dirt-rimmed fingernails. Soil and microorganisms. Dead fathers and protégés, dead birds. Wildfire smoke.

"What are you going to do? What can I do?" Sibley pleaded.

Ava's teeth rattled like bones, her skin blue as blue-footed boobies dead on the beach. A reckoning.

"Are you still going to the Galapagos, the cloud forest, the Amazon? All the places we talked about? Find all those birds that you love?"

"Yes…" Ava said, but what she wished to say was *come, come, come, I'm sorry, I'm sorry, I'm sorry,* sorrow rising like a tidal wave.

The wave overtook her, pulled her body out into deep cold dark.

EZRA

The atmosphere on board told Ezra they were nearing land. A sudden shift in energy, like wind bearing a scent of things tropical—sea and earth meeting under sun.

Even Tiny walked faster, his proportions tipping him forward. Domingo came by the kitchen to drill Ezra on the plan: dock, unload, hit the town. Find the ladies.

"What will you do?" Angie asked Ezra as he brought in the last of the eggs.

He met her eyes, brazen. "What won't I do?"

She flushed red, fiddled with her toast. Chad prattled on while she kept her eyes down. He talked about their plans to find a surf shop and learn to ride the waves. "Angie's a marathon runner," he added, "an endurance athlete. She shouldn't have any problem at all."

"I bet she won't." Ezra watched as her blush deepened.

"The first thing I'm going to do," Penny said, "is find somewhere to take a bath. Then I'm going to wade in the ocean."

"You and your wading," Mary said. "I'm swimming! It's like being in a giant hot tub. Who needs a bath?"

Everyone was cheerful. The weather was good. The ship had made good time.

Ezra let himself think about what it meant to approach another shore, another country, another continent. What it would mean to make it—to step off the ship and disappear. Start again.

Joel was unusually quiet as they stowed the pans, sorted supplies, and made lists. He would be only taking a short stop at Manta—enough to resupply, maybe get the tattoo of his dreams.

"You're not coming back, are you," Joel said, his hairy hands strangely feminine as he measured what was left in a bag of rice.

"Coming back?" Ezra said, careful.

"I've sensed it since the beginning. You're a one-ride wonder. We get them often enough, but that's usually because they don't have the stomach for it or they find something else they'd rather do. You, on the other hand, you had a plan since the beginning. Waiting like a baited lion to jump." Joel stopped, rice in hand.

Ezra met his eyes with a steady gaze. "I don't know what you're talking about. I'm going in to catch the sights, just like the rest of you. And I'll be back, just like the rest of you."

Joel studied him. "Sure," he finally said.

Ezra didn't know what Joel had been hoping for—a confession? A sharing of secrets? A stewards' pact, best buddies forever? Ezra had no idea how Joel had survived this long, on the ship or off.

"Hey, you ready to get that tattoo?" Ezra smiled.

Joel had his back to him, putting the rice away. "I've been thinking I'd wait," he said, his voice muffled. "Heard stories about dirty needles down here. Be safer back home."

"Yeah," Ezra said. "That's probably best."

"We're taking in coffee, some cocoa. The ship will smell like mocha," Joel said. "Too bad you'll miss it. The food going home is always my best. So much fresh fruit. It's mango season. My mango-peach cobbler…you don't know what you'll be missing. The fresh fish too." He smacked his white hands together. "Now that's something a person can appreciate."

"I can't wait to try it."

◆

The preparations for making port kept everyone busy, and Ezra was glad for that. He worked with his head down. Did what was asked. Rooms cleaned. Mess deck cleaned. Linens sorted, washed, stacked, organized. The kitchen to Joel's specifications. Everything prepped for offloading, and onloading, even if he wouldn't be around.

At the crew meeting, Ezra kept a low profile, which in terms of seniority wasn't hard to do. He stood next to Joel as the captain addressed their route plans, gave orders for maintenance and checks, watch rotations. Quick and to the point.

When the captain finished and they were dispersing to their duties, Tiny sidled up. "Easy, buddy, you making out okay? Your duties suiting you?"

He looked around to make sure he had the audience he intended. "Need anything, Miss? A massage perhaps?" Tiny mimed, grabbing his crotch, pumping his hips, "Uh, uh, oh yeah, that's what I'm talking about. *Cabin. Duties.* Maybe I'll demote myself just for the end of this trip. But I'm sure the holy angel has plenty for all of us, right, Easy? She'll be begging for it after the pathetic cock she's been stuck with."

Ezra's stomach lurched.

Joel was just ahead of them, still in his tank top. He turned toward Tiny, reproachful. "She's religious. You shouldn't talk about religious girls that way. Plus, she's a married woman."

Tiny bent over laughing. His face was red when he stood up. "Did you hear that, Easy? Joel says she's *religious*. Goddamned if that ain't the funniest thing." He slapped Joel's shoulder hard enough to leave a red print. "You're a funny bitch, Joel."

Ezra positioned himself between them and turned to Joel, his voice cool. "So you needed me in the kitchen?"

Joel took a moment to process.

"Uh, yeah. We need to prep."

"Better get going then," Tiny said, addressing Ezra, a vein twitching near his left eye. "Fix us our last meal like a good little kitchen bitch. Don't forget the cherry pie."

Ezra walked down the deck reminding himself what was at stake. One wrong choice, one planted fist. One call is all it'd take. He made himself picture the ocean—a silver bowl met with sky. Reminded himself what freedom was—beach sand beneath his feet, birds soaring, fish waiting to be caught, boats and cabanas, seashells clanking in the wind. What stretched beyond.

◆

They made port at dusk. Ezra stood watching as the shore appeared—a mirage, indistinct and hazy—and then solid. Tall masts rose in the fog.

Domingo clapped him on the back. "Ah, home sweet home." He inhaled deep. "You smell it?" He closed his eyes, breathed, then looked at Ezra, eyebrows lifted. "You smell all the ladies in waiting? I do, hombre, and they smell good, real good."

The general cargo berth was at the end of the wharf, with a gantry crane waiting. A quay studded with rock ran alongside. A cruise ship docked parallel to them, fishing boats of all sizes, shapes, and colors dotting the water on either side of the wharf.

The Port of Bahia de Manta, Ecuador.

Ezra could indeed smell the husky depths of the city, the port, the deep earthiness of his own desire meeting the shape of this place. Overhead, enormous birds sailed like kites, dipping so low they became earth shadow and dusk. Black with pointed wings, long beaks, bellows of red for throats.

"What are they?" Ezra asked Domingo.

Domingo looked up. "*El rabihorcado soberbio*—the magnificent frigate bird."

Silent as shadows they drifted, grouping, falling away, sailing low, tilting their heads.

"They're waiting for fish," Domingo said, pointing to all the fishing boats. "The pelicans too. Doc always starts cackling when we get to shore, says 'más pescado, más pescado,' like he's some damn blue-footed booby instead of a talking, seed-eating parrot. Clown birds, all of them."

"Smart birds," Ezra said, glad the magnificent frigate birds were wild and concerned with fish instead of tattooed humans. Glad for a new shore to set foot upon, finding his way under these outstretched wings.

◆

Tiny came around the deck and Domingo threw his cigarette in the water.

"We need the containers readied," Tiny said to Domingo. "You done cleaning, mop boy?" he added, looking Ezra over. "Got your little knickknacks in order?"

"Yes, Sir," Ezra said, clicking his heels together, hands stiffly to his sides. "Anything else you require, Sir?"

He stared Tiny in the eye.

"Nothing you can satisfy. Although, you never know. I hear prison bitches soften up pretty nice." His shoulder hit Ezra's as he walked past, knocking Ezra sideways.

Ezra made his way back to his berth for his rucksack. The ship already seemed abandoned, empty and creaking. A hunk of metal. Rucksack retrieved, he stopped at the deck to look out one last time.

Silver-gray and as large as a pony, a dog emerged from the morning mist. Birthed from fog. The creature approached Ezra, sleek and gleaming, rhinestone-collared and warm-bodied, sniffing him stiffly before padding by. Hip-high and muscular.

"Queen's Reich, sired by Leprechaun Dreaming," Mary said as the dog lifted its leg to the railing, golden piss pooling toward Ezra's feet. An anointing.

"He's syndicated, out of champion lines."

A silvery creature bred of queens and leprechauns. "What *is* he?" Ezra managed.

"A Great Dane," Mary said, stroking the dog's smooth, wedge-shaped head. She and the dog regarded Ezra with the same imperial reproach.

"I've never seen one in person."

"Well, you have now," Mary said, patting the dog as she leashed him to her wrist. A diamond-studded accessory. "This is one is Mama's Boy—not one of those skinny greyhounds who chases fake hares for a living. That's business. This boy's just for fun, aren't you?"

The dog looked up at her with brown-eyed appreciation, understanding how special he was.

So that's what she'd been smuggling—greyhounds. Racing dogs. And one jewel-bedecked Great Dane she called Mama's Boy.

"Maybe we'll see you around, E-Z," she said, tilting her head at him. "Although something tells me you'd rather not be seen again."

Ezra met Mary's eyes, gave her a little index-finger salute. "I hope you and your dogs make out well."

He shrugged his rucksack straps over his shoulders, headed for the lower deck stairs, then walked the ramp down to the docks. When he looked back, Angie was standing with Mary and Mama's Boy on the upper deck, looking down, watching him go.

Find the Malecón, find your way.

The waves washed against pilings as he strode down the dock, as he breathed in the salt air, as he set his feet to land again and turned his face to the southern wind—warm as breath, warm as the sea, warm as fresh blood coursing through a new body.

GREER

She dug through the llamas' packs, trying not to displace too much, even if everything was already *torn asunder.* She'd heard that in a story about a giant and it'd stuck in her head. Might as well *tear it asunder* more. She dumped everything out and burrowed through her damp, dirty gear to find the Baggie of stale hard candy she'd mostly eaten her way through. She'd been dreaming of butterscotch since early morning.

They'd ascended into the high country now, nights frosted, days brilliant with sun and heat. Wildflowers of every shape and color. Greer thought about that little girl in the Dr. Suess book, with a flower growing out of her head.

They climbed trails that drew them up steeper and steeper terrain, following clear-flowing streams cold enough to make their teeth ache. They ate fat huckleberries on hillsides scattered with bear scat and clumps of bear grass spiked with tall, creamy blooms. Watching out for competitors, Greer picked every huckleberry she could, gathering them in her cup and bowl and cookpot, her fingers stained purple. *Nature's candy,* Mr. Estmund called them.

But the air teemed with biting flies, mosquitoes, and no-see-ums from dawn until dusk. Steep trails and cold nights were bearable, but the vicious bugs made her want to give up. The llamas' ears and eyes crusted at the rims. Sirius constantly snapped. Every part of Greer's exposed skin was a bloody constellation of scabby bites.

She tried not to scratch herself raw, but she was being eaten alive. She woke herself with her thrashing and slapping, her body a giant seething itch. She took to wearing every piece of clothing she had, leaving only her eyes unprotected, but still the devouring bloodsucking hordes found a way in. She'd emptied her only vial of bug dope, slathering herself with DEET, but it only lasted half an hour and the bugs came back, seeming to like the new flavor.

She pawed through the heap: map and compass, sleeping bag and wool blanket, matches and fire starters, fire-blackened pot, plate, bowl, cup, collapsible bucket, water filter, poncho, wool sweater and socks, sewing kit, first-aid kit, sunscreen, peppermint soap, toothbrush, washcloth, slingshot, fishing gear, parachute cord, and field guides. Everything Mr. Estmund said was required for an escape "into the bush."

She set aside the tape recorder and tapes, not wanting to think about what they'd captured—Mr. Estmund's life stories and then his ending, too. She placed Icarus's skull on top of them, guardian.

When she found the last fat yellow butterscotch loose in the folds of Mr. Estmund's moth-eaten wool sweater, she drooled down her chin before she could unwrap it and put it in her mouth. Sirius barreled over, sniffing and licking Greer's face. Another sugar desperado.

"Mine," Greer growled as she pushed Sirius back. She felt like snarling and snapping, turning into a wild beast herself, but then Sirius sat up pretty in her best begging position, her long pink tongue dripping, her right ear folded back on itself. Pathetic.

"Fine," Greer sighed. She cracked the butterscotch in half and fished out a wet chunk. Sirius gulped it down and licked Greer's hand for more.

"So greedy." Greer righted Sirius's soft ear. "No more messing around. It's time to get organized and take action. We need to take stock, think ahead, plan for a life on the lam." Juan and Greer loved saying *life on the lam* after their history unit. They'd run around the llama pasture, hiding out behind trees, pretending to be old-time bank robbers escaping the law.

The real thing was so much harder than playing afternoon games.

She'd been meaning to go through all the gear, but after each day's hike—trying to put distance between herself and Headquarters, between herself and anyone who might be searching for her to make her go back home, trapped with her mom and Rory, with no Mr. Estmund to escape to anymore—she was too tired. As long as she was here in the mountains, leading Mr. Estmund's llamas, speaking to him in her mind about plans and routes and survival, it felt like he was still with her. Going home, she'd have to face the truth of what had happened to him, and why.

Sirius trailed her, hopeful for more candy as Greer sorted their gear into the "room" to which it belonged—bathroom, bedroom, kitchen—just as Mr. Estmund had taught her. Luckily, she'd been wearing her basketball sneakers when she ran away, and the days were still warm. There was still a bit of food left. They'd had enough to get by so far—weeks? months?—but she wasn't sure what they'd do later. The nights were freezing, the food was almost gone. Llamas, dog, and girl all bony and disheveled.

"We'll just have to figure it out," she said to Sirius and Kelly and Yavell. She was the head of the family now. It was up to her to take care of them. "If you put your mind to something, there's no telling what you can do."

Something Mr. Estmund used to say.

When she re-packed the llamas' dynamite boxes and soft panniers, she found an unfamiliar brown paper package in a side pocket. Bulky but light and jingly with the tinny sound of small bells, it felt like finding a present forgotten underneath the Christmas tree. She could hardly contain herself when she unwrapped a tangled mass of color, rainbow ribbons and straps covered with pompoms, tassels, and bells—llama halters Juan's family must have given Mr. Estmund.

Greer had seen photos of decked-out Andean llamas and had wished she could dress Kelly and Yavell that way, too. So flashy and cheerful. Like a *jamboree*. Overjoyed, she ran to the llamas, dancing around them with all the ribbons and bells.

"What do you think?" she asked, jangly bright gear looped over her arms and shoulders.

Yavell eyed her with suspicion, sidestepping away. Kelly hummed nervously.

"You're going to look so handsome. Everyone's going to be so jealous."

Illustrating her point, Sirius came running over to sniff the halters, tinkling the bells with her wet nose. Greer patted her head. "I know, I know. We need something to wear, too."

Greer ran back to the tarp and got busy. She used her pocketknife and sewing kit to cut off a bit of extra strapping. She fashioned one part of it into a tasseled collar for Sirius. The other part became a belled headdress for herself. She tied the collar around Sirius's neck, and then tied on her own ornament, dancing around camp jingling.

"Oh yes, we're the pretty ones now," she said, twirling about. Kelly hummed his sweet high-pitched questioning hum and Yavell hummed his deep guttural hum and Sirius whined her excited whine. A happy little family of four.

But she shouldn't have let herself feel any feeling so strongly, because out of nowhere Greer was crying and couldn't stop. She wished she were dancing around a campfire with Juan and Mr. Estmund. She imagined them holding hands as they whirled through the fire's sparks, tassels and pompoms and bells strung from their arms until they transformed into streams of light and color and became a flock of rainbow-colored ravens cawing their way back home, laughing together like they used to before everything went so horribly wrong.

She wanted to show them what she'd done, how far she'd come.

But she was glad they couldn't see her crying.

She climbed into her sleeping bag and shivered herself to sleep.

◆

The next morning the llamas were squirrelly as Greer fit them with their new halters. They circled around and yanked their heads, flattening their ears and gurgling their long throats. But when she was done, Greer stood back to admire her success, each llama transformed into a celebration of color, tasseled and pompommed and belled.

She led them around camp, making sure everything was secure before they hit the trail. At first, they pulled and balked, but then they capitulated to the jingling and bright colors strung along their necks and noses and foreheads. Sirius wore her collar proudly, the whole family matching, like a party of pretty parrots.

The trail angled up again, headed into the clouds.

She wondered how high they would have to go before the mountain guided them down to the river. She started singing her and Juan's favorite Mr. Estmund hiking song. "Hey ho, here we go / off to the woods we go. / Hey ho, here we go / like a flock of crows, ho-ho."

They rounded a bend along a sharp ridge. Sirius stopped, growling at something in the shadowy trees. A man-shaped creature stepped into the sunlight, abrupt. For a moment, Greer thought he was a hairy, disheveled Bigfoot, his face green and brown. What she first thought was a strange kind of fur turned out to be a tasseled ghillie suit.

He stepped closer, looking her up and down with dark hooded eyes.

"Well ain't you the cutest little thing."

Now Greer knew exactly what he was. A man like Rory, a man who meant harm.

Sirius understood it too. She started barking in her thunderous wolf voice, hackles mohawked from neck to tail. The llamas bunched behind her in consternation. Yavell let out a high-pitched clacking alarm call so loud it pealed over everything else, startling Greer enough to drop the lead ropes, but it didn't matter. Kelly had taken up the unearthly sound as well. The Sirius-Yavell-Kelly racket caused the man to back away, holding up his hands, saying "Whoa, whoa, there," like he was the one who needed to be afraid.

Greer cataloged the knife on his hip, the bow in his hand, the pistol on his waist. Sirius charged, teeth bared. Greer grabbed the llamas' leads and ran for the trees, her heartbeat a crescendo in her ears. A chorus of pine squirrels screeched together, and then the whole forest rippled with warnings.

She ran so hard she almost tripped and tumbled down a slope before she reached the thick timber, dodging and leaping, fleeing into terrain so wild it seemed impossible that any human had ever stepped foot there.

She ran until her legs felt like lead, the llamas holding her up.

Ran until she finally fell, skinning her palms and knees into welts of bright blood.

Sirius caught up to them, whined, and licked Greer's wounds. Her new collar was full of sticks and lichen, the llamas' colorful tassels and pompoms all askew, Greer's headdress lost along the way.

Greer imagined the ghillie-suit hunter picking it up, sniffing it, tracking them like animals. She pushed herself up, fear reviving her strength to run further and further into the wild as night fell, until she collapsed in a stone outcrop, making the llamas kush out of sight. She and Sirius scented the air, listened for cracks in the brush, watching for dark shapes to emerge. No fire, no warm dinner. Nightmares of slithering hands like snakes, reaching.

◆

They followed one ridge after another, day after day, until Greer didn't know where they'd come from or where they were headed. No trails, nothing but wild country growing wilder, the ground hollow underfoot, wildfire smoke cloaking mountain shoulders in every direction.

On the fourth night after fleeing the hunter, Greer hid on a stony ledge dressed in every scrap of clothing she had. She risked a small fire and sat with the map and compass in its flickering light. She couldn't make sense of anything, despite how much Mr. Estmund had tried to teach her: longitude, latitude, topography, elevation, coordinates, compass points like a foreign language. She could barely tell if she was speaking or thinking words anymore, but for the first time ever she felt angry at the man she'd left behind, unmoving in his living room chair. *I'm only in fourth grade, Mr. Estmund! Didn't you ever notice that?*

She gave up and pulled out the tape recorder instead, torn between hearing Mr. Estmund's voice again and depleting the batteries.

She put in one of her favorites—the story of Billy Rhodes. Even though it was sad—about an old-time gold miner who lived and died in these mountains—it captivated her with its promise and tragedy.

She lay back against the llamas' panniers, covered by Mr. Estmund's wool blanket, Sirius curled tight against her side.

Greer pressed PLAY. Mr. Estmund's voice unspooled like water running over stones, carrying them all along.

"Billy Rhodes bent over clumps of spent bear grass and mats of flowered heather and cut into the ground, each scrape of his shovel echoing hollow in the high-mountain earth. Mule deer came at night, hungry for salt left from the men's urine, but when the miners turned in their bedrolls or the low campfire sparked, the deer bounded off. Their spring-loaded hops made the same hollow echo, as if there were an excavated world beneath them. Billy hoped it was full of the rich silver ore they'd come for.

Only these mountains sounded like that, smelled like pitch and hemlock, damp mineral rock and thrashing trout. The mountains took and gave in equal measure, didn't matter what the rest of the world saw. Mulatto. Black Billy. Blackie Rhodes. No place for your kind around here. He'd made his way, though—staked the richest placer gold lode claim in Pierce's 1860 gold rush. Rhodes Creek named after him now, twenty-five years later, but those payouts were long gone. California, Arizona, then back to Idaho, flat broke.

He planted the snow pole—a limbed spruce—and tamped it in solid. It towered over his big-man bony height, scored at every foot. Tall enough to measure the coming snow load. Hard to imagine now—baking dust-hot summer—but come a few weeks and the first flurries would blow down the rock-barren ten-thousand-foot slope of Rhodes Peak. Goat Lake would turn from indigo to iced silver overnight.

He called the dog to admire his work. He walked around the planted snow pole as if it were a maypole—just attach some ribbons and call Frank and Hass in with their boyish enthusiasm, tell them it was good luck to *dance for gold and silver, plentiful game and a light winter.*

Down in Lewiston, Risse and Silcott had furnished him a grubstake and equipped him for prospecting. They hired Frank and Hass, both eighteen, to help him develop the mine after less intrepid speculators pulled out, saying it would cost too much in such remote country. Especially for silver ore, although it was the only thing left.

Billy and the dog walked back to the cabin site. The dog chased pikas as they gathered their sun-dried summer grasses. Billy fit one hauled stone after another into the cabin's foundation, readying it for logs—each wrestled stone, each felled tree, each chinked gap one more step toward shelter in a country soon to be solemn with snow.

A moose and her yearling had dropped by again last night, their great long faces streaming water and reeds, wary of the dog. This evening the cutthroat leaped high for flying insects, their bodies fatly slapping the lake's surface. Another cast-iron fish fry for supper, after fishing from the house-sized rock half in and half out of the lake.

Each day he crossed the log-studded outlet, walked the wildflower meadow to fill the water bladder at the spring seep he'd dug where the steep mountainside sloughed shale into the lake. The water tasted like snow, icy enough to numb his throat, to leave him forever wanting more. He called the dog in close as he wandered the inlet's winding flow—one bend after another doubled on itself. The water magnified each pebble, each grain of sand—frogs, garter snakes, and water skippers swimming undisturbed.

Billy and the dog climbed the fishing rock, settled on the far ledge where they could see the cutthroat darting through the lake's green depths. He was still fishing when the boys came back, their voices carrying across the water. He heard them washing themselves at the shore—Billy's rule, a measure of civility although their quarters were only a dirt-floor foundation.

He'd just secured the roof shingles when the first storm hit, snow blowing sideways, banking against the planked door. Now, November, the cabin was buried in snow, tunnels branching from the entry. They had snowshoed a path to the mine, muddy rivulets flowing from the dark mouth. The tunnel was deep but they'd found no ore. Still, they dug and hauled, braced walls and floor, cribbed into the mountain as the snow bore down—three feet one night, two the next, trees bending under the load.

Hass had a good eye, a steady trigger pull. The big mule deer he shot was enough to feed them another month. Roasts and chops and stews and bones Billy seasoned with black pepper and cayenne, laughing as the white boys' faces beaded with spice-sweat. But now the meat was gone, the mine unyielding, snow past the twelve foot mark. Game gone to lower ground. Cutthroat resting under ice in frigid stupor.

For Christmas he carved them slingshots like he once did for his nieces and nephews—before the gold, before the jewelry and dresses, before the high-backed coaches and papered ponies and dogs the placer mine afforded. And Billy made Hass and Frank antler handles for their forks and knives—gifts they opened eagerly, whooping around the cabin, the dog barking joyously as they shot each other with dried beans. High mountains made them family.

Almost the New Year, he told the boys it was nothing more than a bad case of cramps, blamed it on underdone beans and rice. But it was something with jaws, eating him from the inside out.

Billy stayed in. Left off the tunneling. Did all the cooking to make up for it, swept the frozen dirt floor, boiled pots of snow to wash their utensils and clothes.

To wash himself, private.

It wouldn't un-grip his guts. His nerves sparked with each cramping wave, his body and mind in equal distress. He wore the path to the privy into a deepening groove, his knobbed bones distinct as they'd been when he was a Missouri child raised in a passel of hungry children.

March first, he sent the boys to work on the tunnel, said he would cook them a hot lunch. Another pot of snow set to boil on the wood stove, his guts clamping, his knees wobbly, his insides roiling as though he were on a snowy sea, preparing to sink.

He was glad no one heard his guttural cries, his body purging with such violence that there was nothing more to expel. The snow pole over fifteen feet. He slept, dreamed he was being buried alive, awakened. He curled like an infant on the bed, the dog whining and nuzzling his hand until Billy closed his eyes and thought of this: pounds and pounds of gleaming silver ore, a world gone green, sweet water and fish jumping, as hungry and alive as he was."

Greer pushed STOP. She told herself it was to save the battery. But also maybe this wasn't the right time to hear Mr. Estmund finish the story.

She knew the ending already.

AVA

Ava slept like death. Lost track of day and night. Shivering, clanking, hallucinating from one couch-bound position to the next, the ceiling fans sweating equatorial air, mosquitoes buzzing bloodthirsty, the water cooler rattling its death rattle.

The phone ringing unanswered.

When she heard knocking, she thought it was coming from inside her head. But it didn't stop. *Bang, bang, bang.* Ava pushed herself up and stumbled to the door, pulling its heavy wooden weight.

A woman stood in the blinding morning light, tall and windblown.

Ava blinked. Un-slacked her hanging jaw.

"Oh, hola!" the woman said, startled, smiling, her teeth perfect white, her sun-streaked brown hair waving down to her bare waist. An ocean-blue sarong over her bikini, gold bangles tinkling on her wrists. She tucked a beachy strand of hair behind a shell-shaped ear and squinted at Ava.

Two tousled carbon-copy boys stood on either side, clinging to their mother's legs.

Ava, groggy and muddled, took a moment to process. Identical twins.

"I am Gabriela," the woman said. "This is Adan and Ail."

She put a hand on each boy's head. "Some kids down at the beach told us you were a bird doctor. La Chica de Aves?"

"They call me that," Ava said, flickering in Gabriela's golden gaze.

"We have found an injured bird with which we hope you will be able to help us," Gabriela said, her accented English proper, unlike the surfers' clumsy slang.

Ava straightened, trying to recall that other version of self who an ancient time ago on another planet had been a scientist, author, professor. Someone with a life of meaning and sense, who knew how to comb her hair.

"A blue-footed booby?" she said, glancing at the spot where she'd buried Bluebell, ants swarming now to take him home.

"Sí, sí, piquero de patas azules," Gabriela answered. The little boys mouthed the name, practicing with plump rosebud lips. Gabriela's eyes filled with sorrow. "We found it on the shore. I am afraid that there were many more we could not save."

Sula nebouxii. "Is it with you?" Ava asked.

"Sí, we took it to our finca. Please, can you come see?"

Ava smoothed her matted hair. "Yes, yes, of course. Just give me a moment. I'm sorry to not invite you in, but I've been ill. I'm feeling better but I don't want to endanger the boys."

She wished she had refilled the water cooler, wished she had food to offer, wished to erase her imprint on the thin couch cushions, sweat stained and limp.

"Come, come my niños." Gabriela settled the little boys in a porch hammock. Ava brought them what was left of a bag of tafi leche rhum—the cupboards empty but for white rice. Ava filled three glasses of tepid tap water and took them out before scurrying to the bathroom to wash her mottled face. She pulled her lank hair into a hasty ponytail.

Once Ava changed her clothes and collected a few bird-saving supplies, they climbed into Gabriela's old Land Cruiser and drove. Ava felt like she'd stepped from a dire infirmary into a feel-good movie: warm dry coastal wind gusting in, a children's song playing on the stereo, Gabriela and her little boys singing along in their thin, sweet voices. "Fly, fly, fly, can you teach me how to fly / Pobrecito guacamaya, we can leave the world behind / Vuela, vuela, vuela, can you teach me how to fly? / Pobrecito guacamaya, we can leave the world behind."

A flock of magnificent frigate birds sailed overhead.

"You live here, in Cayo?" Gabriela asked, her long hair blowing, gold-rimmed aviators glinting with the bangles on her wrists.

"It's my great-uncle Alfred's place, but I live here—for now."

Ava looked out at the passing scenery, wondering what that meant—*for now.* Would she ever find her way home again?

Gabriela smiled and held her hand out the window. "Ah, this is good. A new friend."

Ava wished she could share this moment with Sibley: Gabriela and her beautiful twins singing about hungry little birds and learning to fly, driving to their finca for the sake of a blue-footed booby, the sun beating down, a smell of silage and hot sand. An old donkey braying beside the road.

They reached the finca at the end of a bumpy lane, winding through an orchard laden with strange fruit. Gabriela drove the Land Cruiser into an open shed and parked, dust boiling up. Adan and Ail climbed out and pulled Ava to an oversized barn noisy with goats and roosters, fluffy rabbits and free-range hens, a messy brimming garden outside. They led her to a straw-filled stable encased in chicken wire. A blue-footed booby nested in the back corner, beside a shallow dish of fresh water.

"Oh poor thing," Ava said, and the little boys nodded, their lips trembling.

"We will do all we can to help it," she added quickly.

"We named her Clio." Gabriela flashed her golden-sun smile. "She is our new friend. Like you," she said, nudging Ava's side, the fresh beach-scent of her hair and skin wafting close.

"La Chica de Aves."

"Clio, daughter of Zeus, goddess of memory." Ava said, regarding the bird.

"Sí! How did you know?" Gabriela said. Ava tried not to be distracted by her shapely eyebrows.

"I memorize names and their meanings for a living." She looked down at the shimmering boys. "*Adan*, from the red earth. *Ail,* from the stony place."

The twins grinned at Ava with baby-teeth replicas of their mother's perfect smile.

Gabriela's golden eyes opened wide. "Who *are* you, La Chica de Aves?"

"Avanthe Estmund, PhD, Professor of Ornithology, commonly known as The Bird Girl."

"A profesora! Oh, buena, buena," Gabriela said. "And a bird doctor, sí?"

"Of types." Ava regarded the ailing blue-footed booby in its straw-heaped corner. A wild bird displaced.

"An ornitóloga, like Señor Louis Agassiz Fuertes?"

"Yes." Ava smiled, surprised. "I study Fuertes's work. He was an amazing ornithologist."

Ava admired Jewish birders like Ryan Tomazin, president of the Brooks Bird Club—one of North America's oldest birding groups. Brooke Barker and Boaz Frankel, who proved that crows had the ability to identify individual humans, remembering who aided or threatened them. But Fuertes was one of her favorite ornithologists.

Gabriela grabbed Ava's arm and shook it gently. "You are our Señora Fuertes. Our special bird girlfriend. Can you help our poor little boobies?"

Ava suppressed a laugh. "I'll try my best."

The boys hovered behind Ava as she examined the bird, their small sweaty heat and fidgeting attention distracting. Clio watched Ava's every move with black-bead eyes.

"I think she'll be okay," Ava said. The bird was in much better shape than Bluebell had been. "I think she'll be okay!" she said again, relief like a suddenly remembered thing.

She used a sterilized dropper to feed electrolyte water down Clio's throat.

She would have to determine more with research, contact with scientists, and whatever tests she could perform without her lab, but she had a pretty good idea the source of malady: a pathogenic malarial blood parasite, often affecting blue-footed booby populations.

"Let's mash up some fish, let's work until we save her. Let's make sure she's never hungry so she can leave this sad time behind," Ava said to the twins.

The little boys took up the cue, and this time Ava sang with them.

Pobrecito guacamaya, I'll share my food with you if you'll only help me, too.

Fly, fly, fly, can you teach me how to fly?

AVA

Blue-black house wasps hovered above the tiled porch, the swaybacked hammocks striped with sunlight. Garrulous green Pacific parrotlets, *Forpus coelestis,* frolicked in the lanky overgrown lime tree, birds the same size and color as its fruit. The outdoor shower on the side of the house dripped from Ava's rinse-off.

She rolled the little blue 1970 motorcycle from the guest room where Alfred stored it and pushed it out to the sun-beaten street.

After Alfred called to tell her that he and Persephone were headed off to the North Fork, Ava had gone to the sea for solace, swimming as the fishermen returned from their early run. Floating on her back, gazing up at sky, she'd imagined the winding drive to the river, Persephone visiting the fire-changed land from which she'd come—her broken wing nearly healed now, her health regained, almost ready to be set free, find her life mate, find a way forward.

Sibley would be on the North Fork now, too, completing her fieldwork, laboring to protect everything Ava loved there—the river and its plants, birds, animals, and trees.

Infused with something she couldn't name, Ava followed the instructions Alfred had given her over the phone. *Mix fresh fuel, put in the new spark plug, open the choke, and kick, kick,*

kick.

She kicked until her leg nearly fell off, but finally, after a sputter and pop and a frantic feathering of the throttle, the two-stroke engine fired. Revving, she jumped astride, toed down, opened the clutch and rode—shaky at first, then gearing up with more confidence. The engine progressed from a choked coughing grumble to a wide-open roar.

Ava remembered learning to ride motorcycles on old overgrown logging roads as a child, neighbors with garages full of motorcycles and chainsaws and all the tools it took to keep them tuned. Remembered well what that form of freedom had felt like as a child. The same as now.

She tore around Cayo's sleepy daytime streets, nobody out but a few rangy roosters and rattling moto taxis. Guard dogs charged her, yanked back by their chains and barking like maniacs as she jammed by. Made their day.

She liked the way the way the enduro surged forward with just a tiny twist of the throttle, how its throaty engine smoked and snarled, but she especially liked the way the wind blew against her face, lifting her hair, cooling her in the stifling heat.

She cruised along the Malecón, the morning surf choppy and glinting with sun, the turquoise fishing boats lined up on the beach. Then she rode up to the overlook spot, all of Cayo nestled in a tidy C below, the cluster of cabanas, sandy shoreline, and barren cliffs dwarfed by the Pacific's silver expanse. The horizon empty but for the dump's distant pillar of smoke. Heat waves shimmered the air. Little lizards and sooty-crowned flycatchers scuttled by. The sun bore down like a malevolent god-eye.

Hot wind peppered her face as she descended back into Cayo and continued north, speeding past empty-gated and guarded gringo housing developments, their investors hopeful for a flood of expats with bottomless IRAs. She rode past rich Ecuadorians' white stucco vacation homes gleaming with windows, rising from yards of raked sand, their swimming pools enclosed by tidily trimmed palms and concrete walls studded with broken glass. Prisons of wealth.

Overloaded trucks tooted their horns, well-worn men leering as she rode past acres of brushy land, twisting the accelerator until the motorcycle popped and tore. She thought about riding up the coast to Manta, an hour and a half away, and then beyond—to Columbia, to Panama, to Costa Rica, Nicaragua, Guatemala, Mexico. Riding all the way home, the North Fork calling her like a siren's song.

Come, my love, come.

A pair of vultures made lazy circles in the hot air. Ava gazed up, giddy. And then the engine sputtered and died.

She coasted to a stop.

Eared doves called from the brush. Other than that, dead quiet.

Balanced on the soft dirt shoulder, she tried to repeat the steps she'd rehearsed with Alfred, checking all she knew to check and then kicking, and kicking again, until there was nothing more her legs could give.

The day's heat built like a furnace around her.

The turn to Gabriela's finca wasn't far, a few miles back, but the last thing Ava wanted to do was push the dirt bike along the highway in the heat, facing every vehicle she'd just blown past. A reckless gringa, a bird girl gone awry. Gabriela had warned Ava that she needed to carry a burner, that it wasn't safe for her to go so far out, birding all alone. But Ava had taken no precautions other than to let Gabriela know when and where she was going.

Except—not this morning, all full of spontaneity and whatever madness had seized her.

She rolled the bike over to scant brushy shade and fretted. Should she wave down a passing vehicle? Hitchhike back to town? Hope the motorcycle would still be here when Gabriela drove her back?

A rickety truck whooshed by, its wake nearly knocking her over. The ogling driver looked like the kind of man who would be more than happy to pick up a woman alone. A woman with no way to call for help.

She pushed the bike further along the shoulder then gave up as the road climbed up into a miasma of sun. As she set the kickstand, she jumped at the sound of a man's voice behind her. An American accent, heavy and slow with heat. She stiffened in fear, then forced herself not to show it.

The man said, "What a beauty," and Ava said, "Don't *even*."

He said, "When I was growing up, CT1s were *the shit*. Haven't seen one since I was a kid. My little brother, Timothy, and I used to dream about riding them. Classic dirt bike crossovers. Don't make them like that anymore, everything plastic and electronic now."

He took form as she turned—shaggy, deep-tanned, tattoo-sleeved. Worn jeans and a plain t-shirt. He sat in the shade, leaning on a faded green army rucksack, looking like a 1970s hitchhiker. Had he been watching her this whole time?

"Sorry, didn't mean to startle you," he said, pushing himself up slowly to lanky height. He came over to shake Ava's hand. "Ezra Kittredge. Nice to meet you. Have to say, I didn't expect to run into someone like you tearing around on a CT1 down here. But then again, I've lived enough to know not to rely on expectations. You gotta be loose and go with the flow when you leave it all behind, you know what I mean?"

Pobrecito guacamaya, fly, fly, fly / can you teach me how to fly?

She summoned her most formidable professor voice. "I do, in fact."

"Broke down?" Ezra rubbed a hand over the stubble on his cheek. He crouched to examine the CT1 with genuine reverence.

"Was running great before, then it just up and died. I've

tried everything."

"Mind if I give it a go?" A bashful kid, yearning.

"Please. God knows I'm not the mechanical type. I'm here for the birds."

Ezra gestured toward the thick mass of thorny roadside brush. "Lots of birds chattering up in there, although I still haven't spotted any. Shipped into Manta with the magnificent frigate birds though, along with flocks of tiny green parrots. The boatswain's talking African Grey parrot, Doc, smart as hell. Swear that bird could see all the way inside my soul."

Ava laughed. "Well, African Greys *are* at the top of the animal intelligence list, along with corvids like ravens and crows, and all the others of course—orcas, dolphins, dogs, elephants, pigs, octopi, rats, great apes, chimpanzees…"

Ezra gave her a wry look. "Zoologist?"

"Ornithologist, actually. And a professor."

"Bird people," Ezra said. His face a sudden wash of sorrow. "I knew one of those up north. Good person…"

"Birds are *everywhere* down here," he said. "I've been around ravens and crows before, but never parrots, before Doc, unless parakeets count. Sister Gonzaga used to keep this little parakeet named Simon in our classroom and he loved Father Riley's story time as much as the kids. He'd fly over to Father Riley's shoulder, waddle around his clerical collar until he could lay his little blue head on Father Riley's lips as he read, and close his eyes in bliss. Whenever Father Riley stopped reading, Simon would squint his little beady eyes and bite Father Riley's lower lip, hard, and then say, *Simon's a good bird.*"

Ava laughed. "Sounds like you've met plenty of smart birds in your life."

A kinship already between them. Was it simply the circumstance of two hurt humans stranded in the brushlands of an adopted refuge? A likeness to a lost and beloved brother? A recognition from a prior life? Ava believed she'd left this kind of magical thinking behind with her father and his fairytales, his starry mythologies. Was there space in her to bring it back, weave the long-ago child into the now? She sensed, here, standing with this unexpected and striking man, an intertwined fate. One soul's experience recognizing another's.

"That's my life goal," Ezra said, rubbing at the flames and skulls on his arms. "Meet smart birds."

She wanted to ask where he'd done his time, but she didn't want to scare him off. Adonis was sensitive about it, his pride at war with his reality. Ezra reminded her of Adonis more than she was ready to contend with. As if Adonis had taken flight from the sweltering Huntsville prison the same time she did. Feathers and wax.

Ezra pulled the CT1's plugs and dipsticks, checking what she'd already checked. But whatever he did worked because when he straddled the bike and gave a few powerful kicks with his black lugged boots and long legs, the engine roared back to life.

He held the accelerator wide open and yelled over the thunder, "Persnickety SOB." His face creased as he grinned.

She took the throttle, revving it like Ezra had. Oily exhaust boiled around them. The engine's percussion sent up a flock of startled slaty spinetails—another Ecuadorian species for her life list, brown as the brush.

"Looks like you're set to go," Ezra yelled, backing off and giving her a thumbs up, releasing her to the road. *Ride or die, motherfucker, ride or die.*

She twisted the throttle but held the clutch, glancing at Ezra's oversized duffel.

"You want a lift?" she shouted. "Puerto Cayo's just down the road—that's where I'm at. If this thing makes it back."

"Are you kidding? This trusty little CT1 will go anywhere you want and beyond. Just needs a little love every now and then."

"Great—you're driving then. I'm afraid I don't have the right kind of love to give. And I don't trust myself to ride both of us with your person-sized pack. Of course if I were Ecuadorian I could ride a whole family and a donkey."

Ezra grabbed his duffel and grinned. "I've been waiting my whole life to ride one of these beauties. If only my little brother could see me now."

She climbed on behind Ezra, tightening his duffel straps over her shoulders, the weight balanced behind her like a hefty man-child. She wrapped her arms around Ezra's waist and peered over his shoulder, nervous as he revved and shifted up to highway speed. But he was a confident rider.

His body shielded hers from the hot wind as they flew.

As they passed the turn to Gabriela's finca, Ava spotted Gabriela's old beige Land Cruiser barreling down the dirt road, a plume of dust in its wake. Gabriela all speed and wind and blaring music. "Like a bat out of hell," a surfer boy had said, proud to know the idiom.

Gabriela honked and waved and swerved, hanging half out of the driver's window as she skidded to a dust-rolling stop where dirt met blacktop. Startled, Ezra slowed and then stopped in the middle of the highway, planting a foot to hold up the overloaded CT1. He and Ava and the bike nearly tipped sideways.

"What are you doing?" Gabriela yelled. She eyed Ezra with wary suspicion, but interest too. Her bright eyes glittered. Her hair was a beautiful windblown mess.

"I broke down," Ava yelled back. "I was taking a ride. This is Ezra."

Gabriela gave him a long hard look. The boys stretched their necks from the back seat like baby birds, trying to see.

Gabriela said, "Do you want to come up to the finca? I can give you a ride back to town."

Ava shook her head. "We're okay. We're heading back into Cayo now."

Gabriela looked skeptical. Her features relayed her thoughts like a boldface message. Concern. Intrigue. Attraction. A good-looking stranger man with her bestie. As Ezra took off again, Ava could feel Gabriela's eyes burning into them like a dual-beam laser.

Ava smiled, the wind in her teeth. "That's my friend, Gabriela."

She leaned with Ezra's lean. "She's a swimsuit model and ecotourism ambassador. Sadly, she's straight. I think you two would like each other."

"Is that so?" Ezra twisted the throttle and the CT1 roared.

GREER

Greer held her hands cupped to her mouth, yelled "Billy Rhodes!" into the abyss—a cliff so steep it made its own wind, blowing her snarled hair straight up.

The name echoed all around her. *Billy Rhodes-Rhodes-Rhodes-Rhodes.*

She imagined him wandering the mountains with a knapsack full of silver glitter, sprinkling it about like fairy dust. She looked for shiny bits as they hiked but it was all brown and gray shale interspersed with nuggets of milky quartz that glinted white in the rushing creeks.

For days now Greer had hiked through high country—a strange planet of barren rock, silvery dead trees like bones tossed aside by a murderous giant—traversing steep mountainsides, rocks pinnacled into witches' peaks, wind whistling through them like voices of the dead, calling and cackling in ghost-speak.

Eager to escape the Witch Caverns and the Giant's Lair, faced with storm clouds and the daunting stone peak of Shale Mountain, Greer decided to risk a shortcut. Shortcuts were cunning tricksters bent on the demise of the foolish, Mr. Estmund said. But maybe if he were here to see how steep Shale Mountain was, he'd tell her to go around.

On the map, the shortcut looked like a good route, saving

miles of treacherous terrain. But sure enough, halfway, the path became a tiny ledge on a perpendicular mountain flank. Open air beneath her. A trickster's trick. A petrifying route fit for mountain goats, not tired, anxious girls and dogs. Not llamas with protruding dynamite boxes.

But now it was impossible to turn back. The ledge wouldn't allow it. Greer coaxed the llamas forward, cliff wall on one shoulder, emptiness on the other. Sirius whined behind them.

Just as Greer thought they'd survived the worst of it, Kelly balked, refusing to move. Greer put all her weight into pulling him ahead. Loose pebbles skittered off into space. A dead branch caught the pannier's bungee cord, pulling Kelly back until it broke like a lethal rubber band, nearly slingshotting the llama into the abyss. His eyes white-rimmed in fright, only Kelly's mountain-goat agility kept him, and Greer, from tumbling to their deaths.

Quaking and breathless, they finally crossed to broader terrain. But the wind was gusting so hard that Greer thought it might lift her into the purple clouds, bunching and boiling, sparking with electricity. The sky was a giant bruise, thunder rolling ominous. They scurried along the barren ridge, wind lashing, until they dropped mercifully down, side-hilling as the rain came in pelting sheets.

She wanted to sink to her knees, cry, give up, but there was no recourse except to follow decades-old tree blazes so grown over they were nearly invisible. Soaked, night falling, Greer fought the urge to strip off her cold wet clothes, to lie down in the beating cold rain and sleep, but Mr. Estmund said *No. This is real. You know what to do.*

She stopped to pitch an emergency camp, but the tent failed to keep the deluge at bay. She huddled with Sirius to keep warm, marooned on a sodden sleeping pad and bag, and for all the water around them, Greer felt a sudden desperate urge to drink. For Sirius's sake, Greer shoved her poncho into her sneakers outside the tent and as the rain filled them, they put their heads out together to slurp smoky-poncho rainwater.

She didn't know where the llamas were in the dark and the rain, but she thought she could hear a quiet humming behind the tent. There was nowhere for them to take shelter.

"At least no mosquitoes," Greer whimpered, to console the dog.

◆

The next morning, after the storm abated enough for them to crawl out of the sagging tent, Greer discovered she had pitched camp a dozen feet from the brink of a sheer precipice. A breath away from tumbling into the dark. The llamas stood well away, appalled.

As Greer packed up, Sirius ran up with a bloody bit of fur in her mouth—a dead pika dangling by its stubby tail.

"What did you get?" Greer said hopefully, her stomach rumbling. But there was nothing to build a fire with, no way to roast the small scrap of meat, so she patted Sirius's head.

"Good girl. Eat it up."

Along the south-facing vales, the snow was mealy and pink-hued. Watermelon snow, Mr. Estmund called it. Greer's mouth watered at the thought. She almost scooped up a handful to see if it tasted like its name, but remembered the word "algae" and changed her mind.

Before the "shortcut," she'd managed to squirrel up a pock-etful of linty almonds from the bottom of the panniers. She'd intended to share them even-Steven with Sirius—"One for you, one for me," but now Sirius was chewing on her pika. Greer ate the almonds slowly, one at a time, drinking from stone pockets of rainwater until she felt stronger.

◆

She'd meant to get up and load the llamas, but she must have fallen asleep. Now the sun was high, hot on her face. From where she lay on the tarp, Greer saw a plane pass overhead, and as she struggled to sit up it let loose a long shower of red on a distant mountain.

Then another being appeared above, its black wings stretched wide as the world. A raven, cawing to wake the dead. Greer stood up and waved her arms as if it were a spotter plane come to find them. The bird kept flying and cawing, calling to her.

Come and see.

Greer whistled Sirius up from her hunt. "Wait, wait—we're coming!"

The raven circled and dipped above something beyond a low ridge. It kept its eye on Greer, flying back and forth, adamant.

The raven wanted her to cross a field of hardened snow, but not too far. The llamas would stay put.

Greer hiked up the slope as fast as she could, which wasn't very fast. She and Sirius were lightweight enough to mostly stay atop the crust, but when Greer did break through, the ice scraped her ankles and legs raw and bloody. One time she lost her shoe; she reached deep to fish it out, tied it tight—the other one, too—before struggling on. Her feet and lower legs were purple and numb, almost an anesthetic to the throbbing pain of stillness the night before.

The raven vanished and reappeared. Called.

She cleared the ridge top, looking back toward Kelly and Yavell who seemed happy to stand quiet and pack-free. Sirius pitched herself down the other side, following as the raven glided over a snag burned in a long-ago fire. The raven circled, landed, and perched, chortling and clicking and clucking and cawing and bobbing, its throat feathers rising and falling.

Dragging her frozen legs and feet like blocks through the snow, Greer struggled toward it. The raven quieted and fluffed as it watched her progress, reaching down to clean a toenail and preen a wing feather back into place before polishing its beak.

When Greer reached the snag, the raven bobbed its head rapidly and let out a series of deep-voiced hump-backed feather-fluffed *gaark-gaark-gaarks*. It looked down at Greer as she stared up—a dark blob on a silver branch against a pale sky.

Sirius was like a bobblehead, tilting her head back and forth, trying to understand. Greer's eyes watered, blurred by light and snow. She looked down to blink away the tears and that's when she saw it—what the raven had led her to.

Sirius was already digging.

A deep bowl had melted around the snag trunk, rainbow prisms dripping from its dead branches. A bit of muted green canvas peeked from the snowpack, pink florescent flagging wrapped around its fraying straps. Something from the human world. Something that said, *You are not alone. You will not follow Billy Rhodes.*

At least not *yet*.

Sirius helped Greer dig. Both pawed until the snow flew, until Greer could grab the duffel's straps and heave it from its icy bed.

The canvas was marked with a faded black name: Hemingway Maclean.

Greer peered into the snow hole, hoping there wasn't a body in there too, hoping whoever Hemingway Maclean was, he wasn't wandering the frozen mountains as lost and desperate as her. Worse, a ghost in the wilderness looking for his lost gear. She knew that smokejumpers sometimes did lose their gear in drops. In school, they'd watched a documentary on wildland firefighting after the North Fork Fire had started up.

She opened the duffel slowly, pulling out each item with reverence: a green wool Filson Mackinaw coat with a chest full of wildland firefighting badges—a North Fork USFS shield with side flames, an Idaho City Hotshots buck in front of a mountain and tree with flames, a Grangeville Smokejumpers parachute over a tall evergreen.

A wool beanie, gloves, and socks. A tin of pretty hand-tied flies. Two worn paperbacks, *A River Runs Through It* and *The Old Man and the Sea*. At the bottom, granola bars and freeze-dried dinners, oatmeal and jerky, trail mix and powdered Gatorade, a bag of bright jellybeans, and a package of watermelon bubblegum.

Greer was too tired to dance, her legs too numb to move, but she looked at Sirius and grinned. "I think we're going to be okay."

Until this minute she'd never admitted, even to herself, that perhaps they would not.

◆

She put on the heavy wool coat, gloves, and beanie, and pulled out two fat strips of jerky: "One for you, one for me." She and Sirius drooled, smacked, chewed. Sirius sniffed for more, but Greer knew better.

"We have to wait," she said. "Too much for our stomachs."

They sat for an hour, dazed with relief, then hiked back to the llamas and laid out a new, luxurious camp for the night.

Greer remembered the raven. She looked up, but it was gone.

◆

Next day, they followed an exposed ridge down, down, down its sharp backbone. First there were spots of lime-green lichen, a sprig of withered leaf, a crumbling of black soil. Their footprints pressed into its thin skin like voile. As they stepped below the snowline, an explosion of color: emerald trees, jade bushes, olive lichens, sage-toned grasses. The llamas snatched green mouthfuls, feasting on fir needles, tufted bits of snow-flattened grasses, and hairy beards of lichen, chewing as they hummed, their mouths and lips stained mossy in a glorious gorging of chlorophyll.

Then came the swarms of insects again—mosquitos and gnats, biting flies and bees. Greer slapped and Sirius snapped. The llamas shook their heads.

They came upon a clear-flowing stream and a meadow of tall waving grass, green and gold and succulent in evening light, the gilded sun sinking. Greer built a fire, fanning fir fronds through the smoky billow, banishing the bugs, bathing herself in the mountains' gifts.

Hemingway Maclean's wildland fire gear hung floppy and warm on her frame. She imagined him a man like Mr. Estmund, like Billy Rhodes. Lost fathers calling her forth.

AVA

Stretched out on the couch under the ceiling fan, she lay with her head on Ezra's lap. Both sipped cold cervezas to cool down after the morning's labor. It was Cayo's big carnival weekend. Tourists and summer vacationers flocked in, filling the beach and cabanas with noise and fresh energy.

Ezra had been helping Ava with her to-do list: pruning the overgrown lime trees, fixing the janky showerhead water heater, patching the concrete fence. This morning, they'd gotten the undersized washing machine churning again, the loose kitchen floor tiles secured and re-grouted, the window AC drained and cleaned.

When she was investigating blue-footed booby deaths, going to Gabriela's finca to visit the twins and Clio, Ezra stayed home and worked on reinforcing the bars on the windows and doors. He said he slept better that way—every opening to the house secured, welded iron bars cemented into stucco. Ava had seen him reefing the reinforcements as hard as he could, testing their strength—to keep out rather than keep in.

Seeing Cayo's barred windows and doors, its high fence walls topped with shards of broken glass, an outsider might think the town was overrun by crime. But other than pretty thefts of convenience, it was mostly a peaceful place.

Early one morning, Ezra—bunked in the back bedroom

where she'd invited him to stay as long as he needed—was awakened by a rustling in the back yard. He saw a man walk past his window. Ezra leaped out of bed and charged to the backyard in his underwear, brandishing the baseball bat Ava kept by the back door. The intruder jumped over the crumbling back wall.

By the time Ava came out, the man was crouched behind the wall, holding up his hands and speaking rapid Spanish neither she nor Ezra could understand. He waved a pair of Ezra's socks that had been hanging out the window to dry. Ezra pointed the bat at him as he advanced into the backyard saying, "What the fuck do you think you're doing, asshole? Stealing my fucking socks?"

The man shook his head vehemently and pointed at the ground, making swiping motions with the socks and rattling off another long sentence in Spanish.

Ava started laughing.

"It is okay, Ezra," she said. "You can put the bat down. The man just needed some toilet paper."

"What? He's using my fucking socks as toilet paper?"

The man grimaced and lifted his hands and shoulders. The universal shrug of sheepish apology.

Ezra glared, blood pumping visibly in his neck, his muscular body still primed to fight. It frightened Ava a little. This man in her house was packing a lot of hard history. But she watched him get a grip. He looked down at himself, standing in his striped bikini underwear with Ava's too-small baseball bat in hand. He ran his free hand through his bed hair, poking in every direction. The thief held out the stolen—still clean—socks.

Ezra stepped back, lowered the bat. "Get your own goddamned socks," he grumbled as he walked back to the house. "That was my favorite fucking pair."

Ava looked at the man and saluted him off.

Later that day when Ezra was working outside, Ava had stocked the bathroom with piles of Ezra's socks, a sticky note beneath them. *For use in case of emergency.*

◆

Ezra's body was giving off enough heat that Ava wanted to lift herself off his sweaty legs, but they'd been talking about ravens and Adonis and she couldn't make herself move.

Here was Ezra, escaped and living free in Ecuador as Adonis served two life sentences, deluding himself about a future in South America. She wanted it so badly for him. Every moment she spent with Ezra, she wanted it more, imagining Adonis in Ezra's stead.

"Thanks so much for your help—don't know what I'd have done without you and Gabriela and the twins," she said, trying to change direction. Everything still raw. She realized anew what Sibley meant to her. Sibley made life good and full and real and right.

"Count birds?" Ezra said.

"Yeah," she said." But she knew that wasn't true. She'd already betrayed most of what made her Ava.

"Have you found out what's killing the blue-footed boobies?"

She took a long guzzle of cerveza, sharp fizz lighting her sinuses. "*Haemoproteus sp.*"

"Oh. That doesn't sound good," Ezra said, even though Ava could tell by his tone that she was already losing him. *La Profesora,* he called her when she started down those paths, citing scientific terminology and bird research. He said he wasn't her student. True.

But she rattled on anyway. "It's not good. A pathogenic malarial blood parasite that causes mortality and morbidity in birds. The Galapagos Islands blue-footed booby populations have declined by at least fifty percent compared to recorded numbers in the sixties. *Haemoproteus sp.* is likely responsible. Yet another effect of climate change and human population growth. Twin pandemics."

"Well, shit."

"Yeah, exactly. That's part of the study—looking at blue-footed boobies' blood and fecal samples, investigating the relationship between infection status and physiological condition and breeding success. I finally bought a ticket to go over to the Galapagos. I have to be there if I want to dig into this. Start making the required research connections."

"And you do? Want to dig into that?"

Ava nodded her head hesitantly on Ezra's legs. "I think so."

"You don't sound very convinced."

Both fell quiet.

"How is Adonis?" Ezra asked.

"Breaking my heart, one piece at a time—what's left of it to break."

She sat up and swiped her finger around her sweating beer bottle, catching the drips before flinging them off. "His hepatitis took another turn for the worse. He's been in the infirmary. He said since he already has hepatitis anyway, he's going to get his guy to give him a new tattoo—a raven perched on a tree. Remind him of being set free."

"That sounds like a worthy tattoo."

"I wonder if your pal Joel ever got his," she said, and Ezra laughed.

Ava imagined herself and Sibley, Ezra and Gabriela hanging out, redefining life together. She wished she was brave enough to call Sibley. To explain how everything that had happened, all she'd put into place, led to a new understanding of herself— and that understanding had everything to do with Sibley.

She finished her beer, warm and flat now in the casa's heat.

"So, surfing later this afternoon?" Ezra asked, getting up.

"I was never any good at sports. Unless you call birding a sport."

"Surfing isn't a sport," Ezra said. "It's a meditation. It's spirituality."

"Okay, guru Ezra," she said. "Maybe it's a religion I can believe in? Although I still can't understand how you learned to surf, growing up in Idaho."

"Only a one-day drive to Oregon, Washington. I went whenever I could. It was my only real escape. It was all I cared about for a long time. I wish it would have stayed that way. Wish I would have kept my focus on the horizon, Pacific against the sky, feet dangling in the deep, the sea lapping as I floated on my board, waiting the next swell. Chasing the sunset."

"I mean, who wouldn't dream of that?" she said. "Beautiful."

"It was. All I wanted to do was surf the world's best waves, globetrot with a backpack and my board. Australia, South Africa, Tahiti, Ecuador. Surfing was the only way I could imagine myself anywhere other than the backwoods, leading a different life. But then it turned into the same old cliché: troubled boy, too much hardship, ACE count off the charts. Turned to drugs and alcohol and ended up in trouble at school, with the law, with everything. Tried to kill myself but killed someone else. When I landed in prison, I was the least surprised of anyone."

Ava put her hand on Ezra's. "You are a person who should be free to live life, not be locked from it."

"You too, Professor Ava," he said, squeezing her hand back. "You need to quit hiding from your own life. Seize the freedom that's yours. Don't lock yourself up. You already know too well what that leads to."

Ava went to the window.

"Promise me," Ezra said.

First Adonis, and now Ezra. Men who knew what it meant to be barred away.

"Okay. I promise," she said, although she didn't know how to redeem what she'd already ruined, damage fanning behind her in a widening wake.

GREER

She woke to a scream, sharp and echoing, halting and then carrying on again. This time she knew it was a mountain lion's haunting ghost shriek, its murdered cry. The soft fur on the back of Greer's neck rose. Her breath came in shallow bursts. She lay awake in the starlit dark until the dim wash of galaxy light gave way to sunrise and bird song, the return of voracious insects.

They hiked into flat country following the bends of a clear rushing stream, Greer smacking bugs despite having applied most of the firefighter's supply of DEET. She blew watermelon bubblegum into big pink bursting bubbles and picked little bouquets of mountain flowers. They entered dense forest, climbing over fallen trees, and the constant buzzing became a deep droning vibration.

Greer thought the droning sound was a trick of her ears.

She tilted her head back and forth like Sirius, trying to clear the noise, but then she saw it, nearly stepped on it: a cougar's log-stashed deer kill teeming with a seething pelt of feasting bald-faced hornets. Swirling stink of rotting flesh.

The vibration suddenly became bright spots of pain, searing metal shards.

She stumbled backward as she batted black-and-white flying bodies stinging her lips, neck, ears, hands, tangling in her hair, still boiling out from the hollow log.

She sprinted away, leaping deadfall, her skin welting, a contingent of angry bald-faced hornets pursuing. The llamas galloped into the woods, lead ropes dangling. Sirius dashed out of sight.

Greer reached the stream and plunged face first into the icy water—bubbles rising from her blistering skin, silt clouds rising beneath her grasping hands, the current waving her hair, releasing hornets. She raised her head to gasp before immersing herself again, holding her breath until her body grew numb, until the hornet hordes moved on, returning to their feast of putrid venison.

When she rose dripping from the water, Kelly and Yavell were standing beside the stream, humming happily, their lips wet and green. Greer tried to whistle for Sirius, but her lips were puffed fat and airy. Her eyelids drooped, narrowing her vision. Her tongue a salted slug fat against her teeth.

She gathered the llamas' lead ropes and called and called for Sirius, her voice raspy as she wheezed through her swollen nose and throat. She heard a hammering thunder—*clallump, clallump, clallump*—something coming, but it wasn't her dog. The beat drew nigh against the hollow earth, and then a distant answer: Sirius barking, calling back to Greer as the hoofbeats sounded. Closer and closer.

From blurry, heavy-lidded eyes, Greer peered upstream, trying to blink away her disbelief: a naked old woman astride a bareback silver horse. White mane and long gray hair blew in tandem as they leaped the stream in a silver flash.

Sirius emerged from the brush, her big tail whapping as she ran up whining and barking, nudging Greer with her cold wet nose, her coat covered in burrs. The little family reunited. Greer squatted down to hug her and pick the prickles out of her ruff.

"Did you see that?" Greer asked in awe. "A woman. And a horse." If she was real, the first human they'd seen since the ghillie-suit hunter. A lifetime ago. Mountains and ravens and snow ago.

Sirius led them back to the trail, the horse's hoofprints deep divots in damp soil amid waffled motorcycle tracks, spits of sprayed dirt disrupting deer and cougar paths, coyote scat tufted with rabbit fur and grouse feather. The way marked with broken fern fronds, leaves, and sticks, but Greer closed her swollen eyes and held on to Sirius, trusting her to guide.

By the time they reached an open flat, Greer could hear motorcycles, their whining growl not unlike a swarm of hornets.

She didn't know whether to hide or try to flag them down, but it didn't matter because they popped out onto the trail. The llamas startled and pulled back. Sirius stiffened into her alert stance.

Three boys on dirt bikes—tidy stairsteps from smallest to largest.

They hit the brakes when they saw Greer and the llamas, planting their boots and peering through their visored helmets, their engines popping and surging as they idled.

Still straddling his bike, the oldest turned off the engine and pulled off his helmet. The two others followed, the woods suddenly still around them. Three tousle-headed brothers in triplicate.

"Hey, you okay?" the smallest one asked. A brown-haired boy no older than Greer.

She put a hand to her tight swollen face, her cheeks covered in hot blisters, her lips fat-fish puffy, her eyelids drooping, her tongue and throat thick.

"Bald-faced hornets," she slurred. Dizzy.

The brothers jumped into a blur of unified motion.

"Grab the first aid kit and water," the oldest brother directed in a surprisingly grown-up voice. Dirt bikes fell to the ground as the brothers rushed to Greer's side.

Greer sat blurry in the grass as the youngest brother took her pulse and checked her respiration. The middle one coached her through careful swallows of water as the oldest tore open sting pads and wiped down her arms, hands, neck, and face before smearing on thick layers of hydrocortisone. They wetted rags to lay over her swollen eyes as they spoke quietly but intensely to each other.

"Is she going into anaphylaxis?"

"Do you think we need an EpiPen?"

"How many antihistamines should she take?"

"Should I ride to get Mom and Dad?"

"No!" Greer said, struggling to sit up.

The brothers sat back on their heels in surprise.

"You look pretty bad," the middle brother said, a dusty shank of blonde hair in his eyes.

"Our dad is a backcountry wildland fire EMT," the oldest brother said, his hair a curly halo. "He can make sure—"

"No. I have to get going," Greer said, trying to stand. "I feel better. Thank you."

Sirius licked goop from her face, whimpering and panting.

"Take it easy," the youngest brother said, holding his hands up.

The middle one smiled, a little. "We can keep a secret." Sirius flopped into his side as he ruffled her ruff.

"You should definitely rest. You have a lot of stings," the oldest brother said. He eyed her filthy clothes, her ruined basketball shoes. "And—"

Greer sat back in the trail's damp dirt, her hands finding divots.

"There was a woman. Naked. On a horse..." she murmured.

The brothers exchanged quick, sheepish glances.

"Yeahhh, that was our grandma."

"She has dementia."

"We were trying find her and bring her home."

"*Again*," they chorused.

Greer pictured the woman and her silver steed galloping along the river. Mr. Estmund's fairyland.

"Are we close to the North Fork now? I lost my map."

"Not too far from here, as the crow flies."

"We go there all the time."

"Where did you come from?"

"The mountains," Greer said. "The snow. A raven. A long, long ways ago."

The boys looked at her, and then at each other.

"You need to rest, get hydrated," the oldest said.

"Yes, rest," Greer said. A smokejumper who'd missed her landing, fallen from a great height. Like Hemingway Maclean's green duffel.

"There's a nice campsite not too far from here."

"By the creek."

"Would you like us to take you there?"

"Yes," Greer said, swallowing the pink antihistamines pressed into her palm.

The llamas munched fir needles. Sirius leaned against the brothers who stroked her fur.

◆

Beyond that, Greer didn't remember much: a feeling of floating, the sound of water, rustling and bustling, the warmth of a sleeping bag tucked around her neck. Kelly and Yavell humming. Dreams: ravens flapping through snow, steaming waffle squares dripping with buttery syrup, thundering stallions. Glorious, naked old women. A tousle of dusty handsome boys.

When she came to, Greer found herself in a creekside glen, a campfire crackling. Sirius by her side. The llamas unloaded and kushed into soft brushy beds, content, chewing their cud. She sat up and found a folded note tucked under a rock next to her: *We'll check on you again soon. Drink lots of water. We left you a map and sandwiches. Feel better.*

Greer opened the bread bag full of smashed sandwiches—peanut butter and jelly spread thick on seed bread. She wolfed down her two as Sirius woofed down hers.

Sucking peanut butter from her fingers, Greer carefully unfolded a new map, her campsite circled and starred. Just like the brothers said, the North Fork was only a stone's throw away. A winding blue map line, a few days' hike for a family of runaways. Mr. Estmund's fairyland awaiting. Cedar frond and fern. Driftwood and white sand. Clear river water, birds, and wildflowers. A new life. Away.

Greer drained one of the dusty water bottles, then retrieved Icarus and the tape recorder from Kelly's pannier, selected a new story. "The Ridgerunner."

She checked the battery.

She knew the story, almost by heart. The Ridgerunner was an outlaw hero, sometimes living off the land, sometimes stealing from cabins and campsites. He had a special fondness for raiding Forest Service stations; he'd made a master key and made a mess of them whenever he had a chance.

Thirty years he haunted the North Fork, sometimes leaving, always returning. He believed he was a special government agent, spying on the crimes of lawmen, disrupting poachers, shielding the vulnerable from sex crimes.

Maybe he was.

Or maybe he was just lost. A little crazy, in a crazy world.

But who, Greer thought, wasn't a little crazy? Maybe even Mr. Estmund, teaching a little girl that she could survive in a place he called Fairy Land. Maybe she was, too, believing him.

She touched her swollen face with her fingertips. Winced. Wondered if she'd recognize Fairy Land when she saw it.

Maybe she was just growing up, like Wendy. A mother of lost boys.

Kind of.

She pushed the fast-forward button further into Mr. Estmund's story. Just a bit of battery, and she'd turn it off. And just like that, Mr. Estmund was with them again, his voice as close as the rushing stream beside them, rumbling and resonant.

"That night, after the chili mac, the Ridgerunner feasted on blackberry jam—glistening purple lumps melting against his raw, empty-socketed gums. But despite all the new supplies and the cabin's warm space, the next morning he decided to keep moving on. They would be after him. They were always after him, tracking him down, trying to lock him away.

They didn't know what he knew. They hadn't seen what he'd seen—everything captured there in his mind, like flashing movie reels—murders and poisonings and theft. Running and running and running until someone could understand just who he really was. He imagined the medals of honor they would bestow upon him when they did finally know—the President thanking him for his life of selfless service, for saving them all from themselves.

He climbed up further and further into the unknown, until he reached his final coming-home: a rock high above a deep rushing stream. The Ridgerunner stepped into air, crying for everything he'd never known, all of them come circling and circling to claim him as their own, his spirit sent soaring, making this river country forever home."

Tucked into Hemingway Maclean's wool coat, Sirius curled tight into her, Greer put the tape recorder away and cried for the Ridgerunner, for Billy Rhodes, for Mr. Estmund. All of them lost to the wild country, where she huddled now, trying to survive what they had not.

She would build a cairn for them when she reached the river. A place to lay flowers and feathers.

◆

Early the next morning, the sound of motorcycles sent Greer's heart beating. That deep-droning whine and roar. The brothers came to see her again as they'd promised. They leaned their dirt bikes against cedar trunks before pulling off their goggles, helmets, and gloves.

Sirius ran to them, whining and yelping and knocking into their knees.

"You look better," the curly-haired brother said in his manly voice.

"Yes, *much* better," the blonde-haired brother said, petting Sirius's head.

"Fabuloso," the light-brown-haired little brother said, grinning.

"I feel much better," Greer said, her cheeks and lips tight as she tried to smile back. "Thank you for the map and sandwiches and water and the super nice camp."

"We're just glad you're okay. You must've had a dozen stings."

"It was a cougar kill—a dead deer that the hornets were eating," Greer explained.

"Yikes."

"I hate those bees."

"Did you find the trail you wanted?" the tallest brother asked, gesturing to the open map.

"Yes," Greer said. "That's where we're heading today."

"There's a fire between here and there. The North Fork Fire."

"A girl wildland firefighter died on it."

"Our dad was there."

"Can I get around it?" Greer asked.

The brothers looked at each other.

"You'll have to go through a logging job."

"It's pretty steep."

"It's not too bad."

"Did you ever find your grandma?" Greer pictured the naked, gray-haired lady on her silver horse galloping all the way to the river, flying over creeks and fires, swimming through clear waters.

"Yes," the three boys said in unison. "But she'll probably just do it again."

"Thank you for saving me," Greer said.

Because it was the best thing she had left to give, she handed them Icarus's skull. "To remember me by," she said. "Raven Girl."

A new name. A giving for a taking.

"Good luck to you, Llama-Raven Girl," one of the boys said. "Maybe someday we'll meet again."

"Yes," Greer said, smiling shyly, fiddling with Sirius's burr-ridden fur. The llamas hummed and chewed behind her.

The boys waved as they rode away.

Greer watched until they were out of sight, out of sound, dirt spitting from beneath their knobbed tires, hands raised in salute.

"Goodbye," she said, dust drifting on drafts of fresh, cool air, the creek singing its watery song, currents calling them forever forward to the river.

AVA

Gabriela and Ezra arrived at the same time. Gabriela pulled up and parked on the street. Ava opened the slatted gate for Ezra, who parked the CT1 in the casa's narrow driveway. Ava looked for the twins, but Gabriela was alone. Her long legs gleamed under a white frilly dress, her sun-streaked hair curled into loose spirals.

"Whoa, Ms. G." Ava gave her a quick hug. "You smell as good as you look." Scents of lavender and orchid wafted from Gabriela's skin.

"Oh, stop it." Gabriela batted Ava away, but Ava could tell she liked being seen, especially when she looked this good.

"So *where* did you find him again?" Gabriela whispered, standing outside the gate with her little vulpine smile.

"Wouldn't you like to know," Ava said, grinning. Not her usual gig, but she knew she'd been right to play matchmaker.

Ezra strode over and shook hands with Gabriela as she and Ava came through the gate.

"Ezra," he said, all manly and brusque, "nice to meet you."

"You as well," Gabriela said, her English more formal than usual. She smiled. Batted her irresistible eyes.

Ava grimaced. "Oh, *stop it*. Let's at least go inside where it's cooler for the rest of your straight mating rituals."

Ezra blushed and Gabriela gave Ava's shoulder a light punch.

Gabriela leaned toward Ezra as they went inside, the ceiling fan blowing stuffy heat, the water cooler rattling again. "So, Ezra, what are you doing here in Ecuador?"

"Oh, making my way around. I've never been here, but I've been planning on coming for a long time."

"Nearly his whole life," Ava added. Ezra and Gabriela perched on either end of the couch, their bodies turned toward one another like homing beacons.

As Ava filled sweating water glasses, Gabriela continued her inquisition. She pressed her pink manicured fingertips against the tops of her tanned thighs.

"So, from where did you come?"

"Idaho," Ezra said. "North-central. Born and bred, fourth generation."

Gabriela leaned back, eyebrows up. "And now both of you in Cayo."

"A crazy set of circumstances," Ezra said, looking at Ava. "We—haven't talked about, all of that. Yet."

"Mystery. Adventure. Just what I like," Gabriela said, settling back.

Ava rolled her eyes again, but she couldn't help smiling.

"Shouldn't you two beautiful women be wary of a stranger like me?" Ezra asked, his words loose-flung. "You ought to run me off with a shotgun."

"Ah, but who doesn't have skeletons in their closet?" Gabriela said.

"Yes, even birds," Ava said, handing out water glasses. "For instance the northern shrike—*Lanius borealis*, like the northern lights—is a predatory songbird. It hunts, catches, and impales other songbirds and small rodents on thorns and barbed wire, saving them to consume later. Whole fence lines of skeletons. Nature just doing what it needs to survive."

Now it was Ezra and Gabriela who rolled their eyes.

Ava sat, heartbeat staccato in her chest, in her throat, in

her head, thinking again about Sibley. Sibley's words playing on loop in her head. *Please, come back to me. Please, let me come to you. I'll leave right now—I can be there tomorrow...We can go to the Galapagos, find all those birds you love....*

Ezra dropped the levity. Darkened. His face spoke before his voice did. "You don't know anything about me."

He stood, scanned the barred windows. Looked about to flee.

"I know enough," Gabriela said. Solemn. Wise to the world and its sorrows.

"I do too," Ava said.

Gabriela put her hand on Ezra's leg. "We cannot know everything there is to know. We cannot see everything there is to see. We cannot live all the lives there are to be lived. All we can do is be here now, know we are doing the best that we possibly can."

For Ava, something came full circle. Some small, beautiful thing unfurling beyond the loss. Ezra sitting there on her kind uncle's couch. The ceiling fan's lazy turns, the little green parrotlets chattering outside in the lime tree. Ground doves croaking. Cicadas calling.

Ava sat back in the chair to steady herself.

"We are here, with you. You are here, with us," Gabriela said.

To Ezra? To Ava?

Ava pictured the wildfire's blackened wreckage sprouting with new growth in the years to come. Wildflowers filling the blanks as tree seedlings pushed tender roots into their ancestral soil.

"A toast." Gabriela jumped up and grabbed a bottle of rum from Ava's kitchen cabinet. She poured three shots in their now-empty water glasses, then lifted hers as she nestled back toward Ezra. "To us—the broken birds."

They clinked glasses then tipped them back.

Gabriela poured a second round. "To Ezra and Ecuador," she said.

Ezra held his glass in the air. "To two beautiful women who rescued me."

"Here, here," Gabriela said.

"Here, here," Ava said.

They drank to themselves as the birds and insects called forth in a riot of noise.

EZRA

Ezra had picked up enough Spanish—especially from Domingo on the ship—that he could follow along as Gabriela's uncle, Edwardo, detailed the 1974 Lada Niva's peculiarities. Of which there were a multitude.

Edwardo spoke about as much English as Ezra spoke Spanish, but cars were a language they both spoke fluently. Edwardo demonstrated how to make the Lada run and drive, fairly arduous skills—the army-green, humpbacked, two-door, 4x4 Russian beast never imported to the US but known abroad for its unreliability. Unyielding and ornery as a mule. But when Ezra had seen it jouncing along the beach at sunset, he had to have it. When he found out it belonged to Gabriela's uncle, he knew it was meant to be.

He'd put away savings while incarcerated, and since he wasn't planning on ever leaving Ecuador, he figured he needed some wheels sooner than later. Plus, he liked a vehicle that made a man work for every drive, something he couldn't take for granted. It was more satisfying that way—earning each mile he didn't have to walk.

You had to respect something with that much quirk, personality, and gumption.

Finally, hemming and hawing and dragging his feet—maybe in show, maybe in earnest—Edwardo accepted Ezra's handheld fan of one-hundred-dollar bills. It was clear how much Edwardo loved the car, but it was equally obvious that his wife and children did *not* and were thrilled that someone wanted to buy it.

They toasted the deal with homemade starfruit liquor, like what Domingo had served Ezra on the ship—syrupy, bright with flavor. The taste of Ecuador.

Driving with Gabriela down the Malecón, Ezra could see why Edwardo had been hesitant to part ways. The Lada's little engine chugging, the wide silver ocean stretched and broke just beyond them. Windows down, Ezra soaked in the smell of salt and tropical blooms. Gabriela's hair blowing around her face as the radio played a melancholy Spanish love song. At the curve, the scrappy stray dog they'd jokingly named Tuko ran barking at their tires.

Every time he let himself sleep, Ezra feared he would wake still trapped in his sweltering prison bunk. Forever. But here he was.

"So, you like it?" Gabriela smiled at him, her teeth brilliant against her sun-bronzed face, her hair in her eyes, her beauty taking his breath away.

He wondered if a person ever could get used to such a thing.

"Not as much as I like you," he said.

She shook her head and rolled her eyes at him. Laughed.

"We should pick up Ava and go to Playa de los Frailes. I have been wanting to take you both there. The boys are still with their abuela in Jipijapa. We could stay late, watch the sunset?"

"I'll take you anywhere you want to go," Ezra said. He downshifted the Lada and revved.

In the prison rec room, Ezra had gotten flak for watching every rerun rom com. But he'd never thought he wanted to live in one. But here it was, he and Ava and Gabriela and the twins almost always together now.

Adan and Ail reminded Ezra so much of himself and Timothy that it was bittersweet. He was surprised the kids had accepted him so readily, always hanging off his arms and neck like happy chattering monkeys. He didn't take their trust for granted. They were very young, but they understood how the world worked more than they let on. Sorrow had touched them early—a father and stepfather drowned, a beautiful, gifted mother shunned and alone.

He pulled up to Ava's gate honking the Lada's rusty horn—a wheezing heehaw that sounded like a cranky donkey getting its tail pulled. Then he did his "secret" raven call—a loud *ca-caaww* he used to call the twins in from surfing. Their little answering *ca-caws* made him happy for hours.

Gabriela leaned out her window and yelled, "Come, Ava, we are going to the beach!"

Ava came out looking startled, a well-stuffed beach bag slung over her shoulder.

"You already got the car?" She crawled past Gabriela into the Lada's tiny back seat.

"Welcome to the welcome wagon." Ezra gassed the Lada, chirping its tires as he took off.

Gabriela banged her hand on the passenger door and whooped, throwing her head back. "Another adventure for the three amigas!" she yelled in her lovely rolling Spanish accent.

It was what Ezra loved most about Gabriela—her unending adventurousness. Her willingness to make a good time out of anything, to rise above heartbreak.

"Wow. I think you just achieved honorary amiga status," Ava said.

"Screw amigos. Amigas are where it's at."

Gabriela hooted and banged the door again.

"Here, here," Ava said. Ezra caught her in the rearview mirror, grinning like a little girl.

Gabriela turned around playfully. "Ava, just wait until you see all the pretty girls in their skimpy bikinis at Los Frailes. We all went there for photoshoots."

"Of course you did," Ava said. "You and all the other sexy world-famous beach models."

"Well, I can't imagine any prettier women in the world than the two of you," Ezra said.

Ava and Gabriela said *Awwww!*

"Such a schmoozer," Ava added. He met her eyes in the mirror and smiled.

He meant it. He couldn't believe he was there with Gabriela and Ava, driving in the sun, wind through the windows. Each day it hit him anew, knocked him off his feet, sucked the breath out of his lungs. Sometimes he could hardly stand upright.

It's real, he would tell himself. Until he believed.

◆

The drive south from Cayo was canopied with deciduous trees. Each tiny town they drove through swarmed with uniformed kids coming home from school, the girls perky with their sleek ponytails swishing against the backs of their white shirts, the boys looking rumpled and ready to rumble.

A toothless old man stared as they drove by and Ezra wondered what they looked like—the three of them in the Lada Niva, headed for a world-class beach.

Ava was on one. "So, I say after this, we run away. Go to the rainforest, the Amazon, the mountains, Cuenca and Quito and the Hot Springs of Baños." She leaned up between the front seats like an over-eager kid at the start of a long road trip.

"I thought you wanted to go to the Galapagos—see the birds there?" Gabriela said. She caressed the tiny hummingbird tattoo on the inside of her wrist—the place Ezra kissed over and over, never getting enough.

"And what about the Colibrí Parque, the 'hummer park' as you call it?"

"'Consider the hummingbird for a long moment. A hummingbird's heart beats ten times a second. A hummingbird's heart is the size of a pencil eraser. A hummingbird's heart is a lot of the hummingbird.' That's from 'Joyas Voladoras' by Brian Doyle," Ava said. "'Flying Jewels.'"

"Fabulous," Gabriela said, turning to smile at Ava, covering Ezra's hand as he shifted, the trees a green blur, the air warm and moist.

"Did you know that hummingbirds get their fantastic feather shimmer from complex microscopic pancake-like melanosomes that create the phenomenon of iridescence—the same effect that makes soap bubbles, oil slicks, and seashells glow? Light-shifting structures. One hundred million of them on a single tiny hummingbird feather." Ava said.

"Did you know there are at least a hundred and forty hummingbird species in Ecuador alone? Listen to these names: tawny-bellied hermits, amethyst woodstars, booted racket-tails, black-throated mangos, sapphire-spangled emeralds, gorgeted sunangels, violet-tailed sylphs… I want to see them all."

She reached up and nudged Ezra's shoulder. "You too, right Ezra? Explore all of Ecuador. See all the birds. Hit the road and never look back."

But Ezra knew what Ava was going on about: *Sibley, Sibley, Sibley.* Ava called Sibley's name over and over when she slept, which wasn't often, Ava always padding around the casa in the night so desolate it made Ezra want to cry.

"Anywhere you two want to go, I'll be your chauffeur." Ezra revved the Lada and honked the horn, the noise sending up great clattering clouds of birds that Ava named in English and Latin and Gabriela named in Spanish, a bilingual birding team.

Gabriela pointed out the dirt road into Los Frailes. The park entrance was marked with a tall, thatched bamboo check station with an attendant sitting in its shade.

"This is it!" Gabriela said, reaching over to grab Ezra's hand. "You will love it."

"As long as I'm with you, there's no doubt." He lifted her hand and kissed her fingers.

They drove down the dirt to the parking area, colorful double-seat moto taxis in a line in front of the thatched concessions stand stocked with floppy beach hats and umbrellas. Ezra parked the Lada under a scrappy but graceful bonsai-like tree that only cast enough shade for the little scuttling lizards. The afternoon sun was powerful enough to wither everything else.

Protected by the Machalilla National Park, Los Frailes was one of the most famous Latin American beaches, featured in nearly every Ecuadorian travel ad. There was good reason for the national pride; Ecuador was the first country in the world to grant legal rights to nature, flora and fauna—the same protections as a person. In his cell, Ezra had read about Taromenane men in the Ecuadorian Amazon hunting down loggers stripping their lands of cedar, mahogany, and other timber within the Yasuní Biosphere Reserve—a protected wilderness with the richest biodiversity of any forest on earth.

Wielding twelve-foot wooden spears, the Taromenane warriors attacked the loggers. One logger was wounded, speared in the back. Another was killed, struck by thirty-three spears. It made international news in the early 2000s, igniting a conversation about whose rights were sacrosanct, but really it was nothing new. Ecuador, like every other place laden with natural riches, was pillaged by greedy corporations, regimes, and individuals, leaving destruction and devastation in their wake.

Wasn't it the same in Idaho?

Ezra had fantasized about joining the Taromenane cause, learning how to throw a spear, hunting down loggers and punishing them in all the ways they deserved. Now he thought of Tiny and Vic, what he'd like to inflict if he could get away with it. He pictured their corpses stuck full of spears.

Violent ideation a prison therapist had called it.

Ezra thought of Adan and Ail. Timothy.

Gabriela stood at the trailhead, smiling as she cocked her hip and held her long brown arm toward their destination.

"What do you think?" she asked, gazing down on the famous crescent of white sand lapped by aqua sea. Distant mountains rose on one side, vertiginous bluffs on the other. More stunning than any photograph could capture.

"Breathtaking," Ezra said, but he was looking only at her.

"You two," Ava said, shaking her head as she joined them. "Give me a break. *Brad and Angelina Go to The Beach*."

"Ah, you are the one who looks the movie star, Ava," Gabriela said. "You with your dark hair and red lips and sad, pretty face. Like Elisabeth Bergner or Sylvia Sidney."

Ava laughed. "You always do surprise me, Gabby."

"Oh no! I already tell you—you cannot call me Gabby. Such an ugly name," Gabriela said, hitting Ava in the shoulder with a resounding smack.

"Oh yeah? Who's going to stop me, *Gabby*?"

"Now, now, break it up you two," Ezra said, putting himself between them. "No fighting until we get down to the beach."

"Last one there is a rotten egg, and I am the fastest," Gabriela said, taking off, sand kicking up behind her. Her tasseled beach wrap hitched up her legs. Her hair streamed in light, her ridiculously large sun hat billowed like a sail.

A vision Ezra wished to brand forever in his mind.

GREER

What Greer didn't know was how she would stop it.

Chainsaws revved and roared, giant trees falling like the dominoes she and Juan liked to set up and then knock down.

One goliath and then the next and the next. An airy needle whistle, a thundering thud, a great cloud of sorrow rising. A swath of desolation in each hungry chainsaw's path, the land laid bare.

Greer wanted to run into the clearing waving her arms and screaming *NO! STOP!* She wanted to sweep over the clearcut and smite the loggers down, smash the chainsaws into smithereens. She wanted to lie down weeping.

She knew clearcuts. How could she not, growing up in Headquarters—a logging company town, the surrounding mountains slashed to stumps and tree guts, taken over by thistle and knapweed, hawkweed and cockle-burrs. Yet this felt different. A primeval forest, thousands of years old. The magical fairy trees Mr. Estmund had told her stories about. The kind of trees that had made her want to live at the river.

A massacre taking place right in front of her. Great silent beings slain.

The trail angled toward the loggers. Greer pulled the llamas and Sirius from the path and tucked them out of sight in still-standing trees.

The dirt bike boys had warned Greer about hazards on the trail—the North Fork Fire smoldering as it crept through deep forest duff and evaded the wildland firefighters. The active logging jobs creeping closer and closer to the river. But Greer had not expected to run right into the action, close witness to the titanic felling.

Hidden in the thick-girthed trees, she watched the loggers work. The sawyers cut. The hookers scrambled into the tangled mess of broken limbs and trunks and set chokers before hitting their Talkie Tooter to signal the line-machine operator. The line machine yarded the felled colossuses up to the landing where the rest of the men swooped in to finish them off, limbing and sawing each ancient being into log lengths before loading and strapping them onto the waiting logging trucks, the logs so enormous they could only fit one to a truck.

The day had turned hot, bright shafts of sunlight filtering into even the dense virgin forest where Greer, Sirius, and the llamas were bed down, biding their time. Midafternoon, the loggers halted their work. First, they shut down the machines, then they walked around doing a fire check, and at last they filed into their pickups and drove out the logging road gashed into the hillside like a knife wound. Great billows of dust rose in their wake.

Beyond them, a steep mountainside stood stark and blackened. The North Fork Fire, the last obstacle between Greer and the river, a wasteland of clearcuts and charred ground. Nowhere Greer wanted to tarry.

Greer thought of these loggers. She thought of Rory raging after her. She thought of the hunter in the ghillie suit looking her over with his predatory eyes.

All the violent men merged together in her head—one predator man hunting her down, tracking her through dust and mud and snow, through mountain and creek, through haunted Witches' Cavern peaks and bald-faced hornet flats, through clearcuts and wildfire burns, always right behind her, a revving chainsaw in one hand and a slithering snake in the other. A man who might at any moment find her, even though she'd outrun him so far.

Hunting around the landing, she found what she was looking for.

Making a paste out of powdered sugar dirt mixed with heavy equipment grease, she used a severed cedar limb to leave her message, etching each giant letter in the ravaged dirt.

She stood back, lit the end of the limb, set flame to the spilled fuel, and walked away as it burned, the words she'd left bubbling black.

STOP.

Oily smoke rising behind them, Greer and Sirius and the llamas ran, pushing through layers of deadfall along the burned-out mountainside, the landscape charred as a bomb site. Greer thought about the woman firefighter who died in the fire, her ghost calling from the dark ground just like Billy Rhodes and the Ridgerunner, like Sacajawea, Watkuweis, and York.

Every step Greer, Sirius, and the llamas took sent up soot until they were powdered black. Creatures risen from the dead, formed from the flames of Hades.

Over a sharp rise, the trail transformed into a fire line—a deep indentation of churned dirt. Greer imagined the firefighters, everything ablaze around them, the blistering hell Juan's mother warned about, crossing herself.

"You must always say your prayers to ward off evil," Mrs. Cedeño reminded Juan and his little sisters. Greer too, even though Greer had never been promised to heaven like they had, baptized as babies, anointed in holy waters. She didn't know how to pray other than repeating whatever Juan said, but she wanted to try again now, walking here with ghosts. Not even a bird flew by, although she thought she'd heard ravens croaking from the giant godlike trees where she'd hidden from the loggers.

As night fell, the blackened land merged with the blackened sky until it was one unending reach of blackness. But the fire line was easy to follow. She worried they might run into smolder, but the ground was soft and cool, the sooty billow of their footsteps invisible. But she didn't stop, didn't dare rest, didn't dare do anything but scurry through the dark like a frightened night animal. Her stomach growled and cramped, her legs were lead, feet wooden, her muscles weak and rubbery.

The llamas hummed and hummed, their mournful voices pursuing her like a prayer. Sirius nudged Greer's hand with her wet nose but Greer didn't slow down.

◆

Time returned when she heard the rush of whitewater. The trail fell away from the steep, burned-out country to the sudden flat of a little creek valley. The water shone like moonlit mercury. Sirius and the llamas rushed down to gulp, water running black from their chins. Greer splashed icy water onto her face and sank to her haunches.

This was the creek which led to the river. The calling, beckoning river.

Come, my darlings…You're almost here.

Greer tucked herself under thick bushes and fell asleep. The llamas moaned to each other in the dark. Sirius twitched and made quiet barks, dreaming.

EZRA

They piled in the Lada like sardines in a can—the twins in back with Ava, Gabriela next to him in front, all of them bopping to a love-and-fate pop song looping on every Ecuadorian station. Surfboards tied on top. They parked at the end of the Malecón and walked past the hostel with its scary patio curtains that made the boys run squealing for the beach. Ava and Gabriela followed close behind.

The boys were natural surfers, bobbing and squatting and duck-diving, riding waves as easily as they ran in the sand, though their mother carried herself a little stiffly.

"You look like a stilt-legged shorebird," Ava yelled before eating a breaker. Ezra almost swam after her, she was under so long, but then her head popped up, mouth gaping.

"Oh yeah, well, who is a drowned bird now?" Gabriela yelled back.

To Ezra, it all felt like coming home—the water carrying him, crashing over him, singing underneath him like a hymn.

"You're really good, Ezra," Ava said as they drifted, legs dangling into the deep, waiting for the next good set. "I don't know. It kind of gives me the creeps—looking down at all that depth. What might be swimming by right now?"

"Landlubber," he said, grinning. "You'll get used to it. You've just got to embrace it. That discomfort. Make peace with it. Find your way to the other side."

"Easy for you to say, riding waves like a fish."

"My sexy dolphin man," Gabriela said, tilting her chin.

"Moooomm, grooooss," the twins protested, paddling to catch the building swell, popping up and speeding along its break like there was nothing to it.

"God. They make it look so easy," Ava said. "I truly do suck."

"You have to just keep trying, Ava," Gabriela said, paddling after the next one, crouching in her long-legged bird stance as she rode it in.

"You all need to go to the Galapagos with me," Ava said. "We could find some blue-footed booby colonies, surf around the islands, explore, collect data."

Ezra almost said, "You know who really ought to come to the Galapagos with you?" but he checked it. Probably she wasn't ready to talk about it. Maybe it would ruin a perfectly great surfing day.

A wave washed out with Gabriela in its wake. She coasted with the boys into shore.

"I'm serious," Ava said, and he knew that she was. Still running from what couldn't be escaped.

"This one's yours," he said, pointing at the next big swell. "Paddle, paddle, paddle!"

She did, crouching and bobbling and wiping out before she washed up on shore with Gabriela and the twins. A drowned bird, indeed.

They sand-walked to a cabana for the boys' favorite treat: tres leches cake, made fresh for festival tourists. Every table at every cabana was packed. People thronged the beach, calling to each other, kicking soccer balls, thumping music. Gabriela had warned them that it got crazy in Cayo for festival—people flocking from everywhere in the country, all-night parties. Ezra had tried to prepare himself, take it easy, but he still felt his back tightening as he herded the kids, checking behind them all as they walked. He wished he could stay out on the water, watching the people on shore like a distant bird colony.

On the water he could relax, feel his freedom. But in the cabana's confines, sweaty humans bumping up against him, his body flushed with adrenaline, muscles tightening, ready to defend.

Gabriela reached over and took his hand, gave him a searching look.

"We will stay in for the night. Watch *The Terminator*?" she said, and the boys yelped. She smiled at them. "You must promise to go to bed without a fight afterward, sí?"

The twins nodded, cake crumbed at the corners of their identical mouths.

Ezra saw the girl first, stumbling past the cabana toward the beach as if she meant to walk into the waves without stopping. Blood ran from a cut above her eye, her mouth was swollen, her hair tangled, knees raw. She was eighteen, maybe younger.

When the twins saw her, they froze, eyes locked on her zigzag through the sand. And then the crowd saw her—people stopping to stare from the beach, people whispering and pointing from the cabana.

She kept going, feet bare, skirt askew, the inside of her thighs bloodstained.

People gathered around her in a wide circle, some women holding out their hands to her, but she pushed them off. She turned slowly to look behind her and started keening—a high, wavering cry like a wounded seagull.

Ezra followed her gaze. A young man, her age, followed behind her, weaving too.

The man laughed as the crowd looked on. "What's up? You running away?" He lifted his arms, defying the angry hecklers. "Come on, baby. We were just getting started."

Ezra threw his napkin on his plate and stood.

"No, do not go, Ezra," Gabriela said, gripping Ezra's arm,

her voice a pitch he'd never heard. Fear and warning, tuned to high alert.

The circle around the woman had drawn closer, closing rank. They yelled at the man, their voices high and angry.

"Somebody's got to teach that piece of shit a lesson, teach him what to expect, doing that to a woman," Ezra said, pulling away from Gabriela's grip. But as he walked up behind the drunken man, a white and green police pickup sped in, jerking to a stop. The uniformed driver jumped out—a towering brawny officer glowering like an angry giant.

Suddenly, everyone was yelling at once—every bystander, every cabana patron, every woman in the circle shouting things Ezra couldn't understand. But he understood their angry faces.

The officer ignored them all as he questioned the man.

Whatever the drunk said in reply was all it took. The officer shoved the man into the pickup's windshield, door, and fender, cranking his arms up behind his back until they looked about to break. The man's smashed face streamed blood and his legs buckled. The officer slapped cuffs on his wrists and threw him in the pickup's back seat, slamming the door.

Ezra expected him to drive off to the station, but the cop turned, shielding his eyes with his hand, looking for the woman who'd collapsed in the sand.

The officer went to her and pulled her up roughly.

The circle of women closed in on the officer then too, their faces contorted with anger, all chanting the same word—*cochina, cochina, cochina.*

The officer pushed through their bodies, yanking the injured woman along behind him.

Ezra started after them but Gabriela pulled on his arm with a vice grip, her fingers stronger than he would have imagined.

"Come, Ezra, we must leave now. It is not safe here."

As the officer pulled the woman toward his pickup, he scanned the restive crowd. His eyes locked on Ezra. A cool assessment. An acknowledgement between learned enemies. *You,* it said. *I will take you, too.*

"Ezra. Come. Now," Gabriela said, her voice quiet and sharp.

The officer shoved the woman into the passenger seat of the pickup and only then did Ezra glance down. Saw the twins clutching Gabriela, their faces streaked with tears. He remembered cowering with Timothy as their father raged, that cold wash of terror running down his spine, paralyzing him just as surely as when their father hit him, threw him, threatened to break his neck.

"Please, Ezra, please come with me."

Ezra let himself be led. As they walked away, Ezra bent down and scooped up Adan and Ail, tucked them into his chest, one in each arm.

He held them close, their heads against his shoulders. Buried his face in their damp hair, breathing in the salty-sweet scent of them, their chests rising and falling in rhythm beneath his hands.

GREER

"My god, it's a girl."

Greer thought she was dreaming.

Then she realized that she was the girl.

She sat bolt upright.

"What are you doing?" the woman asked, frowning, peering at Greer through the brush. The woman looked over her shoulder and called to someone Greer couldn't see. "Bring food. And electrolytes. And the first aid kit. Quickly. Get the dog something, too."

She said more about exposure and injuries. There was a scurry of heavy footsteps as Greer tried to push herself up, find the llamas and Sirius. Escape.

The woman held her hands up. "*Tá'c meeywi, 'iin wées Josephine Erdrich*. Good morning, my name is Josephine Erdrich. We're just gonna get you something to eat and drink."

Greer sat back, tensed for escape. But everything hurt, and she was so tired she felt like crying. She *was* crying, a little bit. She ducked her head to hide it.

Josephine handed Greer a bottle of Gatorade and Greer saw the other person—a pudgy guy with binoculars around his neck. He gave Sirius a pile of something to eat and she wolfed it down faster than he could dump it on the ground.

"Looks like you all went through a tornado," he said.

She looked at herself, her arms and legs all scratches and bruises and sores, her clothes dirty scraps. She lifted a hand to her matted hair.

Kelly and Yavell paced and hummed, leaves sticking out of their mouths. The animals seemed happy to see these new people, but Greer wasn't.

"You know where you are?" Josephine asked. She gave Greer a crusty heel of bread, a small chunk of cheddar, and a tart apple—the most delicious things Greer had ever eaten.

"Almost to the North Fork of the Clearwater River," Greer said. She tried not to gulp her food down like Sirius.

"That's where we're headed," Josephine said. "Me and Walter and Dr. Ward, our PI." She smiled a little at Greer's alarm. "Principal Investigator, not private investigator. In other words, our professor," she added. "We're from the university."

"Oh," Greer said as she formed an escape plan. Once she'd eaten enough, she would toss a rock in the creek to distract them. Then she would bolt. Sirius would follow her, but she'd have to leave Kelly and Yavell behind. She and Sirius would move fast through the brush along the creek until they could climb back up to the mountains. Then they'd find a hidey hole and wait these people out. Then she'd figure out the rest.

Josephine pointed to the grease-stained map folded by Greer's side. "Some impressive navigation skills you've got. Looks like you've been on quite the journey. Never expected to find a girl by herself in this country with two llamas and a shepherd pup."

"Sirius." Greer patted Sirius's head and pointed at the llamas. "That's Kelly and Yavell."

Josephine smiled, her teeth a little crooked, her face kind. "Great names," she said. She gestured at the bruises and scrapes and dirt. "It looks like you could use a little patching up though."

Greer shrugged.

"If you don't mind, I can look you and Sirius over and see

what I can do?"

Greer looked more closely at Josephine. She wore big hiking boots and a holey t-shirt that said BLACKFOOT No Reservations. A tattoo on her arm said Josie and Coyotē.

"That's my band," Josephine said, following Greer's eyes.

"A rock band?" Greer asked hopefully.

"Yes ma'am," Josephine said, smiling. "How about this—you let me fix you up a little, and maybe I'll sing for you later?"

Then Greer saw the raven.

It perched in a cage, checking her out, its head tilted like Sirius when she was curious. It looked like the mountain raven that led her through the snow to Hemingway Maclean's duffel beneath the silvery snag. This raven was smaller and had a white mark on the top of its shoulder.

It cocked its head the other way, and then back, looking at Greer with its bright eyes. It fluffed its neck into a mane and shook out its wing feathers.

"A raven," she said, in awe.

"That's Persephone," Josephine said. "She was injured in a fire nearby, but she's nearly healed up now. We're babysitting her for a friend who's camping on the river."

The pudgy guy looked anxious. "Shouldn't we call this in?"

Josephine looked at Greer and Greer met her eye. Steadier.

"One thing at a time," Josephine said. "Right now, food, water, and wounds."

The guy rubbed his soles in the dirt. Fidgeted with his binoculars.

"Walter's the best. He makes sure we don't get ourselves into trouble," Josephine said. "He's right though. Is there anyone we can call for you? You're pretty banged up."

Walter brightened. "We have a sat phone."

Greer couldn't allow herself to think about the safety of shelter. The relief of kindness, the care of capable adults, of good food. Of finding her friends again, telling Juan and his family the stories of her great adventure.

Because behind all of that: Rory.

She tensed herself to take off through the brush. She knew Sirius would follow her. They could survive together, even without their raggedy gear. Kelly and Yavell could find a happy home.

"It's just me and the llamas and Sirius, but we know how to take care of ourselves."

"I can see that," Josephine said. "Is it alright if I take a look at your wounds—get them cleaned up, bandaged properly?"

Greer glanced toward Persephone. If these people were caring for an injured raven, helping it heal so it could be set free on the North Fork, perhaps they could be trusted to do the same for a girl.

"Okay," she murmured. A couple of stupid tears. She wiped them away.

Josephine's hands were sure and strong as she used wetted clothes to clean Greer's skin, administering a salve that felt as good as it smelled. But when Josephine pulled off Greer's tattered sneakers, she clucked her tongue in dismay.

"*Éetxewce*—I am so sad," she said. "You've been long in the cold."

She touched the tips of Greer's mangled toes. Walter leaned over to see, then looked like he was going to throw up.

Josephine said, "You remind me of my niece, Camas. Getting herself into one scrape after another. Tougher than her twin brother, Cedar. But your feet are frostbitten. Do you understand what that means?"

Greer yanked her throbbing feet away. "We're going to the river. Me and Sirius and the llamas." She was crying again. She was so tired, but she couldn't let anyone stop her, no matter how kind and worried. No matter how much she wanted to give in, let them take care of her and eat everything they gave her.

Walter touched the binoculars around his neck. "Would you like to try these out while Josephine doctors you up?" He handed them to Greer, showed her how to adjust them to her eyes.

Josephine started cleaning her feet and the pain made Greer suck her breath in. She used the binoculars to distract herself, training them on the raven. She could see each tiny eyelash whenever the bird blinked.

"Can she fly?"

"She should be able to now, but we won't know until we set her loose," Josephine said.

"She's going to be just fine," Walter said, giving the raven a sassy look. "She's always trying to escape, trying to steal our snacks. Oatmeal cookies are her favorite."

Josephine finished wrapping Greer's feet in gauze and tape. "I bet she'd love for you to give her some treats when you're all patched up. You can eat all you want, too, but be careful. Your stomach will have to get used to it. Too bad we don't have any pie left—Persephone was hilarious with it."

"Yeah, I'd say she liked it a little *too* much," Walter said disapprovingly, just like Juan.

"Sirius loves all the sugary things too," Greer said. "Even Mr. Estmund's old candy. Especially the butterscotches. We ran out of those a long time ago though."

"Mr. Estmund?" another woman asked, pushing through the brush, appearing like a vision. Her arms were covered in tattoos, her hair long and ropey.

There was something powerful about her. Something that made all of them act suddenly different.

"This is our PI, Dr. Ward," Josephine said.

The new woman looked Greer over, her eyes searching, intense.

"I—called him Mr. Estmund, even though he said not to," Greer said. "He wanted me to just call him Philip." She wished if she spoke his name enough, she could bring him back. He would know what to do, here, in this bewildering situation.

The woman knelt in front of Greer, taking her in. "How did you know Philip Estmund?" she asked, gentle but urgent. "You need to tell us."

Josephine and Walter had gone still and watchful too, intent on something Greer could not comprehend.

"He was my friend. In. Ummm…" She sounded like Kelly. "In Headquarters," Greer faltered, sure now that she had spoken too much. What would these people do if they knew what had happened? Her mom and Rory had likely taken off right away, but Juan and his family would have worried about her for sure. Her mom was always threatening to take Greer away without saying goodbye just to punish her. They all probably thought that's what had happened.

"He told me stories."

Greer reached into the llamas' panniers, pulled out the tape recorder, plugged in a tape, and pressed PLAY.

She thought she'd chosen the tape where Mr. Estmund told her favorite story, *How Raven Tricked Trout*, where Ava had swum across to the other side of the river to find the forest fairies and startled sleeping Trout, who Raven caught and flew high into the sky, barrel-rolling and laughing and laughing.

But instead, only maybe accidentally, she'd picked the tape she never wanted to listen to. Because deep down she knew someone else needed to hear it. To know what had really happened.

"I remember who she wanted to be. She wanted to live at the river when she grew up, speak its language, learn its secret fairyland magic. But where is she now? Head buried in her studies, in her data and reports."

"That's life's truest secret, Greer. Pay attention to everything nature says. You've got to listen to nature if you want to know anything about yourself or this earth—breathing its air, drinking its water, eating its plants and its creatures. Nothing else can teach you what you need to know about real things. You must learn to hear it. To see it. To taste it. To smell it. To feel it. To know it. To be it. Only then will you know what it means to be real and alive."

Mr. Estmund's voice stopped, the tape crackling as it whirred on. Greer remembered his expression as he glanced out the window, when they saw Rory storming across the bridge, coming for her. Coming for them both.

When Mr. Estmund's voice returned, it was sharp and urgent. "Go, Greer, now—Run!"

Greer felt the prickle of the hay cave, felt her limbs contracting and quivering, the thump of her heart as she'd sat with her knees clutched to her chest in the enveloping dark, her body quaking, her teeth clanking, her fingernails digging in her palms. Her pants wet and stinking with her own terrified animal musk.

Then there was the sound of Rory pounding on the door. "You little whore you better not be in there with that kike lech, or I'll fucking kill you both."

Then came the part Greer dreaded more than anything else.

The rustling muffled sound of Mr. Estmund throwing the blanket over the tape recorder as Rory crashed through the front door, his voice contorted with hate.

"You waiting for me, old man?" A scornful laugh. "You like my girl? Thing is, I don't like to share, so you better fucking tell me where you hid her."

The sound of movement, the sound of struggle, and then a single gunshot, loud enough that it seemed right here, not back in Headquarters in Mr. Estmund's house.

Greer felt it in her bones, as she had in the hay cave.

Rory's voice came again. "I told you to keep the fuck away from her. I should've put a bullet in your head a long time ago, done the world a favor."

There was a hawking sound of spit, the sound of receding footsteps, and a door slammed shut. Then the sound of nothing at all.

Until the sound of Greer's raw voice crying out.

Josephine pulled Greer close, safe, as Greer remembered the mineral smell of blood, Mr. Estmund's body sagging from the chair.

There was the sound of her sobbing, the sound of her telling Mr. Estmund goodbye.

The tape finally stopped.

"Oh my god," the kneeling woman said, her voice breaking. She held her hands to her face as her shoulders shook.

"Please don't call the police," Greer pleaded, her face streaming with tears. "I can't go back there, I can't go back."

Walter was pale, his shaking hands trying to grasp the binoculars that weren't on his chest.

Josephine released Greer but pressed her hand firmly on her back, anchoring.

"*Qooqox Pit'iin.* Little raven girl. You've gone through things nobody should ever go through."

Dr. Ward dropped her hands. Her face was full of seething rage, her jaw muscles clenched, her fists balled tight. "I'll kill him," she hissed through teeth.

"You can't call the police!" Greer cried. "They'll try to stop me. They'll make me and Sirius and the llamas go back. We have to make it to the North Fork. It's the only place we can go. Please don't make me go back, please!"

Josephine started humming a low song, her voice strong as she brushed her hands lightly down each of Greer's limbs, like she was wiping away clinging cobwebs. She did the same thing over Greer's head, sweeping from forehead to shoulder as she hummed. Greer's body suddenly felt lighter, as though she were floating or flying. She closed her eyes and imagined herself soaring with Persephone, meeting the mountain raven who'd saved her on the snowy peaks. It was just like one of Mr. Estmund's stories. *Ravens and Raven Girl Fly Together Forever Free.*

"You're safe now," Josephine said. "We'll take care of you. We are your friends. That man will never hurt you again."

Greer looked at Persephone and Persephone looked back. Her black eyes made Greer feel like Mr. Estmund was with her, saying she was going to be okay. That she would make it to the North Fork and find her forever home with the river and the trees, with the ferns and the flowers. With Raven and Otter and Trout. That she would learn to listen to nature talk, nature in its terrible and beautiful forms, and learn to answer.

Raven Girl & Her Friends Find Their Way to the Other Side of the River.

AVA

I t was as if Ava was traveling through her childhood.

The long winding drive to the North Fork dropped from the rolling windblown prairie to the heat-struck valley, then climbed back up to thick forest. In Headquarters, haunted and lonely as a nineteenth-century ghost town, she passed the llama pasture and her father's empty house.

The stretch from Headquarters to the river was dreamlike: treelined meadows and meandering streams she knew were full of water skippers, frogs, and water lilies. S-curves climbed into tall trees, the air scented with forest humus, sunlight, and rich soil. Alders and ferns grew thick as the elevation dropped toward the river, blackberries and moss blanketing blacktop and tree trunks, the creek paralleling the road in a whitewater rush.

Alfred had left a message to meet them at Aquarius Camp-ground, the site of Ava's earliest memories: the little wobbly board bridge over the stream where her father had told her trolls lived. The small white-sand beach, the cedar stump where she stood with her father each spring, the North Fork's swollen surge of icy mountain snowmelt swirling around their feet. Her favorite campsite hidden at the end of the loop, nestled back in the ancient cedars' shaggy mastodon trunks. Home of trillium and wood violet, sword ferns and maidenhair; Pacific wrens, *Troglodytes pacificus*; American dippers, *Cinclus mexicanus*;

and Swainson's thrushes, *Catharus ustulatus,* with their beauti-ful, unforgettable trill.

◆

Everything had happened so fast. Yesterday she'd been in Cayo, planning her trip to the Galapagos. When Alfred called—a girl found in the woods with her father's missing llamas, some-how witness to his murder, not suicide—everything turned on its head and spun.

Ezra and Gabriela and the twins came to the casa to send her on her way. She hugged Gabriela, and Adan and Ail, who sang their favorite song about birds flying away. Ava memorized the sound of the croaking ground doves and the little chattering parrotlets, the smell of the overgrown lime tree above the drip-ping outdoor shower, the feel of the warm and heavy ocean air, the taste of salt in the wind. Gabriela's long hair blowing, the twins on either side of her like bookends, magnificent frigate-birds sailing overhead like black kites.

"We love you, Profesora Ava, La Chica de Aves," Gabriela yelled. "We will always love you. No matter how far you fly, you will be forever with us."

Leaning from the Lada's window, Ava blew kisses until Ezra turned a corner and she lost sight of them, and then lost sight of the ocean rolling silver and blue. She sat back in her seat, crying, trying to believe she would return, that this was her home now, too. Forest to ocean, fire to water, earth to air.

They passed flat green fields flooded into rice paddies, heaps of harvested grain spread out on the roadsides to dry in the sun, stilt-legged great white egrets stepping slowly through the murky paddy waters as they hunted frogs and snakes.

Ezra drove at breakneck speed to reach the airport in time for her flight. Guayaquil to Seattle to the Palouse.

◆

All this time she'd believed her father had given up living when that's all he'd ever demanded that she do. She'd been waiting for the coroner's report when the truth—all the truths—had been in a little girl's interview tape recordings all along.

She could hear him still, the timbre of his voice, his disappointment when she said time and again that she was too busy to come see him, to go to the river with him.

Too busy.

Really, she'd been too angry. Too full of guilt and sorrow. Too full of unresolved, complicated emotions. He'd been right. She'd needed to face herself. It was too late for him—had been too late for a long time before his death. But it wasn't too late for her.

She hadn't been able to forgive him for his emotional arrest. A father who was a loving, compelling childhood guide, but couldn't follow her across the river into adulthood and couldn't forgive her for going there. He answered her questions with insistent fairy stories, he couldn't recover from the vicissitudes of adult relationships, he took his lonely daughter to a lonely cabin and, for all his love, was controlling and self-indulgent. Drink and fairy tales. He couldn't see that he had succeeded in instilling a lifelong love for place and wilderness in a daughter who *had* committed her life to it, answering nature with deep education, committed terminology, field experience, creative answers to self-sustenance on the contemporary planet, love, and disciplined passion. Like many adult daughters of dazzling fathers, she had struggled to forgive him for what she first loved most in him. She thought she had to leave the "magic" of nature behind because she'd left the fairies behind. She had to re-learn the value of folk wisdom, the power of story, the possibility of metaphysical forces without having to surrender her acquired scientific paradigms. And she had to come to terms with her guilt—a genuine abandonment of a deeply flawed but beautiful father she loved, long before he was physically gone—without re-debilitating herself.

She could so clearly envision it—her father adopting a little lost girl as his apprentice. A metaphysical "do-over," a second chance at bridging two related but estranged Avas: starry-eyed child/accomplished (and tempered) adult. Taking on a new pupil, teaching her all his life lessons, all his nature and fairyland magic, telling her all his stories of grief and hardship, everything imbued with the same message: *You've got to* live *your life, really* live it. *This is all you get. Right now. This moment. You've got to live like you've got nothing left to lose. Be unafraid to be truly and fully alive. Listen to and commune with nature until you can understand it secrets, until you can speak its language, until you learn from it the reaches of both loss and love, suffering and splendor, darkness and light. Nature will teach you everything you need to know, if you only learn to listen.*

He'd always been a gifted storyteller, able to bring everything to life. Said it was his purpose: to be a weaver of words, a bard of nature, keeper of truth. But even he couldn't have come up with this kind of ending, this outcome: a runaway girl and her dog traversing forest and mountain and waters with his llamas, on their way to the North Fork to live, just as Ava herself had always wanted to do.

◆

On the drive to Guayaquil, she'd checked her travel documents and found her Galapagos ticket. Her long-awaited journey: Darwin's path of discovery, his understanding of life's astonishing—dare she say "magical"—variabilities and adaptations. Sighting his famous finches and the elusive lava herons and gulls, studying blue-footed booby colonies. She was outlining a new book about them, an accompaniment to her raven work. Birds with their hollow air-sac bones, their iridescent feather magic, their exquisite strengths and sensitivities, whether to wildfire smoke or malarial blood parasites.

"Take Gabriela and go to the islands," she said, handing the Galapagos ticket to Ezra.

Ezra looked at the ticket. Then at her.

"Okay. I will," he said. "But promise you'll tell Sibley everything you've told me—how much you love her. If there's anything this place has taught me, it's don't lock yourself up. Seize everything *now*."

"You sound like Adonis. Like my father."

"Put him to rest properly now. Say goodbye the way you need to. Make peace."

She put her arm out the window, let it trace warm air currents. Clouds of smoke rose from the spreading ruins of climate-refugee tent cities leading into the city. Poverty, refugees, desperation, sorrow, loss, rage, confusion, wealth disparity, population growth, food and water and energy shortages, murder and rape and war and death and so much heartbreak. What possibility was there to find love, joy, and peace amid so much struggle and hardship?

When they reached the airport, she climbed out of the Lada, the smell and feel of Ecuador an enveloping presence, wishing her farewell. She hugged Ezra so hard she could feel every part of him, broken and whole.

"You're one of the best things I've ever found."

"Stop that. You're going to Idaho, you're going to figure shit out and take care of business, you're going to tell Sibley you're sorry and then you're going to come back here, to us, and we're all going to live happily ever after looking at birds."

She smiled. "I told Alfred you were going to stay on at the house as a caretaker. He was glad to have somebody there, keep an eye on all the birds for us."

"I'll be here with Gabriela and Adan and Ail, awaiting your

return," Ezra said. "You know I can't come track you down, so you better promise to get back down here before I send someone after you."

"You and Adonis would get along just fine. You speak the same language." She kissed Ezra on the side of the neck, his rough Velcro barb against her lips. She imagined a world that couldn't be: Adonis and Ezra trading stories, surfing together.

"Until next time," Ezra said, pulling away in the Lada. He leaned out of the window and yelled his signature *ca-caaww* and travelers turned in response.

Ava cupped her hands around her mouth and repeated it back. *Ca-caaww, ca-caaww.*

EZRA

"**O**ne more day," he said, and it was like lighting a flare. Adan and Ail screeched, bouncing like caffeinated rabbits, punching their wiry arms into the air, chanting, "Ga-lá-pa-gos, Ga-lá-pa-gos, Ga-lá-pa-gos."

They leaped on Ezra's back, their bony butts digging into his spine, their heels jabbing his stomach, spurring him on. "Giddy-up horsey," they yelled, shrieking as he reared and whinnied and galloped around the floor on his hands and knees. They twisted his shirt into a chokehold around his neck and wrapped their legs tight as they hung on.

Gabriela came inside, line-dried clothes in a wicker basket balanced on her hip. She clicked her tongue. "Ninõs, ninõs, chicos locos, you must finish your chores before we go to Lopez. Remember: no work, no fun."

"Sí, Mamá," they chimed in such perfect unison it sounded like one voice.

They hopped off Ezra's back and went to work, preparing Ava's casa to be shut up for the next few weeks. They'd never been to the Galapagos Islands, although Gabriela had traveled there often as an ecotourism ambassador. All the boys could talk about was surfing, surfing, surfing—finding each hidden break, each new wave set, each new trick they would try out.

Ezra remembered the same obsession, how he'd dreamed of

the water, the waves, the breaks, day and night. He'd promised to take them to Puerto Lopez's surf competition that weekend and they'd become even more impassioned.

They rode their skateboards down to Cayo's beach every day, battered surfboards tucked under their arms, Ezra and Gabriela running behind them, trying to keep up. Ezra finally set up the CT1 so it could carry their surfboards, and then they all rode together to the beach, one boy in front of him and the other behind Gabriela. A family surfing affair.

Gabriela had promised the boys new wax and fins on the Lopez trip before they set sail on their "Charles Darwin Gala-pagos Adventure," named in honor of Ava. The boys sang the parrot song as they did their chores. It made Ezra think about Doc and Domingo, sailing the world together.

At first Ezra hadn't been sure he could step aboard another ship, even if this one was a "cruise" instead of "cargo." But this time he was a paying passenger, not a fugitive, and he would be with Gabriela and the twins instead of Vic, Tiny, Joel, Domingo, Chad, Angie, Mary, Penny, and Grace. Gabriela had promised that the six-hundred-mile, four-day journey was worth it. It would be a family adventure, she'd said, and that's what convinced him—Gabriela calling them that. The berth reservation declared it too: "Family of Four."

A family.

It was still hard to trust this happiness, this life he'd never dared to dream of. Too sweet and beautiful, this found love, this connection, this community that had suddenly formed around him. He tried not to show Gabriela his hypervigilance, pacing and looking out the night windows, eyeing the dark streets.

◆

In Lopez, they sat on the beach, watching the end of the surf competition—the waves and weather perfect, young men and women ripping the water to shreds, performing spectacular moves to the cheers of the crowd.

The boys rode their skateboards to the surf shack, chattering like the parrotlets Ava loved. While they were picking out surf supplies for the Galapagos trip, Ezra followed Gabriela through the outdoor shopping area—a labyrinth connected by tarps and packing-crate walls. As Gabriela picked out last-minute vacation wear from her favorite spot, Ezra stood transfixed by the mannequins. Straight out of a slasher movie: battered blonde gringas with black chokers, grimacing faces scuffed and repainted, eyes cat-amber, blue eyeshadow like bruises. His mother after his father came home—her eyes puffed into dark moons, her wrists ringed red.

Ezra told Gabriela he would wait outside. He made his way out of the of shops, relieved to escape the mannequins' dead-eyed stares. But then he saw the boys.

It was the same oversize officer who'd manhandled the assaulted woman on Cayo's beach. Now his police pickup sat close to the park where all the kids hung out, shooting hoops, playing soccer, and smoking pilfered cigarettes.

The cop was standing over Adan and Ail, glowering down. The boys stared up in fear, holding their skateboards to their chests like armor.

Ezra sprinted. A stray dog tucked its tail and scurried out of his way and a rooster off to the side crowed in alarm. But Ezra saw that he was too late, the officer's stance as aggressive as it'd been on the beach. He slapped his huge hands on the boys' thin shoulders and shook them. Ezra rushed forward, quivering with violence meant for the officer—what he should have done when he'd had the chance, no matter what Gabriela said, no matter the consequence.

Moto taxis honked in cacophony as he ran in front of them, but the officer didn't look up. He said something Ezra couldn't hear over the street noise. He grabbed Adan's skateboard and dropped it to the ground where it bounced on its wheels. The big man stepped on it, positioning his feet and bending his knees in a smooth practiced motion, executing a perfect kickflip. And then an ollie. He popped the board into a manual and rode a car's length before grabbing the end and jumping off, effortless, his laugh booming as he handed the skateboard back to the twins.

They looked up at him in shocked wonder. He patted their heads roughly and gave them a handful of candy before he ambled off, whistling, heading for a thatched cabana whose sidewalk chalkboard advertised "Special Breakfast" in white chalk letters.

By the time Ezra reached them, hyperventilating, the boys were already sucking on the candy, squirrel-cheeked.

"Ezra, Ezra, did you see the policía? He rode my skateboard," Adan said, grinning.

"He was really good!" Ail said, eyes bright.

Ezra restrained himself from scooping them up and holding them safe to his chest; it would wreck their burgeoning street cred. His hands shook as he set them on the boys' shoulders, listening to their chatter as he gently steered them back to the Lada. Gabriela was waiting for them, surprising the boys with new Panama hats and colorful beach hammocks. She smiled at Ezra like he was a man who deserved all she had to give.

◆

Their ship was named *The Simon Bolivar,* a man with an upraised fist astride a rearing horse painted on either side of the bow. *El Libertador*—liberator of Ecuador, Colombia, Peru, Panama, Bolivia, and Venezuela from the Spanish Empire.

Oswaldo Guayasamín prints lined the walls of the berths— figures with haunted eyes and long-fingered hands held against angular color blocked faces. Gabriela had a Guayasamín print hanging at her finca—a brown-bob-haired woman backed in yellow, looking outward, head tilted to one side. Her straight-shouldered torso and the right side of her face were shadowed, but her round breasts, long arms, and upper abdomen were bright and pale with light.

The Simon Bolivar's Guayasamíns were more grim, pain and sorrow caught in their expressions. Something Ezra could understand. Then again—who picked these to decorate a cruise ship? Carrying their bags to their berth, he stopped to gaze at one titled "Tenderness," a mother and child clutched together in suffering. Adan and Ail rushed past him and piled onto the queen bed with its puffy comforter, jumping up and down, laughing and grappling with each other, their joy infectious.

♦

Gabriela had been right. The cruise was as easy as the cargo trip had been hard, each day soft lit and smooth, time passing quickly with each meal together, each sunset ramble around the deck, each nighttime story Gabriela read to the boys.

Ezra would lie back on the bed, a twin nestled on either side, listening to the lovely lilt of Gabriela's storytelling. The boys tensed and relaxed with the different scenes, inhabiting the action as they fought off the deadly foe of sleep. They often all fell asleep that way—the four of them strewn atop the bed, pillows and blankets tossed like flotsam. A *pack of puppies*, Gabriela said.

The other passengers came from around the world: North Dakota, Brazil, Denmark, the Congo, Oregon, China, British Columbia, India, Iowa. A young English man named Titus—small and wiry and ferret-like—claimed he was a relative of Darwin's from Shrewsbury, England. He was following the HMS *Beagle*'s historic path, the Corps of the Surveying Officers from the UK to the Galapagos Islands.

When they arrived at San Cristóbal Island, Titus informed his fellow passengers that it was the easternmost island in the Galapagos archipelago, and geologically one of the oldest, pocked with the ancient volcanoes Darwin had thought he had come to study. Unimpressed, Adan and Ail bolted down the ship's ramp like wild chimpanzees, yelping and whooping and beating their chests.

"We made it, we made it," they yelled, and the other passengers smiled and cheered, all feeling a part of the discovery, part of the glorious origin of species.

Ezra thought of Ava, finding her way back to her own origin. Thought of Timothy, wild and alive like Adan and Ail, brothers swinging high over the St. Joe River. Timothy's hair a halo, hungry fish jumping for bugs beneath them, willow branches waving in the breeze.

Thought of their mother, trying her best to give them what they would never have.

Ezra hoisted their bags on his shoulder and held Gabriela's hand as they walked down the gangplank to join the boys.

"We made it, we made it," Gabriela sang with the twins until they were all dancing on the dock, shouting to the sky.

◆

They went diving on Darwin Island and El Arco, saw schools of scalloped hammerheads, manta rays, and a massive slow-moving whale shark.

They swam with the Galapagos sea lions, the Pacific green sea turtles, and Galapagos penguins on San Cristóbal. Saw the underwater volcano on Roca Redonda and the Cerro Chato Tortoise Reserve and Charles Darwin Research Station on Santa Cruz Island where the boys climbed inside a giant tortoise shell and poked their smiling faces out.

They found a blue-footed booby colony on Española and

stayed the whole day watching the birds do their blue-foot high-step mating dance, their heads tipped back, beaks quivering, Ezra and Gabriela and the boys making a list of each detail to tell Ava.

Gabriela started calling it their family honeymoon. "You and I. Adan and Ail. We are a true familia now," she said to Ezra one night, trailing her hand through his hair. The boys slept at their sides, waves breaking ashore in the dark.

They said their vows on Isabela Island under the ancient mangroves, the trees' roots like earth's arteries pulsing beneath their feet. Adan and Ail stood solemn on either side of them, sun-kissed and brown, their tangled hair combed back, their hands and feet scrubbed clean of salt and sand. They looked suddenly long-limbed and grown, sprouted into a new variation of species beneath the island sun.

"Novio Ezra, tomas tu a Novia Gabriela como tu esposa, prometes amarla, respetarla, protejerla abandonando a todo y dedicandote solo a ella?"

The words translated in Ezra's head as *Ezra, can you believe that this beautiful, amazing, brilliant woman, Gabriela, wishes to be yours? That she believes in you—in the true and everlasting reach of your love for her, your respect for her, your desire to be forever with her and her children, Adan and Ail, abandoning all others, dedicating yourself only to her and her children always? Will you honor this, her belief in you? Will you forgive yourself so that you can move into this love, this family, this new truth? Will you forever believe in her, too?*

"Sí, father. Yes. Forever and ever, always and forever."

They ran down to the island's hidden lagoon and went surfing afterward, as they'd promised the boys—bodies suspended by the Galapagos sea, the water stretching endless around them, flocks of colorful flitting birds mirrored by schools of darting fish.

A family of silvered light. A family of water and air.

A family.

AVA

They followed the ancient Trail of the Nez Perce—the same trail Lewis & Clark's Corps of Discovery had followed west from Montana into Idaho, traversing the sharp-toothed Bitterroot Mountains as winter came in and the snow flew. The explorers fell ill, starving and freezing, the nearest to mass death they came on their 8,000 mile expedition. The Nimíipuu saved them.

The Lolo Motorway was part of the Trail of the Nez Perce—a narrow winding road off the Northwest Passage Scenic Byway. Brown Forest Service road signs pointed them to Imnamatnoon Likoolam, Saddle Camp, and Bear Oil & Roots Camp. They stopped to explore each site, passing wildfire scars along the way—thousands of acres of blackened ground and burned trees growing in with fireweed, foxglove, asters, and paintbrush.

They stopped for a lunch break at Indian Post Office, Bitter-root summits rising sheer around them. Rhodes Peak ringed by Blacklead Peak and William's Peak. Using her birding binoculars—Walter's gift—Greer rotated slowly, zooming in on details, consulting the raft of dogeared guidebooks and historical narratives "Dr. Ward" and Josephine had given her. Wildflowers, waterways, birds, trees, Bitterroot botany, edible plants of the Nez Perce, trails, hot springs, the 1910 Fire, human histories, and ethno-cultural biographies.

Little autodidact that she was, Greer had been spouting factoids the whole trip: by the end of their expedition, Lewis & Clark's journals had identified 134 species of birds with at least twenty-five previous unknowns. Chief Joseph—Josephine's ancestor—had led his people over 1,600 miles through Idaho, Washington, and Montana, outsmarting the U.S. military until he and his people made it safely to Canada. Indian paintbrush—*Castilleja*—symbolized passion, resilience, creativity, and a connection to the natural world.

The girl looked out over the vast green and blue treed mountains and talked about Billy Rhodes and the Ridgerunner. Talked about Sacagawea, Watkuweis, York, and the ancient Nez Perce people who'd lived there, always. *The People.*

Ava could see what her father had seen in Greer—why he'd taken her on as his acolyte, teaching her the amalgam of folklore, fairytales, fact, and sometimes sheer nonsense he'd once taught Ava. More uncanny, though: Ava could see herself in Greer—the eager, precocious child she had been. Saw what her father loved.

♦

Josephine had been generous with her knowledge, too, teaching Greer Nimíipuu history, culture, and language while Greer was laid up for weeks, her frostbitten feet, battered body, and broken heart healing.

As promised, when the foster care agreement came through, Ava threw Greer a big party, complete with a Josie and Coyotē concert. Josephine dressed in boots, cutoffs, and a fringed Redbone "Come and Get Your Love" t-shirt, singing a new song she'd written just for Greer. All of them sang along to the chorus, "Wild eyes recognizing each other as whole."

When Josephine was finished singing, she sat down, said, "Wáaqo' kiiye 'úuyisix—let us begin. 'Eetx tiwatíisa kaa 'óykaloo hipecúukwenu'. I will tell you a story and everyone will know it."

Josephine began by teaching her listeners important Nimíipuu words. Greer shouted each one out after Josephine spoke it:

"In the beginning, there were The People, the Nimíipuu, and The People knew the land. They knew its creatures: 'iceyé-eye—coyote, nacó'x—salmon, himiin—wolf, wewúkye—elk, saq'antáayx—bald eagle, qooqox—raven. They knew its plants: cemiitx—huckleberries, nicka'niicka'—strawberries, qém'es—camas, nánk—cedar tree. Wéet timiipn'ise miniix wées? Do you remember from where you came? Cukwenéewit—know it, hitéemeneewit—learn it, téecukwe—teach it, c'ixnéewit—speak it, titooqanáawit—live it, wiyéeleeheyn—every day!"

Josephine told the story "Yellow Jacket and Ant," where Coyote punished two insects for fighting. "How the Beaver Stole Fire from the Pines," about the origin of fire. "Bat and Coyote," where Coyote played a practical joke on Bat. And as the night wound down, she told her final story, "just for Greer"—a creation story about the relationships between animals and humans called "A Meeting Between Creator and the Animals."

"Creator called to all the animals, gathering them around to tell them human beings were being created. Creator said they—the animals—must argue their qualifications for helping humans or be turned to stone. Crow argued that they would be black and warn others in times of danger, so Creator qualified Crow. But then one Crow came forward and this Crow said that they wanted to be bigger and have a different sounding voice for their warning call—a hoarser and louder voice—so the Creator made this Crow into Raven. Qooqox."

Josephine smiled and looked at Greer. "Raven is a most powerful doctor and messenger. People with Raven's powers can interpret Raven's messages and bring news of great significance over very long distances."

"Like Persephone!" Greer exulted.

Josephine smiled. "'Eehé, yóx c'a'á—yes, that's right. Like Persephone, and like you, too, Qooqox Pit'iin."

"Raven Girl," Greer said. "Qooqox Pit'iin."

"Ta'c, ta'c hitemenew'éet, very good, good student," Josephine said, beaming at Greer. "I am honored to be your teacher, sepehitemenew'éet. Qe'ciyéw'yew'—thank you."

Everybody started clapping and repeating it back to Josephine, saying it to one another, embracing. Qe'ciyéw'yew'. Qe'ciyéw'yew'.

◆

An azure high-country lake sat below Indian Post Office, a blue jewel in a dense nest of evergreens. Bear grass softened boulders stacked into huge ancient cairns. Spired alpine evergreens, silvered snags with gnarled limbs outheld to sky, warm heather-and-hot-scree-scented wind. This place was holy. Ava could feel it in the air, in the hollowed and echoing high-mountain ground. Hushed by bird calls and buzzing insects, wind in the trees, and the singular euphoria of high-mountain solitude, the four of them—Ava, Greer, Sibley, and Sirius—walked quietly, looking and listening, smelling and feeling, as Ava's father had taught Ava and Greer to do.

Mr. Estmund, Greer still called him.

Now all of them said it, including Ava. *Mr. Estmund* this and *Mr. Estmund* that. Telling and retelling his stories—Ava from old memories and Greer with new renditions. *Mr. Estmund* was someone Ava could accept and forgive, even embrace. He was someone different, yet still the man Ava had known. *Mr. Estmund* was washed of familiar failings and lifelong hurt and family grief. A man with a decent heart, with the right inclinations—good things that might eventually outweigh the bad.

With Greer, they had. And because of that, Ava could begin

to forgive the self-destruction, the alcoholism, the emotional absence when his children needed him the most. She found in forgiving him, she could learn to forgive herself. Accept her own failures but acknowledge her own resilience, her accomplishments. Her gifts.

Sirius heeled at Greer's side, as always—self-appointed Greer-guardian, standing in when everyone else had failed the child. Ava felt privileged to be appointed a Greer-guardian too. She and Greer fussed over Sirius as if she were royalty. Queen Dog.

They walked to the large interpretive sign off Lolo Motorway's powdered dirt road. "Indian Post Office: Walking on Sacred Ground." One side Nimíipuu quotes, the other side William Clark's diary entry from the Corps of Discovery. Greer read the words aloud, her voice sure and strong.

"This trail so old it used from time of creation by Nez Perce people to go to Montana to hunt Buffalo and some time to war other tribes of Indians, when Red Bear come to Indians Post Office on this trail, he tell Lewis-Clark and all, stop here, this is very place Indian come to send message—and to get Indian spirit medicine and do Indian worship in Indian custom—Here is where the Monster— the Big Coyote come to make powerful medicine for Indian."

–Sam Lott, Many Wounds

"Tribal members are still using the trail as they did for thousands of years and generations. They are still hunting, fishing, picking berries, and gathering plants for food and medicine."

–Sandi McFarland, 2003

"Indian Post office is still a sacred place to be honored

and respected. It's like walking on sacred ground."

"Lonesome Cove Camp. Steep hills side & falling timber Continue to day, and a thickly timbered Countrey of 8 different kinds of pine, which are So covered with Snow, that in passing thro them we are continually covered in Snow, I have been wet and as cold in every part as I ever was in life, indeed I was at one time fearfull my feet would freeze in the thin mockersons which I wore, after a Short delay in the middle of the Day, I took one man and proceeded on as fast as I could about 6 miles to a Small branch passing to the right, halted and built fires for the party agains their arrival which was at Dusk verry cold and much fatigued we Encamped at this Branch in a thickly timbered bottom which was Scercely large enough for us to lie leavil, men all wet cold and hungary. Killed a Second Colt which we all Suped hartily on and thought it fine meat."

–Capt. William Clark, September 16, 1805

Greer shivered as she read the journal entry.

"Are you okay? Do you need to go back to the car to rest? Have you eaten enough, drank enough water? Are you in pain?" Sibley asked. She leaned down to Greer's height, her brow wrinkled with concern for this small fierce girl, so like her.

Her face buried in Sirius's neck, Greer shook her head. "I'm okay," she said.

But Sibley wasn't convinced. She frowned, as ferocious about Greer's wellbeing as she was the earth's. "We should go back. You've been through too much."

"No, really, I'm okay," Greer said. She stood and squared her shoulders, all gangly limbs and determination. "I don't want to leave. It was very hard, getting here. Please don't make me leave yet. Me and Sirius are so happy."

Ava kissed the top of Greer's maple-sweet head. Greer's green eyes like the depths of the river, trout and ferns and moss and lichen all tangled. Her eyebrows and lashes blonde as her hair. Their plucky little woods sprite.

"Okay," Ava said. "But promise us you'll take it very easy on yourself, and let us keep tending to you and checking in on you."

Greer nodded. "Yes, I promise," she said earnestly. She patted Sirius's fuzzy head. Sirius panted, hanging her long pink tongue, looking happy and hot. "I wish Kelly and Yavell were here with us too. They worked so hard. They were brave and strong, even if they did lay down all the time."

"Their spit is foul," Sibley said, wrinkling her nose.

Greer grinned. "Once, Yavell spit on my arm and it was so green and slimy and stinky I almost threw up."

"That's just plain nasty," Sibley said, ruffling Greer's hair.

"Juan and his family will take good care of the llamas. They gave Mr. Estmund ribbons and bells for them, but I lost them when the hunter scared us."

"Don't you worry—Gabriela and Ezra and the twins will get you hooked up with all kinds of fancy llama duds," Ava said. "Someday we'll all go down to surf and explore with them."

"Will Uncle Alfred and Josephine and Persephone come before we're done with this trip?" Greer asked.

Ava and Sibley glanced at each other over her head.

"They're bringing Mr. Estmund's ashes, right?" Greer asked.

"Yes," Ava said. "They are. I wanted to talk to you about that. I was planning on taking Mr. Estmund's ashes down Isabella Creek Trail to scatter them at the river. Say my goodbyes."

"But you don't have to go if you don't want," Sibley said. "You can stay with me, Josephine, Alfred, and Persephone at Aquarius if that'd be easier for you. Whatever you want, whatever you need, little chickpea."

"I want to go with Mr. Estmund," Greer said, her eyes welling up.

Ava and Sibley hugged her between them. Ava kissed the top of her head again, whispering her lips through Greer's fine hair.

"We'll go together," Ava said. "You, Persephone, and me. It's time we set both of them free."

"Raven Girl, Mr. Estmund, and Persephone Fly Forever Free," Greer said.

"Yes," Ava said.

Yes.

A whip-thin girl with legs like a stork. A girl with a thoughtful adult face, a large flop-eared dog standing guard at her side. A girl Ava had recognized—even though she'd never seen her before—as surely as she'd ever known anything.

◆

They went to Lonesome Cove Camp next. While Greer and Sirius explored, Ava leaned into Sibley, breathed in her fragrance of bergamot, rose, and sweet almond oil.

"I missed you. I missed this. So very, very much."

A mantra: This woman and girl, these mountains, this place.

Sibley wrapped her arms around Ava.

◆

As they drove back down to the North Fork, they stopped at every overlook. Greer brushed her arms though tall bear grass, most of the cream-colored flowers eaten off by black bears, grizzlies, elk, and deer as they followed the hardening season lower and lower, until they too arrived at the river.

Sibley and Ava kept up their bird count, but Greer was the first to spot a party of pileated woodpeckers in the duff under a group of towering trees. She watched them through her binoculars as Ava explained that pileated woodpeckers were almost always solitary, and since they were also nonmigratory, they almost never flocked together.

"You must be good luck, girl," Sibley said.

Greer grinned. She ticked birds off on her fingers. "We've spotted mergansers, mallards, Canada geese, dippers, flickers, downy woodpeckers, pileated woodpeckers, nuthatches, chickadees, kingfishers, wood wrens, house wrens, house sparrows, Steller's jays, violet-green swallows, barn swallows, tree swallows, evening grosbeaks, catbirds, cedar waxwings, red-tail hawks, rough-legged hawks, kestrels, bald eagles, osprey, crows, and ravens."

"Ah, don't forget the red-winged blackbirds," Sibley said, smiling at Ava.

"Oh yes, and starlings and cowbirds and meadowlarks, along with quail, pheasant, turkey, and grouse. Alllll the tasty gamebirds," Greer said, and they laughed.

Greer's appetite was an unstoppable force. She'd already shot up an inch, the clothes they'd bought instantly too small, pants riding highwater, her bony wrists poking out of her long-sleeved shirts. Another bird nerd in the making, stumbling around, binoculars glued to her face.

◆

It was twilight when they reached their night's destination. Ava's father had named it Lean Tree Beach—a camping spot tucked among giant cedars that jutted over crashing boulder-washed rapids and a long, white-sand shoreline.

The River. The North Fork. A place of possibility. The place that had made Ava who she was in every way that mattered, no matter how far she'd strayed from its rocks and rippling waters.

When she'd returned from Ecuador, when she saw the

North Fork's clear green water flowing past Aquarius Campground where she'd spent her childhood summers with her father, wisps of campfire smoke rising from the fragrant cedars, she'd wept. She thought she'd steeled herself, prepared herself for all that awaited: the river, Alfred and Persephone, the girl who'd witnessed her father's end. And Sibley—beautiful, fierce, forgiving. Always and forever Sibley.

But the impact hit so hard she felt like flotsam, dislodged, spinning, loose and drifting on the river's surface. The water's roar pulsing in her. What she'd fled. Her essence in every sight and smell and feel and sound and taste.

Up the steep mountain slopes west of Aquarius rose the North Fork Fire's blackened scar. Choking whiffs of a million smothered campfires. So close she could have hiked there, seen for herself where Claire had died and Persephone was born.

She never could have imagined this journey, although her father might have as he spun his tales of life and death, despair and hope. Gods and their tragedies—and triumphs.

◆

As Ava and Sibley set up camp, Greer stood with Sirius at the river's edge, listening as the water burbled and roared, its dark flow seeming to rise and embrace the glowing dusk. She tossed rocks in the river and Sirius stuck her head all the way under to retrieve them, laying them at Greer's feet like exquisite wild bird eggs.

Greer's cheeks were pink and full, her countenance vibrant although her arms and legs were still mapped with barely healed scratches and scars. When Ava went down and stood next to her, Greer put her thin cold hand in hers.

"Mr. Estmund loved to tell stories about you and Midas and Adonis and the wood fairies and the river. And we finally made it here, me and Sirius, where Mr. Estmund always talked about.

And we love it just like he said you used to."

"Like I still do," Ava said, her eyes filling. She pulled Greer into her, careful not to hug her bony frame too hard. "You made it. *We* made it."

Sibley trotted down to stand next to them, exuding her typical camping energy. "We have a surprise visitor for you," she said, raising her eyebrows and smiling wide at Greer. But it didn't have the effect she intended. Panic paled Greer's face.

"No, no, it's okay, I promise it's someone you want to meet," Sibley said quickly, wrapping her arm around Greer's shoulders in reassurance. Sibley and Ava flanked the girl as they walked up to camp to meet a wildland firefighter, still in his dirty beat-up Nomex. His face was stubbly and creased.

He offered a giant calloused hand. "I hear you rescued my lost firefighting gear. Brought it all the way out of the mountains with some pack llamas and a dog?"

Greer's mouth fell open. "H-how?"

"Exactly," Hemingway Maclean said, and everyone laughed.

"I still have it, your stuff," Greer blurted, flushed. "But Sirius and I ate all your food…"

He smiled, his teeth white against the dark stubble on his face. "I can't imagine a better use for it. Quite the journey you undertook. You're a legend in these parts. When you get a little older, come see me about becoming a smokejumper. You'd get through rookie training no problem. Not many people could make it through what you did, especially without provisions. I was wondering if I might get your picture and autograph, have you sign my logbook for me? It'd be a real honor—"

"Sure," Greer said, pink-faced and grinning.

He handed her a tattered waterproof notebook he pulled from his back pocket. She wrote on its waxy pages: "Greer Groff & Sirius the dog & Kelly & Yavell the llamas thank you Mr. Hemingway Maclean for the use of your wildfire gear, especially the candy. Sincerely, Greer, Raven-Girl."

Ava took photos of them together—Greer tiny next to the big man—and then he shook her hand and thanked her again. Greer was buoyant afterward, helping Sibley build their campfire, expounding on all the best ways to lay the wood. They sat around the fire until late, sparks shooting up into the dark as the coals burned down. The night was streaked and speckled with starlight, one shooting star after another unzipping the inky black sky. A raven sky, Greer called it.

They made s'mores, told stories, talked about Mr. Estmund and Persephone until Greer was finally ready for bed. She crawled into the tent and snuggled between Ava and Sibley. Sirius flopped down and snored at their feet. Ava stroked Greer's head until the girl fell asleep, twitching and murmuring with her dreams. *Comfort sounds.* Ravens bonding together.

A flock that kept growing, despite the ones who'd been lost. Death transformed into life. Persephone, bringing her message of great significance over such a long distance.

Sibley reached over and stroked Ava's face. They listened to the rush of the river's dark green waters. They smelled the cedars and ferns and damp sand. They breathed the cool mineral air. And Ava felt her father there, at the river with them.

A flock made whole.

◆

In the smoky late-summer heat, Ava and Greer stood on the slick pale-orange coffin-shaped rock, submerged to their knees in the North Fork's cold green waters. The towering cedars behind them shaded the hidden crescent of white-sand beach where they'd stashed Persephone in her cage, along with Mr. Estmund's old fly fishing vest, reel, and dry flies, the wool blanket Greer had carried on her long trek, and the velvet bag that had held what remained of him.

Ava had carried the surprising weight of her father's ashes

down the Isabella Creek Trail—Sibley staying behind at Aquarius with Sirius and Alfred—until Ava and Greer and Persephone reached the river's slack water that stretched up from Dworkshak Dam. No roads along that quiet slow section of the river, only cedars and alders, osprey and wildflowers, ferns and trout.

Ava told Greer they would make up the ceremony as they went, act only on instinct, no religious rites or rituals. They listened to cutthroat slap the surface and mergansers and dippers and wrens and kingfishers and osprey call. Then they waded into the river, slipping on the slick rocks until they stood side by side.

They dipped their damp hands into the box and filled them with Mr. Estmund's ashes, holding them above the water and letting them scatter, rushing downstream. Again, and again.

Trout nosed fragments in the silt. White ash spread like shock drawn long down current, a calcium-rich cloud. The fish were curious—this river offering churning at Ava and Greer's submerged feet, shiny bits that glinted like teeth. Bones baked so hot they shimmered underwater like mica.

These were his feet, his legs, his hips and spine. The blades of his shoulders, his arms, his hands, his neck, the bones of his face. What curiosity it all was. A river otter swimming and snuffing near, witnessing this offering of grief, this new shape of him.

This forest like a church, he'd always said. Forest and river, osprey and ravens, otter and trout, honeybees and butterflies, paintbrush and asters.

This orange rock they stood on, casting him loose and drifting.

They worked side by side until it was done, letting the tears come as the last bits of bone and ash sank into silt and sand.

"We love you Mr. Estmund," Greer said.

Ava bent over to kiss Greer's head, held her hand as they waded back to shore.

They made a thick slurry out of the dry Quikrete Ava had packed in, mixing it with cold river water using a green alder twig.

Greer brushed away dried leaves and sticks, then they cemented the heavy brass Army plaque—engraved with his name, a cross, and the dates of his birth and death—into its new permanent place, hidden between a trio of boulders and alder brush, out of reach of the river's high-roiling spring rush.

Laid to rest. Ashes to ashes. Dust to dust. Ava imagined the plaque papered with leaves and lichen, coated with drifting wildfire ash. Her father would never depart from his beloved river. It would hold him, forever always, form after form, and so hold a part of them, his family, here in this sacred place.

Ava and Greer sat beside Persephone in the cedar shade, watching the river go by. Bees buzzing flowers, a dipper bobbing the shallows, trout slapping the current.

Ava looked at Greer and nodded.

Holding her breath, Greer reached over and slowly opened Persephone's door.

Persephone swiped her beak along the length of her perch, tilting her head to look at them before examining the open space, seeming to ask, "*Now?*"

"You are healed, Queen Persephone. You are free. Spread your wings and find your way from the underworld to the sun," Ava pronounced.

Persephone climbed down from her perch and stood at the open cage door. She looked all around her. She hopped out onto the sandy blanket.

She took a few pigeon-toed steps onto the beach, imprinting her tracks. Three long toes pointing forward. One short toe pointing back.

Greer held her hands to her mouth.

"Go ahead," Ava said. "You are strong. You are a survivor. Fly."

And just like that, Persephone took one more step onto the sand and lifted herself into the air, her great black wings flapping, the white butterfly patch on her shoulder cap raising her higher and higher.

Ava and Greer stood, breathless, watching as she flew across the river.

Greer ran into the cold green water, cupped her hands to her mouth, and called out, "*Ca-caawww, ca-caawww.*"

Ava joined in, her voice lifting on the wind. An echo that carried over the rocks, the trees, the water, calling them forth. Calling them home.

ACKNOWLEDGEMENTS

A writer's journey is often long and arduous. Sometimes you get really lucky and have people who gird you up along the way, who bring joy and encouragement and help you reach *The End.*

Will Neville-Rehbehn, Editor Extraordinaire: You give the best hugs—literal and metaphorical—a person could get, along with providing a razor-sharp wit and intellect (and excellent wine taste). Thank you for offering all you do. It's a rare gift indeed. My sincere gratitude to the whole Torrey House Press team: Kirsten Johanna Allen, Scout Invie, Eryon Shondíín Greenburg, Alexis Powell, Kathleen Metcalf (who may have designed the best cover ever!), and Karin Anderson for providing such insightful editorial work.

Kim Barnes, MN, and Brittney Poulsen Carman, MD, thank you for your constant generosity of love and care. Your hearts and minds are golden and awe-inspiring. You enrich the world, and me. Val Vanderpool, Alexandra Teague, Angie Rasmussen, Sayantani Dasgupta, and my family of women: Cathleen Eastman, Michelle Giesey, Deborah Wood, and Vicki Lynn Raine—your kinship and communion mean so much. I'm so grateful to have you all in my corner.

To the OG Lampmen—Steve, Phin, Ben, and Saiah—and all the new amazing Lamp-peoples—Liv, Alex, Amelia, Booker, and Basil—my deepest wells of love, gratitude, and affection. I am the luckiest person alive to have you all as mine.

To the institutions of higher learning that have shaped and inspired my journey: Washington State University—especially the Honors College with Dean Grant Norton at its helm along with all my wonderful and caring colleagues; the WSU Raptor Rehabilitation Program and Raptor Club; the University of Idaho MFA program, College of Natural Resources, and UI Library; and the Lewis Clark State College English Department and Nez Perce Language Program.

Finally, many thanks to all the readers and thinkers out there supporting literature, art, science, the natural world, and the transformational nature of diverse experience and thought. This alone may sustain us, may save us.

My heart to you all.

ABOUT THE AUTHOR

Annie Lampman is a professor of honors creative writing and a faculty senator at the Washington State University Honors College. She lives on the Palouse Prairie in Pullman, Washington, where she bird watches, grows a pollinator garden, and restores a National Historic Registry home. Her debut novel, *Sins of the Bees*, was awarded the American Fiction Award and named a LitHub/CrimeReads Best New Debut Selection, a Popsugar Book Club Best New Thrillers Selection, a Scribd best nature novel, and a Dreamscape Media Trending Audiobook. She is author of the poetry chapbook *BURNING TIME*, and her short stories, essays, and poems have been published in eighty-some literary journals and anthologies and awarded the Dogwood Literary Award in Fiction, the Everybody Writes Award in Poetry, a Best American Essays "Notable," a Pushcart Prize Special Mention, an Idaho Commission on the Arts literature fellowship, and a national Bureau of Land Management artist-in-residence in the Owyhee Canyonlands Wilderness.

You can read more about her and her work at
annielampman.com.

ABOUT TORREY HOUSE PRESS

Torrey House Press publishes books at the intersection of the literary arts and environmental advocacy. THP authors explore the diversity of human experiences and relationships with place. THP books create conversations about issues that concern the American West, landscape, literature, and the future of our ever-changing planet, inspiring action toward a more just world.

We believe that lively, contemporary literature is at the cutting edge of social change. We seek to inform, expand, and reshape the dialogue on environmental justice and stewardship for the natural world by elevating literary excellence from diverse voices.

Visit www.torreyhouse.org for reading group discussion guides, author interviews, and more.

SPECIAL THANKS

As a 501(c)(3) nonprofit publisher, our work is made possible by generous donations from readers like you.

Torrey House Press is supported by the King's English Bookshop, Maria's Bookshop, the Jeffrey S. & Helen H. Cardon Foundation, the Sam & Diane Stewart Family Foundation, the Barker Foundation, the George S. and Dolores Doré Eccles Foundation, Diana Allison, Klaus Bielefeldt, Joe Breddan, Karen Edgley, Laurie Hilyer, Susan Markley, Marion S. Robinson, Kitty Swenson, Shelby Tisdale, Kirtly Parker Jones, Robert Aagard & Camille Bailey Aagard, Kif Augustine Adams & Stirling Adams, Rose Chilcoat & Mark Franklin, Jerome Cooney & Laura Storjohann, Linc Cornell & Lois Cornell, Susan Cushman & Charlie Quimby, Kathleen Metcalf & Peter Metcalf, Betsy Gaines Quammen & David Quammen, the Utah Division of Arts & Museums, Utah Humanities, the National Endowment for the Humanities, the National Endowment for the Arts, the Salt Lake City Arts Council, the Utah Governor's Office of Economic Development, and Salt Lake County Zoo, Arts & Parks. Our thanks to our readers, donors, members, and the Torrey House Press Board of Directors for their valued support.

Join the Torrey House Press family and give today at www.torreyhouse.org/give.